I'M FROM NOWHERE

Also by the author

Stone Cove Island

I'M FROM NOWHERE

SUZANNE MYERS

Published in the United States by Soho Teen an imprint of
Soho Press, Inc.
853 Broadway
New York, NY 10003

Library of Congress Cataloging-in-Publication Data

Myers, Suzanne
I'm from nowhere / Suzanne Myers.

ISBN 978-1-61695-660-8
eISBN 978-1-61695-661-5

1. Secrets—Fiction. 2. Identity—Fiction. 3. Boarding schools—Fiction.
4. Schools—Fiction. I. Title.
PZ7.M9917 Im 2016
[Fic]—dc23   2015028478

Interior design by Janine Agro, Soho Press, Inc.

Printed in the United States of America

10 9 8 7 6 5 4 3 2 1

To my four-legged teachers, Miranda, Stitch, Rabbit, and Gerry,
and to my husband, Adam. You are the best.

The National Horse Show was held at Madison Square Garden in New York City from 1883 to 2001, with a brief stint at the New Jersey Meadowlands Arena in the early 1990s. In 2002, the ASPCA Maclay Finals split off from the National Horse Show and were held at the Washington International Horse Show, then at Chelsea Piers in Manhattan, while the National Horse Show decamped to Wellington, Florida. In 2008, the Maclay Finals reunited with the National Horse Show in Syracuse, New York, before moving to Lexington, Kentucky, where they are held today. For the purpose of this story, I have imagined that the Finals still take place at the Garden in New York City.

"And there you are, at the edge of the world
Dangling with my heart a' pounding . . .

You're right. I'm from nowhere."

—Neko Case

CHAPTER ONE

California

Beginning is the hardest part, don't you think? Or maybe I just have trouble with commitment. Some books make it so easy. You leap on, tangle your fingers in the mane and gallop off into the sunset. The story drags you to the end. You can't let go. And too soon it's over. Others hang back, aloof, like unfriendly guests at a party, pushing you away with too many details about the colors of the grass and sky, the texture of this and that, histories of what came before and premonitions of what's to come. No one talks to you or even notices you are there. You either dig in your heels and stick with it until you find a way in, or you turn away and head back home, chapter closed.

I'll try not to do that. Instead, I'll tell you up front, and you can decide whether or not to come along.

THIS STORY IS ABOUT the year I found out I was not who I thought I was, and also about how I learned to be okay being myself. If those things sound like they are opposites, they are and they're not. You'll see.

It begins in September, back at school. It's about three weeks into my sophomore year, but it feels like the end of something instead of the beginning somehow, despite the brand-new pens and notebooks.

I'm balancing my biology homework in the basket of my bike, and I loop around the parking lot once before turning up Ocean and onto the bike path along the beach. That Aimee Mann song runs through my head:

So I'm bailing this town
Or tearing it down
Or probably more like hanging around

I see girls lined up along the beach like static, mellow cheerleaders, watching their boyfriends surf after school. Or instead of school. Hanging around. None of the girls is surfing. They never do, and I always wonder about that. It seems so boring just to sit there and watch.

Welcome to Ventura, California, beach town in decay.

It made its last big splash in the '60s (you know that song?) before becoming a just-too-distant suburb of L.A. Rincon Beach, which is nearby, is still a big deal in the surf world, but besides that? Not much. There's mini golf. One big hotel on the beach that attracts conventions rather than vacationers. Some outlying strawberry fields. Nice weather. And me, Wren Verlaine, tenth-grade student at Ventura High School. Resident of South Ash Street. Daughter of Hannah Verlaine, journalist. Owner of twin black cats, Spite and Malice.

My mom is what they call a stringer for the *Los Angeles*

Times. That means she basically covers the local stuff that happens, writes for other places when she can and hopes for a big story to break near home. When you're a reporter, that puts you in the strange position of essentially hoping for disaster to strike. Unless a movie star or the next president happens to come from Ventura, my mom's pretty much stuck with high school football in terms of reporting on good news. An earthquake, forest fire or gruesome enough murder, on the other hand, and she's in business.

A few years ago, there was a big mudslide up the 101 freeway. A whole hillside collapsed and buried tons of houses, some of them with people still inside. You might remember it. It was truly, truly horrible. My mom practically camped out up there for a week. I'd see her only late at night or early in the morning, hollow-eyed and pale, strung out on coffee, grabbing a change of clothes. It's a strange way to live, if you ask me. But that's what makes Hannah Verlaine happy.

There's just the two of us, not counting the cats, but I feel lucky, because compared to a lot of kids I know, we have a pretty good relationship. I can tell her things, and she'll help instead of grounding me or screaming at me. Some of my friends even talk to her instead of their own moms when they have a problem. We don't have many secrets from each other.

Except for one. One really big secret.

My mom moved here from the East Coast when I was born. Her parents died when she was about thirty, not at the same time, but within a year or two. They were pretty old when they had her, especially for that era, when everyone married so young. They were old-fashioned. "Dyed-in-the-wool Yankees" is how Hannah describes them if I ask.

I was only six or seven when my grandfather died, and I don't remember him much. I went on his boat once. It was moored in the harbor of a windblown Atlantic island. It was May, but the day was freezing. My grandfather tried to teach me some sailing knots, and Hannah got mad at him, saying he was pushing me and being impatient.

That part about him being impatient I don't remember, but the part about her getting mad I do. She was like a lion in a nature show, how you see them getting in between the cub and whatever's threatening it, her back up, teeth bared. My impression now is that she and her father never quite saw life the same way. Her mother was reserved, Hannah says, always letting my grandfather make the decisions, never complaining. Proper. Tasteful. Quiet. By the time Hannah went to boarding school, she was over it and ready to get away and figure out her own life.

My mom doesn't keep in close touch with her extended family, so I don't have much in the way of relatives, though I'm named after her great-aunt Cornelia Wren, a suffragette back in 1919. When Hannah first moved to Ventura, she found this little Craftsman bungalow on South Ash Street near the beach, and we've lived there ever since. The neighborhood is called Midtown, which my mom thinks is hilarious, because she went to college in New York City, and it's nothing like the midtown there. I always get the feeling she thinks Ventura kind of sucks, but at the same time, she's turned down every chance to go somewhere else.

I've always lived in Southern California, but I'm not very Southern Californian. I'm average height, on the scrawny side, with super straight, dark hair chopped just below my chin and blue eyes—the only thing I inherited from my mom. People sometimes say I look like a cat. And I have been a cat for Halloween, more than once.

Most of the girls at my school are blonde and have long hair. They hang out with surfers or date guys on the football team, play volleyball. They giggle nonstop because they think it's uncool to seem smart . . . You've seen it all before on TV. Or, at the other extreme, they're Mexican. Their parents live on the Oxnard side of town. Most of them work in agriculture or for landscape companies. Or in laundromats or supermarkets. Some are migrant-crop pickers and go back and forth to Mexico, sometimes right in the middle of the school year. They work hard, for the most part, in and out of school and don't have a lot of time for cheerleading and partying, even if they were welcome.

I don't fit in with either group. I have friends, but not a best friend. I think people pretty much like me, but I'm never at the center of what's going on. I'm a good student, but not a star. My scene is no scene. I'm just Wren. Hanging around.

WHEN I GET HOME from school, Hannah's not there. She must still be at the fairgrounds. Right now she's doing a story on the horse show or rodeo or something.

I toss my books on my bed before flopping down next to them, then reach for my guitar. We have a good flea market in Ventura; that's where I got it. It's a beater cowboy guitar, but it does what I need it to. That same song is running though my head, so I try pick out the melody.

All that I need now
Is someone with the brains and the know-how
To tell me what I want . . . anyhow

The cats weave around my ankles. The screen door bangs closed, and I hear my mom in the kitchen, unpacking groceries. Usually she comes straight in to see me. After a while, I get up and go out there to see what she's doing. A few boxes and cans are still sitting out, and her palms are pressed on the counter. She looks up and smiles tightly. Not her usual greeting.

"Hey, Mom," I say, waiting for an explanation.

Her expression is usually open and easy. She's sort of a quiet person herself, but a relaxed and calm quiet, not straining to hold it all in the way her mom was. "Hi, Wrendle," she says at last.

I pick up a can of tomatoes for something to do. I must look expectant because finally she spits it out.

"Okay, sweetie, here it is. It's good. I don't want you to worry. It's a good thing."

"What's a good thing?" Now I *am* worried.

"It's an assignment. The *LA Times* is sending me to Greenland to do a story on the melting ice sheet."

"Amazing!" I yell. This is just the kind of story Hannah's been chasing for years.

"For six months," she adds.

"Oh. That sounds, I don't know, like a long time."

"It's a long time," she agrees.

"So what about school?"

"I wish." She reaches over to smooth my hair. She must really be dreading whatever's coming next. "I wish . . ."

"Spit it out, Hannah. Enough with the suspense."

"Well, it's lucky, really. I made some calls, and it turns out they can take you at Hardwick. A spot opened up in your year, and the timing works out. It's the best possible solution, really. I'm excited for you."

"Hardwick as in Hardwick Hall?"

Hardwick Hall is an ultra-fancy, super-intense boarding school in Connecticut. It's been around for hundreds of years, and the list of famous people who've gone there is a mile long.

Hannah, as it happens, also went there, but she rarely talks about it. She certainly doesn't keep in touch with many old roommates or go to class reunions or anything.

"It's a great school, Wren. It's a great opportunity for you. I know it'll be hard jumping in when the year's already started." She's in all-business mom mode, convincing herself as well as me.

"But I'm already in school. Why can't I stay here?"

"By yourself?"

I guess that isn't such a great idea. I can't even cook spaghetti.

"Wren, Hardwick was great for me in a lot of ways. I think you can get a lot out of it too. Try it for this year. You don't have to commit beyond that."

"What about Spite and Malice? What are they going to do?"

"They can stay with Jonesy. I've already talked to him."
Jonesy is a friend of my mom's who writes for the Santa
Barbara paper and runs a used bookstore on Main Street.
I think he's kind of a weird guy, but I can picture the cats
as happy bookstore cats, lounging in the window to attract
customers, creeping between the bookshelves in search of
a patch of sun to nap in, catching the occasional mouse.
Okay.

"*I* could stay with Jonesy." Hannah gives me a look. Of
course I can't. I know that. "When is this happening?"

"Monday," she says, this time looking right at me. "I got
a flight for you Monday. I can fly to New York with you and
put you on the train. I'll leave for Greenland from there."

"Monday? And you just found this out?" I feel betrayed
having this sprung on me.

She looks guilty. "Wren, it's going to be a good thing.
You'll see."

And just like that, it's done. I'm going to boarding school.

HOW HANNAH SWUNG GETTING me in to Hardwick without my knowing
anything about it—not to mention how's she's planning
to pay for it—remains a mystery. But it's clear she doesn't
want to discuss it.

We spend the weekend packing, buying me a heavy
coat, hats, mittens, a few sweaters: things I'll never use in
Ventura. I wonder what the kids wear at Hardwick. I picture them, blond and ruddy-cheeked from hours spent on
the playing fields, dressed in baggy cords and nubby L.L.
Bean sweaters, circa 1989. I guess that's because I've seen
pictures of my mom from that era.

Sunday night, I dig her old yearbook off a dusty shelf and thumb through it. The campus looks pretty. Idyllic, really. Like a tiny, perfect college.

I hold it out to her. "Mind if I take this?"

She nods without really looking at it.

We fold shirts and underwear, stamping them with my name (when did she have time to get the stamp made? Seriously, how long has she been planning this?) before packing them into a giant navy-blue duffel bag with Hannah's initials on it.

"I don't have to wear a perky little plaid skirt or a tie or anything, right?"

She smiles absently. "No, you can wear what you want. They said no jeans to formal dinner, but that's about it. I didn't see 'perky' anywhere in the dress code."

"Good."

"Well, that's the first positive thing you've said."

"Mom, give me a break. How do expect me to feel?"

She kind of half-pats, half-strokes my hair. "Exactly like you do." Then she looks at me for a long time, but her mind is somewhere else; she's like someone going into a flashback in a movie.

I can feel tears pooling in the corners of my eyes and cut her off. "Hannah? Hello? We still have about a thousand socks to stamp."

"You're right. Listen, I have a going-away present. I guess I should just give it to you now." She kneels on the floor, pulls an old guitar case out from under the bed and sets it in front of me.

"What's this?" I ask.

"A going-away present, I told you. Really, it's a good-luck present. And kind of a 'remember who you are' present."

I unsnap the latches. It smells musty, and the edging is worn along the sides. When I open it, I draw in such a sharp breath that I kind of squeak. Spite and Malice spring off the bed in opposite directions, taking cover.

Cradled in the dented velvet lining is the most beautiful guitar I've ever seen.

It has a tortoiseshell pick guard—probably from a real tortoise, it's so old—and a pearly inlaid bird drinking nectar from a flower. I recognize it right away: it's a Gibson Hummingbird, close cousin of the Gibson J-45 Aimee Mann plays. And left-handed. Exactly the guitar I've always wanted. I wonder how Hannah could possibly have known. She's not a musician. She's one of those people who likes "all kinds of music,'" which to me means not any kind of music all that much.

"It's an old one," she says, maybe just to fill the silence.

"Mom, it's perfect." I hug her.

Now she looks a little teary. She glances at the yearbook, then back at me. "It'll keep you company. Not that you'll need company. I just remember when I was there, it was nice to have something to remind me of home."

"But you hated your family," I say.

"That doesn't mean I never got homesick."

CHAPTER TWO

Hardwick Hall

Hannah rides the bus into New York with me and puts me straight on the train from Grand Central. So much for my first visit to New York City; I get to see exactly one tunnel and one wide, ugly street lined with tall buildings. It seems like a huge wasted opportunity. I beg Hannah to let us stay over, just for a night, but she says no. Her flight for Nuuk leaves later that evening, so her plan is to turn around and head straight back to JFK Airport.

Before she puts me on the train to Wassaic, she scribbles the name and address of an old Hardwick friend, one of the few: Warren Norwood. I've heard his name a few times over the years; I think I might even have overheard Mom giggling on the phone to him. He's a theater director who lives in New York, she tells me in a rush. He has a play opening in New Haven. Maybe I could go one night. He's offered to come to school and take me out to dinner and generally keep an eye on me.

"He's wonderful," she says. "You'll love him. You have the same sense of humor. You two should have met sooner."

As she speaks, I'm distracted by the gold and aqua con-stellations glowing on Grand Central's huge ceiling. My eyes wander to the clock perched high above the swarm of people, huge and bright, just like it looks in every movie. It's confusing, the chaos around me. The surreal dream feeling I have right now, like I've been transported from my own life into someone else's. My mind races. What am I doing here? Why are we doing this again?

"There's your great-aunt Helen too," Hannah says without a lot of conviction. That's my grandfather's sister. She moved a few years ago from Boston to her summer house on Stone Cove Island, and now she lives there full-time. We get a Christmas card from her every year, but she and my mom never really talk. "That's a last resort, though," Hannah adds. "Don't think you'll be needing her number. Unless you want it?"

I recognize her journalist's "trying to be fair" expression and shake my head. Then I stuff the note with the theater director's name into my bag and instantly forget about it.

"Okay then," Hannah says, a little breathless. "Goodbye, my Wrendle. I'll call as soon as I get there, and you can tell me everything. Maybe you can take some pictures for me."

We're not allowed to have cell phones at school, but Hannah and I plan to video chat on my computer.

"Bye, Mom." I hug her, but it doesn't feel like a real goodbye. I don't know what it should feel like, but this isn't it.

A HARDWICK SHUTTLE BUS picks me up from the Wassaic station and navigates the bouncy twenty-minute drive to school. I chew my thumbnail the whole time. I am the only student on the bus, since I am the only student arriving three weeks late. My bags have already been delivered.

It's mid-afternoon when we pull into the long, shady driveway. The campus feels very quiet. A student here or there hurries along a flagstone path. Someone hauls a bundle of lacrosse sticks and a net across the quad. Out the window, I see playing fields rolling gracefully down the hill in one direction; in the other, I see orderly redbrick dorms. They look pretend somehow, copied from and arranged to look like Oxford or Cambridge by men who had only recently left those places and were either home-sick or looking to impress their old friends.

The shuttle groans up the slight hill to the main entrance and stops in front of an elegant white clapboard administrative building: Burrage Hall. I know its name because of the prominent plaque. The whole picture is, to be honest, intimidating as hell.

Once I'm off the bus, a lady in a twinset with reading glasses sliding down her nose appears. In a hushed library voice, she directs me to Selby Hall, a girls' dorm close to the center of campus. Maybe that means I can at least get up late and still make it to breakfast on time.

The schedule I read in the school brochure seems daunting. Breakfast at 7, 8 A.M. chapel (wait—*chapel?!*), 9 A.M. classes, marching along right through afternoon sports (mandatory), twice-a-week formal dinner (also mandatory), pre- and post-dinner study time, and dorm check-in at 10 P.M.

When do I ride my bike around aimlessly? Noodle on

my delightful new guitar? Sit on the beach and stare at the waves, just spacing out? Not that I have a bike at school, and there are no waves but, you know, *conceptually*.

According to the giant packet of admissions materials Hannah dumped on me, I will be sharing a suite with three other girls. She's helpfully included last year's student directory.

Honor Gibson: New York City, field hockey 1, equestrian 1, tennis 1, squash 1. (I figure out the "1" means they played the sport in ninth grade. The seniors have a "4" after their teams. Or a "1, 2, 3, 4," if they were way into it and played the sport all the way through. I have "0" sports.) In the photo she has long, gleaming honey-colored hair and the polished look of someone who never bites her nails or forgets to shave her legs.

Eloise Browning: Concord, New Hampshire, field hockey 1, equestrian 1 and swim 1. Eloise has a big, friendly smile, thick blonde hair in a ponytail and slightly big, very white teeth.

India Alpert: Westport, Connecticut, equestrian 1, arts 1. Hardwick has an option where you can paint, dance or study music as a "concentration," which seems like a fancy way of saying extra credit. India has a round face, medium brown hair in a braid and is wearing a woolly fisherman's sweater. In the photo, she's laughing and making a peace sign.

Perfect, I think. *They all ride horses.*

I flip through the directory. There is only one other kid in the book from California, a studious-looking Chinese boy named Philip Han. And he's from San Francisco (computer 1, video lab 1).

SELBY HALL IS VERY old: dark redbrick and casement windows paned with wavy glass. A twisting wisteria grows up the walls. The whole campus looks much more like a college than a high school, laid out around a perfect green quad, with crisscrossing paths that veer off on either side of the main building past the dorms and drop away down to the stables, tennis courts and boathouse, on a widened part of the Housatonic River.

Our suite is at the end of a low-eaved attic floor at the top of worn limestone steps. It's small but sunny. *Cozy* is my impression the first time I see it. Two narrow bedrooms, each with a bunk bed and a desk, open to a shared sitting room with two desks, a sofa and a bay window looking out over the quad. Outside I can see a few boys playing Frisbee in T-shirts. It's cold, early fall, but one of them is barefoot.

As I turn back toward the door, I almost jump. A tall girl with straight blonde hair is stretched out on the sofa, reading. *Eloise Browning.* I recognize her instantly. Friendly smile, big teeth.

"Hi, I'm Eloise." She tosses her book on the floor and jumps up to shake my hand. Formal, for a kid our age.

"Wren," I say, looking around. I drop my bags near the door, since I'm not sure which room is mine.

"Excellent. You're sharing with India. In here."

She motions to the room on the right. I take in India's pale print comforter spread across the top bunk, a batik tapestry on the wall and lots of postcards and photos pinned on the ceiling.

Eloise catches my gaze. "People always send her post-cards when they go to India. She has a big collection. That girl in the picture with the hat, that's her sister Tabby. She went here. She's at Amherst now."

"Oh," I say brilliantly. "Wow."

I don't think I've ever met anyone in Ventura who's been to India. Unless they were Indian, of course.

"Honor and I are in the other room. Do you want to drop off your stuff? I can show you around a little if you want. We have a quiz in history tomorrow, and dinner's at six thirty, so I don't have a ton of time, but—"

"No, that's cool. Really, thanks. I think I want to just unpack a little and walk around. You know, dive in slowly." I drag my bags to the entrance of my new room and sit down on the faded Marimekko print cushion on the window seat.

Eloise catches sight of my guitar case. "Do you play?"

"A little. I'm still learning. I'll try not to torture you guys too much. What happened to your old roommate?" I ask to change the subject. I'm shy about playing in front of strangers.

"Katie? She got caught partying in the woods. India made it back just in time for check-in. Katie was too slow dragging herself away from her boyfriend, and well, it was kind of three strikes: stoned, caught with a boy, late for check-in." In case I'm worried, she adds, "Don't worry about India, though. She never gets caught. Tabby taught her the ropes while she was still here last year. And even if she parties a lot, she won't care if you don't. She's chill."

"Where are they? India and Honor, I mean."

"At the barn still. Taliesin, the horse I'm riding this semester, has a stone bruise, so I'm not riding today. You'll meet them at dinner. Do you ride?"

I shake my head. "No. I've been on trail rides at home. You know, riding Western. But nothing serious like here. At least, what it looks like in the brochure. Jumping and everything." I have no idea what a stone bruise is, but I don't ask.

"Oh, you can learn. Lots of people are beginners when they come here. Most people ride. At least, the girls do. Not many of the guys. Rowing is bigger with them. You know Corwin Hardwick, who started the school, dug his own lake especially for rowing? His daughter was into horses, so that's how riding got to be such a thing. Of course, she broke her back doing it, but . . . you know. That doesn't really happen much."

"Oh, cool." To be honest, I hadn't considered riding. I figured you were either a horsey girl who showed up, pony in tow, or you weren't. I pictured myself more as the arts-concentration type, skipping sports entirely. Honestly, I'd had a hard time picturing myself here at all.

I start to shake my head, but surprise myself by saying, "Yeah, maybe."

Part of me feels the urge to try something I normally would never do. Nobody here knows what is or isn't me. I could make up anything, really. Be anyone.

"Isn't it too late, though? I mean, everyone's already been here awhile."

Eloise smiles in a patient way that reminds me of a baby-sitter. "Well, you have to pick a sport for the semester. Talk to Mr. Kelley tomorrow if you want to do it. He runs the program."

"Great. Maybe. I think I'm going to go look around. So I'll see you at dinner?"

"'Kay. See you there."

OUTSIDE THE LIGHT IS starting to fade already, and the air has a sharpness it never gets in Southern California. Some of the leaves on the trees glint gold, the light striking from a sideways, angled pitch. Students are hustling back and forth—between dorms, sports practice and Hale Library— but it's quiet, punctuated by an occasional sweaty lacrosse or soccer player's yell of "Duder!" and the slapping high-five sound that follows.

Everyone seems very focused on where they're going and what they have to do. Which is good for me. I'm less onstage as the new girl, showing up midsemester with no horse, no field hockey stick, no lay of the land, no friends.

The path I'm following leads to a row of classroom buildings. Behind them the landscape drops, and at the base I see an old-fashioned red barn with a big, sandy riding ring surrounded by a post-and-rail fence. Three horses and riders crisscross it in even, flowing circles, moving seamlessly from trot to canter and back. Without thinking, I turn onto the path that leads down there. I'm a little mesmerized by the silken, muscular swirl of the horses, their hooves beating the ground in an even, drumming rhythm.

I stop outside the fence to watch. A tall, thin man leans against the red-and-white striped top rail of a jump, frowning with concentration. He's limber but hunched over, like he's trying to take up less space than he needs. A messy wave of red-blond hair falls across his forehead; his face is that ruddy tan of someone outside all the time. His eyes follow the dark horse coming around the top of the ring and turning back in our direction.

The rider is slender, graceful and relaxed. She looks like she's sitting still, though the horse's pace has increased— and then it springs, front legs snapping up neatly to clear the jump. They land together and circle back around to join the other horses standing in the center.

I try to imagine my mom here, jumping a horse like that. I can't. I feel a sudden pang; I should have pumped her for more information. Not about classes and opportunities and all the glossy crap she did tell me, but about the reality of a place where girls are professional equestrians and boys call one another "Duder."

"Nice enough," the thin man says to the girl in an English accent. Not as criticism; the way he says it comes across as high praise.

The girl smiles politely but looks dissatisfied. She smooths her horse's mane, then brushes at something on her knee. I don't have to know anything about riding to tell she's exceptional at it. The way the other kids look at her. The way the trainer treats her. The way she doesn't notice any of it. You can tell she's used to being the star, or at least one of them.

"You next, then, India. Weight in your stirrups right up to the base *and* in the air."

So this is India. She wears her hair in a braid like in her picture; it pokes out from under her helmet. She giggles as she untangles and shortens her reins, already cantering toward the jump. "Mr. Kelley?" she calls from the far end of the ring.

"Organize and keep the chatter for after the fence, missy," he says. India rides a golden horse with a cream-colored mane and tail, the kind you often see in cowboy movies. It looks springy and good-natured as it gathers itself for the jump. When the horse lands, clearing the stacked rails by a good ten feet, India laughs again.

"Distance! Distance! Right around again, and I'm counting with you this time," yells Mr. Kelley. India circles around once more and heads for the same jump. She counts her horse's strides out loud with Mr. Kelley. "Four, three, two, one . . ." The horse pats the ground lightly with its front hooves and clears the jump easily. It's not as sleek and polished as the first girl's performance, but Mr. Kelley seems satisfied. India rejoins the horses in the center.

"Okay," Mr. Kelley says. "You could have used more leg at the base, but much better spot that time. I think we'll quit on that one."

"Honor, wait up," India calls to the girl with the dark horse. They disappear into the barn together.

I hang by the rail a moment longer, absently twisting the charm on my necklace, a tiny anchor set with black diamonds. That makes it sound a lot fancier than it is. The diamonds are like tiny chips, so it sparkles, but it's a dark sparkle, not like regular diamonds. It belonged to my mom until I dug it out of the bottom of her jewelry box one day a few years ago, the summer before seventh grade.

I hadn't seen it before. She never wore it. When I asked

her about it, she said she'd just never really liked it that much. Her father had given it to her as a graduation present, but it didn't really seem like her, so she'd stuck it in the box and forgotten about it. I asked if I could have it; I liked its goth Victorian vibe. She said okay, and I haven't taken it off since. I'm in the habit of wearing it inside my shirt, because in Ventura wearing diamonds—chips or otherwise—would be kind of conspicuous. Probably here no one would notice.

Part of me wants to follow India and Honor and see the horses up close. But I don't.

I'll meet them back at the suite later anyway, in a place that if not exactly familiar, will feel more like neutral turf.

IN OUR ROOM, INDIA is friendly, showing me around, pointing out her favorite belongings, chattering about her sister and some bands she saw over the summer—jam bands, not exactly my thing, but that's fine. She asks to see my guitar.

Honor says "hi" and "welcome." Her voice is bright, but the whole time she's combing her hair in the mirror and not really looking at me. Eloise sits nearby, helping her pick out something to wear. They laugh about something that happened at the barn earlier that day.

Apparently I'm supposed to dress up for dinner. Good to know.

THE HUGE DINING HALL is nothing like the cafeteria at Ventura High School. This looks more like a library, or maybe Hogwarts. Heavy, dim chandeliers hang on thick chains from a high, vaulted ceiling; two rows of old wood tables line each side of the room like church pews. My school's cafeteria was loud and metallic and echoey. This one isn't quiet, of course—it's still filled with teenagers—but the sounds are softer, rounder, richer.

What you are supposed to do is fill the next available seat and sit with whoever's already sitting there—boy, girl; Upper, Lower, Last or First; your roommate, your best friend or a stranger. You can see how this was a nice idea in theory.

On my first night at Hardwick, I so wish the rule was actually enforced. But that's not how it works. Instead kids clump up at the end of the food line, waiting for their friends so they can sit together. Once you are seated, you're allowed to get up and move around, so actually it's worse than having to wander around with your tray looking for a table. The person you sit with can get up at any point and leave you for someone more interesting.

Tonight at least my suitemates don't seem like they'll abandon me. We hover together at the end of the food line. At the last minute, a few other girls hustle through the line to catch up, and we take a big table near the back. With seven we're enough to almost fill the table on our own.

Honor sits across from me. The other girls ask her questions nonstop. She answers but never asks any herself. A few boys stop by the table, say hi to her and then the other girls, but they can't stay because there's no room left. I try not to stare at her. You'd think Honor was a movie star being interviewed about her latest role in one of those behind-the-scenes shows, judging from the way everyone bombards her with such breathless focus. I've never seen anything like it in real life.

It doesn't take me long to figure out that Honor, in fact, doesn't have much to do with real life. There is a magic, invisible force field around her; her effect on others is supernatural. Girls become clones. Boys become slaves. Eloise, her best friend, normally friendly, turns off her personality when Honor is around. Honor is not mean, like the fake, bitchy cheerleaders at Ventura High School. Honor is Teflon. She doesn't need anything or anyone, but she always gets whatever she wants. If she likes you, you'll be friends. If she doesn't like you, you don't exist.

That's the category I fall into. She looks through me. Her eyes glaze over when I speak, so I quickly stop talking to her altogether. I shouldn't let it bother me, but it does. Because as much as I don't belong at Hardwick, Honor does.

For starters:

1. She's beautiful. But more than that, she's *attractive*—in that perfect, not-trying-but-always-saying/wearing/doing-the-right-thing way.

2. She rides better than anyone else at school. Her horse Rainmaker was champion at Junior Hunter Finals last year. When he trots, he seems to float above the ground.

3. Every boy at Hardwick knows who she is and seems to have her on some kind of radar. I haven't seen a boy walk by her without saying hi at least, and usually trying to come up with an excuse to stick around.

4. Her father, Edward Gibson, owns the famous depart-
    ment store in New York. He went to Hardwick too,
    and has a building named after him.

The girl seems to have her own gravitational pull.

But the truth is I don't want to be friends with Honor.
I'm alone in that sentiment, clearly. What bugs me is not
that the feeling is mutual (which it is). It's more how she
manages to communicate with everything she does that I
will never—*could never*—be a person like her. *Sorry, Wren.
You're not. You can't be. You should give up now and go back to
wherever you came from.*

AFTER A WHOLE WEEK of being invisible at dinner—in fact, of being
invisible for most of every day—I realize another reason
I will never quite fit in. Everyone else has been here for
a month, yes, but at least half of the class has also been
here a full year for ninth grade. There's a whole language
between them I don't speak. I'm like a foreign exchange
student. Hardwick Hall will never feel like home.

Alone on my laptop at night, I let my mind wander. I
still can't quite work out what strings my mom must have
pulled to get me in here so last minute. Or how she would
even have strings to pull. She never really talked about
high school. It seemed like she was always trying to get
away from the East and away from her past—to make a life
as different as possible from the one she grew up with.

I remind myself that I'll be able to ask her those questions soon enough. Hannah won't be gone forever. It's a
six-month gig. I just have to make it through this year. That

helps a little. I promise myself that I won't call her every day. I check the website for Jonesy's store, Pacific Books, looking through boring snapshots of a book signing from last week, hoping to catch sight of Spite and Malice. I do see Malice in one, tail floating up above him and kinking back under as he stares at a patron with his glowing yellow eyes. Spite is in another, sleeping in a window. It looks like they've settled in, at least.

Mostly I find myself in a constant state of both wanting to call my mother and not wanting to talk to her. If I had a cell phone like a ton of the kids here do, despite the rules, I think I would be texting her all the time, those pings satisfying this impulse to reach out, find her there, but not have to come up with anything to say.

ABOUT MY SECRET: IT'S really my mother's secret, but since it's about me, that makes it mine too. She has always refused to tell me who my father is.

Hannah's never been married. She has many friends who are men, and I've certainly gotten the impression from a few that they would have been happy to stick around. There have been one or two "boyfriends," I guess you'd call them, though that sounds weird when you're talking about your own mother, and she never acted in the slightest bit like I feel when I like a guy. She was just okay about it. They could leave. Or stay. Nothing was going to rock her world. None of the boyfriends is my father. None of the friends is my father.

I have tried to figure out the timing, the similarities—were they in the same place that summer? Isn't my hair kind of like this one? Do my hands look like that one's? And of course, I've asked. Nothing will make her tell me. She says it's not important. That I'm my own person. I should feel free to invent myself instead of follow or reject someone else's mold. Inevitably the conversation goes something like:

Me: "What about *your* mold?"

Hannah: "That you are stuck with. Feel free to follow or reject."

Me: "But what if I want more options to follow or reject?"

Hannah: "This person is not able to provide you with any options."

Me: "Is it someone I know?"

Hannah: "No, it's someone from a million years ago."

Me: "Why didn't you stay together?"

Here she always gives me the pained look. "We're from different worlds. Well, not exactly. But we live in completely different worlds. It was impossible, Wren. It *is* impossible. You'll just have to take my word for it."

"Impossible because he's dead?"

No answer.

"Because he's married?"

No answer.

"Because he's your long-lost twin brother?"

"Wren!"

I get nowhere. She won't budge. If I push her, I get a cliché. "When you're older. When you're ready. When it feels like the right time. At some point. Not now. It doesn't matter. Wren, just trust me." All shorthand for "no."

Usually what happens—or at least what happened

before I ended up at Hardwick—is I give up and go back to my room to write a song. (Not about that. How lame do you think I am?) About a story I read that day. Or the way the beach looked in an earthquake. Or some guy in my history class. A lot of times I listen to other people's songs and take them apart and try to figure them out. It's like doing a crossword puzzle, if you like that sort of thing.

The point is, there is always this vacuum between me and Hannah. She'll never tell. And I will always wonder. I've spent a lot of time wondering already about this other half of who I am. But I've kind of given up talking about it to her, or to anyone else. Not that there's anyone here I could to talk to.

THAT FIRST WEEK, I look for Hannah everywhere, trying to compare my Hardwick to her Hardwick. Did she have friends right away? Were the classes hard for her? Did she wonder what she was doing here? Or did she accept that it was the place she was supposed to be?

In the chapel, I scroll down the list of senior prefects. In the gym, I scan photos of the girls' sports teams from the '90s, though I have no idea what sports Hannah played. I walk along the flagstone paths, picturing her steps under my steps, imagining I can see what she saw.

I get used to some things: the breathy half-snores of India in the bunk above me; the odd salad I take to concocting for lunch, exactly the same ingredients in exactly the same proportions every day; studying, *really studying*, for hours every single night, whether I have a test or not the next day. The classes are hard, much harder than I'm used to at home. On the plus side, I don't really have anything else to do.

But there's already so much I know I won't get used to: how low and metallic the sky can look on an overcast day; how the sun keeps setting earlier and earlier each day, earlier enough to notice; how there really are girls who have their own gravitational pull.

CHAPTER THREE

Horsey Girl

Have I mentioned Nick?

The day I meet him, I'm on my way to the stables for my second riding lesson, and I'm nervous. The first lesson was amazing. Mr. Kelley had me on a quiet, thick-necked chestnut named Chester, with a Roman nose and a white blaze down his face. The saddle felt different from the armchair-like Western saddles I had sat in before. This one was thinner, flatter. Not exactly uncomfortable, but more like you were wrapping yourself around it than it was wrapping itself around you.

Chester's walk is slow and rolling. His hoofs hit the ground with a dry thud, as though they are heavy, and with each step it is a relief to put them down. We walked around and around in the still-warm September sun. By the end of that first hour, I could already stop, start and turn to make small circles in either direction. My hair was matted with sweat under my borrowed helmet, my nostrils coated with dust, and when I slid to the ground and drew the reins over Chester's head, my thighs ached so much I couldn't imagine ever standing up straight again. I absolutely loved it.

The next time—today—we were going to trot. Before I took that first lesson, I hadn't even wanted to ride, so I didn't care how it went. Now all I can think about is how long it will take me to get as good as Honor and Eloise, if that is even possible. I am impatient, the way I felt when I was first learning to play the guitar. I want to canter, to jump, to be invited to ride in one of the interschool horse shows that Hardwick either hosts or visits.

At the same time, I am terrified to canter or jump. Hell, I am terrified to trot. My legs still feel like jelly from the first lesson two days ago. How will I hang on at all?

This is what I am thinking as I pass the boathouse on my way to the ring. Crew practice is ending. A scull with four boys, all in gray sweatshirts with HARDWICK HALL printed in green across the front, pulls up along the dock. One of the boys jumps onto the dock in a practiced way.

He is slim, with straight, light-brown hair falling in his face. His eyes have the kind of crinkles in the corners that connect to his smile. The other boys hop out, and together they flip the boat out of the water and upside down. It's a light, thin, fast boat; you can carry it easily, especially if you have muscles hardened from hours of rowing on and off the water as well as a thousand other painful exercises required for the sport.

I take in his eye crinkles sort of absentmindedly. I guess maybe I am even staring. Normally I would pay more attention to looking like I wasn't looking, but I am more focused on Chester and Mr. Kelley and whether

I will be able to trot well enough without falling off to be allowed to canter and jump someday.

The boy catches my gaze and walks right over. "Hey," he says, "you looking for the women's eight? Coach is on the other side right now."

I don't know what he's talking about, but I gather from context that it has to do with rowing. The teams compete in boats of four or eight, I later learn. At schools that are really serious, they often divide the teams into lightweight and heavyweight. Hardwick is a very serious rowing school, but not a very big school, so our team is divided only into boys' and girls' teams.

"I'm not rowing," I answer, nodding toward the stables.

"Got it. Another horsey girl. Too bad." He winks. Some guys can really pull that off, and with others it's completely cheesy. He can pull it off.

"Too bad?" I say.

"Heartbreakers."

It's a line, I know, but like the wink and the crinkly eyes, you know it's a line, and you don't care.

"Right," I say doubtfully. "I just started, so I don't think I qualify."

He looks me up and down and smiles to himself. "Give it some time. It's kind of inevitable. It's okay. It's not a bad thing. I'm Nick, by the way."

"Wren."

"Okay, Birdie. See you around."

CHESTER IS READY FOR me when I reach the barn.

Mr. Kelley reminds me how to hold the reins (not the

Western way I'm used to) and sends me out to the track along the rail. "Wren, keep your inside leg on him, steady contact on your outside rein. Don't let him duck in toward the center of the ring. And look up. Look where you want to go."

I find even just walking takes such intense concentration that I stop thinking about Nick. So that's another plus to riding. When Mr. Kelley tells me we're ready to trot, I nudge my heels against Chester's sides. After a few tries, he breaks into a jagged, bumpy gait. It feels a little like someone grabbing me by the ankles and shaking me. The more I brace myself and try to sit still, the stronger the earthquake effect. I try to relax like Mr. Kelley says and let my weight sink down through my heels. Now I feel more like a swaying, sloppy belly dancer, but at least my bones have stopped rattling.

Mr. Kelley is patient. He explains how to post, rising with every other beat of the trot. It's much harder to get the rhythm right than it looks watching other people do it, but by the end of the hour, I catch it a few times. It feels like rattle, rattle, rattle, soft bump, soft bump, rattle, rattle. I end up sweaty, dusty, exhausted. My thigh muscles are shaking from holding on so tight. But mostly I just feel like I could sing right here in the middle of the riding ring and not care who hears me. Not even Nick.

AFTER MY LESSON, I stay to help feed and water the horses, so I'm late for dinner. There's no time to change. It's not a formal night, so that's okay. Sort of. When I sit down at the table with my roommates, the expensive shampoo smell rising off their wet, sleek hair seems to amplify my own horsey musk, and I wish I'd washed my face properly instead of just splashing hose water on it at the barn.

Lauren Benaceraf, one of the day students, is sitting at the table. She has musical theater practice some nights and stays for dinner. She's friendly with Eloise, but Honor ignores her, just like she ignores me. Still, Lauren puts a lot of effort into trying to make Honor like her. Or convincing herself that Honor likes her.

"If you guys want," Lauren says, "my mom says I can have some friends stay over Saturday night. We could do pedicures and watch a movie or something."

Honor smiles into her plate.

Eloise, off Honor's look, bows out. "Honor and I are going to the city. But thanks. That would be cool some other time."

"Bummer. I don't have a weekend pass left," says India.

I haven't been at school long enough to have one, either. You get one a month, and the first six weeks as a new student don't count. Besides, I'm not sure I'm included in the invitation anyway.

"I've never been to New York," I say, mostly to fill the silence. "Well, except for about five minutes on my way here. But that doesn't count. What are you guys going to do?"

I'm asking both Honor and Eloise, but Honor is suddenly too interested in who's entering the dining room to register the question. Eloise answers for her, like she's her translator or assistant or something. "Honor's dad is getting some big city award, and there's a party for him.

We're taking the train down with Ned. You should really go sometime. It's the best."

Ned is Honor's little brother, a First Year. The term is self-explanatory: they are the kids just starting Hardwick Hall, what in a normal school would be called ninth grade. The next year up is called Lower Year—my class—then Upper Year, then Last Year, the kids who are graduating. I've only met Ned once. He's a blonder, friendlier, spacier version of Honor. They look a lot alike.

India joins in. "I can't believe you've never been to the city. That's, like, seriously crazy. You totally have to go."

I shrug, staring at my plate. "My mom's kind of stuck with the West Coast since I was born. She's come back a few times for work. But I could never come with her. It was for investigative reporting jobs, not really a good time to go sightseeing."

One time was when she was covering a murder trial in San Diego that had a connection to a drug ring in New York. When she came back, she seemed really shaken up. I kept catching her staring at me in this really worried way. I asked if something happened while she was there, but she said no, it was just the details of this trial and worrying about me, out in the world, when I got old enough to be on my own.

"I think Greenland must be super amazing," India says. "Your mom is so lucky. It's so right on that she gets to go." India likes to makes a very big point of her interest in travel and environmental causes. She did some kind of junior Peace Corps thing last summer, so she asks me a lot about what my mom is up to. I've tried to explain it the best I can, though I don't completely understand it myself.

Mainly it has to do with this huge ice sheet. Scientists are looking at layers built up in the ice to try to figure out how the climate is changing and how fast the ice sheet is melting. The sheet is so big that if it melts too much, the sea level could rise almost twenty-five feet, and every coastal city in the world would end up underwater.

What's pretty clear from what Hannah says is that it's very cold—between minus twenty and minus fifty-five— and dangerous. The Explorer XO-565 lab is underground, under the ice, and there's a giant drill that digs down and removes layers of ice two hundred thousand years old.

"I don't know about lucky," I say. "She's stuck with ten scientists in a mobile lab way out on the ice sheet. It's risky. The ice can break, so they have to drill slowly, or else they could get buried."

"I can't imagine my mom ever doing anything like that," says Eloise. "First of all, something dangerous like that. She hates to drive in even an inch of snow. And she would never leave me and go somewhere that far away." She looks up abruptly. "I don't mean *leave* you. I just mean, my mom never really wanted to do anything besides have kids and stay home."

"It's okay," I tell her. The truth is, so far there have been many nights with me lying in my bed or up late studying when that was exactly what it felt like. A better offer came up, and poof, just like that, Hannah couldn't wait to go. No discussion of what I wanted.

When the feeling comes up—usually in the form of a

tightness in my stomach, a closing of my throat, a kind of tingling where my neck joins my head—I try to shake it off. I remind myself of the facts: Hannah has worked hard to become a journalist. She's been frustrated for a long time, feeling like she's not making any advances. She was brave to leave her family and start her own life with her own rules. She's always taken care of me.

I know this. I have always admired this. I've always thought that being independent is the most important thing. Living your own life above all else. In Ventura, I never thought about the other choices she might have made or what she left behind. And now here I am, flung into her past, walking in her footsteps. Footsteps she couldn't wait to erase, as far as I can tell. Did she really think Hardwick would be the best thing for me? Or just the most convenient thing for her?

It's new, this anger, this questioning her choices. I keep feeling around the edges of it like it's a loose tooth.

Honor is picking at her salad, bored, ready to move on to more interesting topics and more interesting people, when Nick walks up with his empty dinner tray. He's changed out of his crew clothes. His hair is wet, washed, still flopping across his eyes. Honor looks up and smiles like she hasn't been watching the door for the past few minutes. I'm done eating. I sit on my hands, trying to cover up the horsiest bits of exposed skin. There's not much I can do about my hair.

"H. You ready? We need to be in Baldwin in five."

"Yeah, yeah. Let's do it." Honor scrapes her chair back and picks up her half-eaten dinner. "See you guys back at the ranch." She nods to Eloise and India.

Nick smiles at the rest of us. "Girls. Birdie. Later."

"Bye, Nick." Eloise, India and Lauren wave.

I sit frozen. My face feels hot, sunburned, like it did the time I fell asleep on the beach in sixth grade. I see Honor take it in, half amused, half annoyed. I can still feel it after they're gone.

India looks at me. "Uh-oh. Another one bites the dust, huh?"

"Why, are they—?" I'm clearly the only one who has no idea what's going on. I need to find out if they're together as much as I need everyone not to know about my crush. "Are they in a study group together?"

"They're on the committee to pick music for the winter dance," Eloise says. "Or are you asking if they're together?"

"Um, both?"

"They went out last year. Now they're just really close friends."

"What does that mean?"

"It means he's not over Honor." India laughs.

"They're *friends*," insists Eloise. She must have the dirt on some more current conquest of Honor's. "Really."

What bugs me is that Honor doesn't even like music. I mean, she listens to the same, lame boarding-school classic rock that everyone else does—the same stuff my mom probably listened to when she was at Hardwick—and she's also up on current stuff that's considered cool, but she doesn't *like* it. She doesn't even think about it.

"Who are they getting? For the dance?"

"Don't know yet," says Eloise. "Tonight's the first meeting. Last year it was Brandon Collins."

Yikes. Brandon Collins is a "soulful" John Mayer-alike. "Really? For a dance?" I can't picture it.

"It was awesome," says India.

Eloise practically spits out her water. "India, how much of it do you even remember?"

They both laugh. I guess you had to be there.

I keep thinking, *Girls. Birdie. Girls. Birdie.* Meaning I'm not part of their group. Or meaning I'm special. I don't know.

LATER AT THE LIBRARY, it's too hard to concentrate. *Girls. Birdie. Girls. Birdie.* The words bounce back and forth across my brain like a tennis match. I push my books aside and start to wander, looking at the class photos that line the walls of the entry hall, going back to the 1890s.

I quickly home in on my mom's class photo from the year she graduated.

She looks pretty, freckled and relaxed, with that long, sleek, layered hair you see on actresses from that era. Julia Roberts and Uma Thurman and Claire Danes.

I start reading the long list of names along the bottom, looking to see if there's a Wren (there never is), or just to find out what kind of names the kids in my mom's day had. I try to guess which ones might have been Hannah's friends. Studious, bespectacled Esme? Sharp-eyed Caroline? Dreamy, distracted-looking Victoria? Paige, with her neat, no-nonsense bob? If they were her friends, she doesn't talk to or keep in touch with any of them now.

Then I notice something funny. Hannah's name is followed a little farther down the list by the name Edward

Gibson. He's handsome, but that's not why I'm drawn to his image. Honor's father? I can see the resemblance, or I think I can. He definitely shares her confidence. He seems anchored, relaxed, like he belongs where he is, and the rest of the picture has formed around him. And it's pretty common for alumni to send their own children to Hardwick. Still, that would be the craziest coincidence if our parents were in the same class, and now we are room-mates.

Instead of going back to the study carrel and my art history book—we're studying Mannerism, meaning ladies with olive skin and long, curvy necks staring out at you sideways—I sit down at the closest computer terminal and look up Edward Lawrence Gibson of New York, New York, Stone Cove Island, Massachusetts, and Amagansett, New York. Graduate of Hardwick Hall. Graduate of Princeton University. Married in 2000 to Annabelle Gibson née Bromley. Heir to the family business, the L.W. Gibson department store in New York.

Two children, Honor and Edward, Jr. Ned. I was right.

Divorced 2007. Lots of society party pictures, first with his wife (blonde, thin, knows how to pose for a photo), then without her. Some more recent party pictures with Honor alone, and with Honor and Ned.

I'm suddenly irritated that I'm spending time on this. Do I think somehow that because Hannah was classmates with Honor's father, Honor will like me now? Why can't I just not care that she doesn't? I stand up with resolve—not that anyone is watching—and force myself back to the study carrel.

Rosso Fiorentino, Alessandro Allori, Agnolo Bronzino, Benvenuto Cellini. I try to memorize the names in the book, turning them into a song in my head *Allori, Bronzino, Cellini . . . the Mannerist ABCs . . .*

THE NEXT NIGHT, I skip the library and go back to the barn after dinner instead. A bunch of girls are getting ready for a show the next day, and the horses need to be braided and have their legs wrapped in big padded shipping bandages before getting loaded onto the trailer in the morning.

There are about ten of us. I don't know how to braid—it's apparently a finicky, particular skill, requiring patience and precision—but I have offered to help clean tack and polish boots. It seemed like a good way to get out in the night air, away from studying and away from my room.

The moon is so full it lights the dirt aisle that runs down the center of the barn. The show horses are tied on each side of their halters to hooks outside the stalls; girls in rolled-up jeans stand on overturned buckets, their mouths and fingers deftly juggling bits of yarn, rug hooks and seam rippers. Eloise is among them. There's a crappy radio tuned to a classic rock station. The mood is festive. Mr. Kelley said good night an hour ago after making sure we all were assigned tasks.

In the tack room, Honor, India and I clean bridles. Actually, India and I clean, while Honor taps away at her cell phone and shows pictures to India. They giggle and gossip, and I listen, scrubbing the leather and squeezing out my sponge in the soapy water, wishing once again I wasn't one of the only students without a cell phone. My mom decided to be a big rule-follower on this, unlike just about every other Hardwick parent, apparently.

"Hey, hey there." I hear a husky voice, coming from outside the barn. A boy's voice. The rowers from the first boat are on their way back from double practice and have made a detour. We wander out to meet them, drawn like moths. I spot Nick first. Then his friends. Bennett Hale. Van Rowen Alder. They start chatting up the girls who are braiding; they joke around, threatening to splash us with dirty, soapy water. Nick grabs a polo wrap and starts tying Honor's arms to her body. I watch it all from my perch on a tack trunk.

"Who wants a ride?" Honor asks, untangling herself. She unclips Rainmaker, snaps a lead rope to his halter and swings her leg over his back right there in the barn.

"Honor," asks Eloise, "what are you doing?"

"It's fine," says India. "The floor's not hard. It won't hurt him."

"What about you, though?" says Missy Holt, a First Year. She's uptight, prissy, so this comes off less as concern and more as a scold. I learned from India that Hardwick recruited her as a champion pony hunter rider.

To answer, Honor wheels Rainmaker around and sets off down the dirt aisle bareback, at a trot. At the far end, they turn and canter back, stopping short in a cloud of dust.

"Dude," says India. "We just gave them baths, you know."

"Sorry." Honor grins, not looking sorry. "Who wants to ride with me?"

India snaps a lead onto a large pony named Sparkle

Plenty and hops on. "Whoa, he's sooo bumpy. I'm totally going to fall off."

"Your feet are practically touching the ground," says Honor. "El?"

Eloise shakes her head. "Two more to braid after this one. I'm going to be up all night."

"I will," says Nick.

"Yeah, right." Honor laughs.

"Hey, my uncle has a ranch out west. I've ridden."

"Take Jasper," says Honor, pointing to a skinny chestnut horse known to be cranky but reliable. He tries to nip Nick's leg as Nick grabs an overturned bucket to scramble on top of him.

Honor and Nick ride up and down the aisle, laughing at each other, pretending to race, Nick clinging to Jasper's mane. He pulls up near the tack room. "How about you, Birdie? Care for a ride?"

"I can't," I say, shaking my head. "I'm a total beginner." I know enough to tell that what they are doing is dangerous. And against the rules. It feels mischievous. I start to smile.

"Hop on," he says. "I'll take care of you. Jasper won't mind, will you, buddy?"

"I'll give you a leg up," says India. She's already returned Sparkle Plenty to his stall. Before I can answer, she's grabbed my knee and boosted me up so I'm sitting behind Nick on Jasper's smooth, warm back.

As I settle myself, I catch a flash of annoyance—or did I imagine it?—from Honor. She turns her attention back to Rainmaker. There is nowhere to hold on except around Nick's waist. I sit close to him and circle my arms around his stomach. It's hard to breathe. I'm trembling a little—so many things about this situation to feel nervous about—and I hope he can't tell.

"Ready?" he says. "Don't worry. I'll take care of you." He nudges Jasper, and we walk slowly up and down the aisle. I hang on. It's easier than I expected.

"Okay?" he asks.

I nod.

"Good. We're going for a trail ride. Be right back." Before I can stop him, he's steering Jasper through the big barn doors and outside into the warm night. It's beautiful. We circle the barn once in the dark. I watch the giant moon instead of the ground. It's utterly quiet except for the shuffle of Jasper's hooves through the grass.

When we reach the front of the barn again, Nick stops. "Nice. Thanks."

Is that it? I think as he signals for me to slide down. He hops off after me and hands me Jasper's lead rope. Then he walks back into the barn.

"Showing off your cowboy skills?" Honor calls. There's general laughter. I stand there in the dark, holding the horse. I'm not trembling anymore, but I have no idea what to do.

"Here," says India, coming out to meet me. "Want to put him back? He goes next to Sparkle. And then we should go." Only the braiders are allowed to stay past ten tonight. "Don't let him barge in past you. Walk in first and show him who's in charge. Make him wait."

I can't help but feel like Nick just did the same thing to me.

I follow India into the stall and learn how to take off Jasper's halter, where to hang it, how to check his hay and water.

"Bye, guys," calls India later, locking the tack room door. "Eloise, don't wake us up when you get back."

"As if," says Eloise. India not only snores, she is a ridiculously sound sleeper.

"Should we wait for Honor?" I ask.

"She went up already," says Eloise.

When I look around for Nick, he's gone too. "That ride was so crazy," I tell India, smiling to mask all the uncertainty bubbling inside me.

"Right?" she says, looking delighted. "Don't you just love it here?" She doesn't bother to wait for my answer.

CHAPTER FOUR

I Make a Friend

Friday nights at boarding school are a total washout. On a weeknight after dinner, kids are either studying or doing a club activity like campus radio or the theater group or chess; the list feels endless.

There are a cappella groups—Madrigals for boys and Chickadees for girls. Usually they perform under the echoey arches of the old buildings, which make everything sound prettier. The members appear to take it super seriously. I can't imagine anyone in Ventura being able to watch them with a straight face, much less wanting to join. But I always stop and listen.

Why does the boys' group get the respectable name and the girls' group the goofy name? That I can't tell you, except to say it figures.

Like every other night, the ultra-studious pore over schoolwork. Everyone else watches a movie in Baldwin Hall or TV in one of the dorm common rooms or just hangs out. A favorite activity: experimenting with the microwaves in the common room kitchens to see who can create the most gooey, extreme, gross-out dessert. None of it feels like my scene. The movie is usually some sucky Sandra Bullock romance, and the Selby kitchen just makes me homesick for good California food, like the tacos they make in the back of this liquor store on Ocean Avenue: warm and fresh, in tortillas some little old lady baked that morning, with spicy tomatillo sauce and crisp slivers of radish. Completely the opposite of goopy, hydrogenated, choco-corn-syrup crap whipped up by a bunch of giggly girls with flannel nightgowns and greasy hair.

By my fourth lame Friday, I decide there's no point in hanging around. I retreat with my new guitar, Humming-bird, to an empty common room on the first floor and puzzle out some songs. We're allowed to hang out in other dorms at night, as long as they are girls' dorms. The penalty for getting caught in a boys' dorm common room at night is not nearly as severe as getting caught in a boy's room with the door closed after visitation, which usually results in an immediate and permanent trip home. Not that I have to worry about that.

The armchairs and sofas—worn tweed and plaid with saggy centers—are terrible for guitar playing. I perch on the end of one sofa, close enough to the wall that I can brace my toes against it and balance the guitar. I stare out the window absently. I'm about to strum when a pale, panicked face pops up against the black nothing. I almost jump out of my skin.

It's a boy about my age or a little older. I don't recognize him from my year. He has dark hair and an impish face. All at once he starts banging on the window—*loudly*. It's enough to disturb anyone in Selby who's trying to sleep or study, not to mention our housemother. I open it just to keep both of us from getting in trouble.

"Thanks," he says. He has the subtlest hint of a Southern accent. He scrambles in and somersaults awkwardly onto the sofa beside me.

"Hi," I say, for lack of anything more inspired.

"I skipped Madrigals. I'm supposed to be in bed sick. Just saw Rivington coming across the quad and had to go into major avoid mode. I hope I didn't scare you. It's a little Halloween or something, appearing in the window like that."

Rivington is the housemaster of Meade House, which I just happen to know is Nick's dorm. "But you're not sick."

"I'm sick of warbling show tunes with a bunch of pansy-asses." This seems funny coming from a boy who—now that I get a better look at him—is slender, only slightly taller than me and has a ruby-colored mouth that could only be described as pretty. I bet he was mistaken for a girl all the time until he got zits and his voice changed.

"I'm not interrupting, am I? Chazzy, by the way." He shakes my hand, formal but relaxed.

Who does he remind me of? Peter Pan, maybe? Little Jackie Paper, who loved that rascal Puff? "Wren. You're not. Interrupting, I mean. I'll try not to warble."

"And I'll try not to make any bird jokes, Wren."

"Much appreciated."

"So go on," he says.

I'm not used to an audience. I hesitate.

"Go on." He sits up straighter. "I'll even sing with you if you promise no *Frozen* or *Phantom of the Opera.*"

"What about Baird?" I whisper. Mrs. Baird is our house-mother, unpredictably attentive, but not to be crossed in the wrong mood.

"I'll sing falsetto," he says. "She'll never notice. Or maybe she'll join us?"

"Yeah," I say, laughing at the mental picture. "She's awesome. You've seen her at vespers. She really rocks."

"No doubt. So, what have you got?"

I start in on "Red Vines," an Aimee Mann song that's one of her bigger hits. It's weirdly intimate to sing in front of a total stranger, but for some reason I surprise myself and don't care. Maybe because it all feels a bit surreal: a pixieish elf somersaults into your life and demands music.

He nods in time as I strum. "Cool," he says. "I only know the chorus of that one, but it'll work."

I sing a little of the first verse quietly, because I'm still not convinced we're safe from Baird. Chazzy joins in on the parts he knows and fakes the others. He harmonizes in an effortless way that makes it clear he either has perfect pitch or years of training or both. No wonder he's in the Madrigals. It's fun. I usually don't have anyone to play with.

Midway through, he stops.

"I know. Oh, I know what we need to do. This is brilliant. Follow me." Before I can answer, he's up and climbing back out the window. "Pass me the guitar."

"What?" There's no way I am sending Hummingbird out into the darkness with this strange boy.

"I'll be careful. Trust me. This'll make your Friday night."

"That wouldn't be hard," I tell him.

He laughs. "And I promise we won't get caught."

In hindsight, I wonder why I believed he could make a promise like that. But it was also the first actual invitation I'd gotten to do anything in the four weeks I'd been at Hardwick, other than an occasional "we're going to dinner" from my roommates. And that qualified more as an announcement than an offer, since they didn't care that much whether I joined them or not.

I hop out and land a little awkwardly half in a bush, struggling to protect Hummingbird and not lose my balance.

Outside the air is cool. There's a mist creating halos around the campus lights peppered here and there. I can hear muffled laughter from Baldwin Hall, where the Friday night movie is playing.

I brush myself off and look around. "What's Chazzy short for?" I ask.

"Charles Moorehead Robinson the Third."

"Oh," I say.

"You asked."

"So where are we going?"

"It's a surprise. But you'll need the guitar."

I'm wishing I had a jacket. I'm still getting used to the cold weather, and I never have the right thing on. Like now: I'm wearing faded paisley-print pajama bottoms, low-top sneakers (no socks), and a long-sleeved black waffle-knit T-shirt. My hair is still wet from the shower I took after dinner. But Chazzy turns out to be such a fast walker that I soon warm up. By the time we reach the woods on the west side of campus, I'm almost sweating.

"I thought you were worried about Rivington," I whisper,

peering into the blackness beyond the trees. "Seriously, where are you taking me?"

"We're halfway there. Promise. I just didn't want to go out the main driveway to the road. We can get there through the woods. It's really close."

"Out? We're leaving campus?"

"Wren, I got it. Really."

I trip after him along a narrow but worn trail. I'm feeling more confident that he's not a teen serial killer or vampire now that I see other kids have used this same route to break out. Soon we're walking along the two-lane road into Falls Village, ducking back under the trees whenever we see headlights. Only a couple of cars pass us. It's quiet. I take in the lacy iron gate of the Grassy Hill Cemetery as the road dips down and forks: right, under the railroad bridge and to the river, or left, past the inn onto Main Street.

"I think we should practice on the way," says Chazzy.

"Practice what?"

"Do you know any less obscure stuff? Beatles? Neil Young? Something popular like that?"

"Sure. 'Cowgirl in the Sand?' Or 'She Said, She Said?' Elliott Smith? The Civil Wars?"

"Fine. Can you walk and play at the same time?"

"Not really. Maybe if you slow down a little."

Now I can see the center of Falls Village where our road meets Main Street, a street too quiet to require a stoplight. A few old-fashioned storefronts glow dimly. It's a short block, with only a handful of businesses, the town hall, and the former savings bank, pretty as a doll's house. You feel like you're in one of those old Christmas movies or something, and Bing Crosby or Barbara Stanwyck is about to walk out of the general store. Chazzy has a nice voice. I sing along, kind of forgetting where I am.

"Nice," approves Chazzy when we finish.

"Too poular?" I ask.

"Nah. Just because it won a grammy doesn't mean it's not good. They'll love it."

They?

I'M STANDING WITH CHAZZY in front of the coffee house on Main Street. It looks pretty busy for Falls Village, even by Friday night standards.

"You ready?" he asks.

"Guess so, since I don't know what I have to be ready for." I follow him in.

A girl in a fringe cowboy jacket and long hippie hair walks over to us with a clipboard. "Name?" she asks Chazzy.

He hesitates. "Uh, Birdbrain."

"Okay," she says. "You can be next." And walks away.

"Next?" I say to Chazzy, but he's already dragging me toward the "stage," two bar stools pulled in front of the barista setup. It looks suspiciously like an open mic night. Oh, God. Suffice it to say, at this point I have played for my mother, my cats and friends I can count on one hand—including Chazzy. An entire room of people turns to stare at me while the cowboy coat girl introduces us as Bird-brain.

"I could kill you right now," I say through my teeth.

Chazzy gives me a huge grin. "Isn't this fun?"

I don't bother to answer, because it's too late to do anything about it. Suddenly we're on, singing our one half-practiced-on-the-way-over song.

At first I'm not sure who bothers me more, the people watching us, or the people not watching: drinking, talking and laughing as though we're not up here exposing our deepest, darkest souls. But after a minute, some of them start watching instead of talking.

When a few people start to sing along, something shifts. It feels amazing. Amazing, like nothing I have ever felt before. I feel like I'm floating above my own head, watching myself sing, hearing my voice outside and inside at the same time. I can hear how it joins and separates from Chazzy's, as though I'm watching the show through my own eyes and from outside, like a movie.

And then it's over.

Everyone claps. I squint under the lights, unable to keep from grinning. One person yells, "Wooo!" and someone else, "Play another one!" The cowboy coat girl nods, and Chazzy and I look at each other. We only practiced the one song. But I don't want to stop yet.

"'Red Vines'?" he mouths.

I shrug and start into it. It's not until halfway through the first verse that it occurs to me that Chazzy doesn't know the words, and it's only my voice I'm hearing both inside and outside my head. Panic flutters in my belly. My voice wavers as it hits one of the upper range notes, and I know I have to refocus. I force myself to look at one thing, a red candle flickering on a table near the center of the room. I consider picking a person to look at, but

I'm worried they will get wigged out thinking I'm singing the song to just them, and that will in turn wig me out. I keep singing.

The rest of the room recedes, and the inside/outside voice thing stops. Chazzy's voice comes in at all the right places, and before you know it, we reach the end, and there's more clapping and it's all okay. More than okay.

AS I FOLLOW CHAZZY to the door, people smile, nod or pat our shoulders, saying, "All right. Nice."

Outside I'm beaming. My skin feels hot. "I can't believe we just did that," I say.

"I know." He's grinning again too. "Now we just have to figure out how to get back to school on time."

"What? You promised we wouldn't get in trouble." My glow evaporates. I've only been at Hardwick for a month, and whatever mixed feelings I have about being here, I do not want to get kicked out. I *can't*. Where would I go?

"It's trickier once it's this close to check-in. But we'll be fine. Will your roommates cover for you if we don't make it?"

"Oh my God. What time is it?"

"Quarter of ten."

"Check-in is in fifteen minutes. I have no idea if they'll cover. Maybe India. I don't think Honor would. I don't know about Eloise. If she's with Honor, no."

"Well, let's go. We can be there in fifteen."

"Chazzy, no, we can't!"

"We have to be," he says, starting up the main street.

On the way back, every car sends us hustling into the

brush; it could be a search party from Hardwick. Stumbling through the woods, I skin my shin and scrape my arms on branches. I hug Hummingbird protectively, trying not to ding her against a tree.

Chazzy finally leads me back to Selby and gives my hand a squeeze. "That was excellent. I wish Gigi could have seen us."

"Who's Gigi?" I ask.

"Are you kidding? I thought you were into music."

"That doesn't answer my question."

"More on that next time. Okay, try the kitchen door. Best of luck." I make out his smile in the dark, and then he's gone. Silently, like Peter Pan.

I sneak in through the kitchen door, hoping not to catch Mrs. Baird mid–tea preparation. The coast is clear on the stairs and in the hall on our floor. Mrs. Baird must be in someone's room. Hopefully not in *our* room. I'm in pajama bottoms; maybe I can pretend I was just in the bathroom. Except I have a guitar, not my toothbrush. Best just to run up the stairs and pray. I manage to reach our room without seeing her and open the door as quietly as I can.

India is asleep, breathing loudly. The door to Eloise's and Honor's room is almost closed, but I hear someone sit up in bed. The light stays out.

"Eloise?" I call hopefully.

"She's asleep," Honor answers. No surprise. Eloise goes to bed the earliest of any of us, unless she's studying for a test or finishing a paper.

"Oh, hi. Did Mrs. Baird come by already?"

"Yeah. She was just here."

"Did you say anything?"

"What was I supposed to say?"

"Oh. Will she come back? Should I go tell her I'm here?" Would that be worse? To leave our room after check-in? I really don't know.

"If you want. Night," Honor says with finality.

"Good night," I say, climbing into bed. I roll over on my belly, wondering how much trouble I will be in tomorrow.

CHAPTER FIVE

I Make an Enemy

The next morning, there's nothing to do but wait for the ax to fall. It's quiet in our room. We have half-day classes on Saturdays, so we're expected to be up bright and early and at breakfast just like any other day. When I come out to the sitting room with my bath bucket, only Honor is there, pulling on her coat. She gives me the tiniest nod, barely raising her head.

"Hi," I say, my voice coming out at half its normal volume.

"So where were you last night?" she asks. Her cold look is contempt mixed with something else. Could she be curious? Threatened? Impressed? It's impossible to know.

Ridiculous, I tell myself, feeling angry I'm more afraid of Honor than our housemother.

She doesn't bother to wait more than a second for me to answer before she turns to go—until something stops her. Her eyes flick in a momentary double-take. "Where did you get that?" she snaps.

"What?" I ask.

"The charm. On your necklace." Her voice is even harsher than usual.

"My mother," I answer, not understanding the sudden storm behind her eyes. She's furious. It makes no sense.

"Are you kidding? Are you kidding me?" I can see tears rising, pure rage. I haven't seen that much emotion in Honor's face ever, and I have no idea where it's coming from now. She closes her eyes, tenses her jaw and swings away from me, letting the door slam behind her.

I stand in the room alone, shell-shocked. Crying seems reasonable, except that I wouldn't know what I was crying about. I decide I'll call Hannah, because even though she has no connection to my roommates or what just happened, she *is* connected to Hardwick. She's responsible for what happens to me, isn't she? Even if she's not here? Even if she has no idea what's going on in my life? And I have no one else to talk to.

Outside there's a steely chill, a preview of winter. Sorry; I said up front I wouldn't harp on details about the weather, but when you come from California, where there is no weather—only the occasional natural disaster—these things stand out. I'm curious about snow and looking forward to it, though it's only October.

I wonder if I'll still be here for the first snowfall.

IN THE DINING HALL, Eloise and India are sitting together with some girls from the field hockey team whose names I don't know. Honor joins them with a tray of granola and coffee. It seems glamorous to me, drinking coffee. I don't like it, even the smell of it, but I feel like that's something I should work on.

The table's only half full. I head for the line slowly and take a tray. If I seriously dawdle, maybe some more of Honor's acolytes will fill the empty seats, and I won't have to sit with them. On my way I pass a table full of teachers, and Mrs. Baird is one of them. She looks up as I go by and gives me the same half-encouraging, half-pitying smile she always gives me. And that's it. I nod hello and take a stack of tepid pancakes, even though they're only good if you seriously smother them in syrup.

From across the room, Chazzy catches my eye. He's sitting with a bunch of boys from Madrigals. They all have this particular look, scarves draped around their blazers, hair parted to one side and pushed back across the other, obviously requiring gel of some kind. Smooth skin. Expressive, theatrical faces. It's all very Gatsby. Chazzy raises his eyebrows at me. He looks concerned rather than impish this morning. Well, maybe a little impish, perhaps mixed with a little guilt? I shrug my shoulders to say, "Seems okay."

I have no choice. I sit next to India, positioning myself as far away from Honor as I can. I consider sitting alone, starting a new table, even though it's against the rules. But that seems like admitting guilt, and I have no idea what I'm guilty of. Honor doesn't look at me as I sit down. She's telling a story to some field hockey girls, blonde girls, the kind of New England blonde where the hair seems washed of color, thick, dry and straight, like bleached wheat. They are engrossed, their faces pale and soft, pink blotching their cheeks, and they laugh in unison at Honor's story when she gets to a good part.

Why do they look alike? They aren't related. They

probably aren't even from the same state. All three of them are wearing their team sweatshirts and jeans, half ready for the game against Taft this afternoon. Honor's dressed in layers of thin, ruffle-edged T-shirts and a cashmere cardigan. A long, complicated necklace of ribbons, knots and pearls dangles around her neck.

She always has a city gloss the other girls don't, hair that falls and swings just right, a sparkle to her eye where the field hockey girls' eyes are pale ice blue and blank. Honor has been to debutante balls, nightclubs, parties in unsupervised Park Avenue apartments. This particular story seems to involve all three.

When she gets to the part where her shoe heel gets stuck in the taxi and she leaves it there, walking barefoot to the after-party at Daniel Boulud's restaurant, I find myself laughing with the rest of them, though I don't want to. Honor's a good storyteller. The maître d' tries to stop her on the way in, but luckily Chef Daniel himself walks out, and since he knows her father, he tells her she can stay— but to hide in the coat check if anyone from the health department shows up.

Then, a boy shows up with her shoe. He saw it fall from the cab onto the sidewalk, and he chased after her—so here he is, crashing an after-party at 2 A.M., trying to find the girl with one shoe. Of course, it turns out he's really cute, and the older brother of a boy in our grade at Collegiate, so she lets him put the shoe back on. They dance, with Honor as Cinderella, hobbling and tipsy and radiant (she doesn't say "radiant," but you can tell you're supposed to picture it like that). Then they end up at his place. They're still friends; he might come up to a dance later this month.

"Oh, yeah? Does Nick know about that?" asks a field hockey girl.

My ears prick up.

"Sure. Why would he care?" Honor asks with faux innocence. "We're just friends." Is it her fault if she leaves a wake of broken hearts? All she wants is to *be friends*. With boys, with girls, with everyone except me.

AFTER BREAKFAST, I HAVE American history with Eloise, so we walk together to Baldwin Hall. I want to ask her what I've done to make Honor so angry, but somehow it seems like a better idea to try to figure it out myself. Besides, I'm embarrassed to admit to Eloise that I've done something wrong and don't even know what it is.

"Where were you, anyway?" Eloise asks. "India and I came back from the bathroom and you weren't there. We told Baird you were brushing your teeth."

"Thanks." So that's why Baird was okay with me this morning. I want to tell Eloise where I was. I want to trust her, but I don't trust her not to tell Honor.

"What happened with Honor?" she asks as if reading my mind. "She's in a real snit about you."

"I have no idea," I tell her truthfully. So much for keeping it to myself.

Eloise purses her lips, looking sorry for me, like Honor being mad at me is about as bad as failing math or getting diagnosed with mono. "I'll try to find out. I'll talk to her."

"Thanks," I say. It's implied that it's up to me to figure

it out and fix it, which annoys me. We walk in silence for a few minutes.

"Wren, I feel bad about that thing I said the other night about your mother abandoning you," says Eloise. "Lots of kids are here for lots of reasons. I shouldn't assume things about your family. It sounds like you and your mom are really close."

A month ago, I would have said, "We are," with no hesitation. I say it now, but the words sound hollow. Since I've been here, I've started to feel like I'm looking at everything in my life backward, as though I've seen it reflected in a mirror in one direction, and now I'm looking at it from the other side.

Before Hannah left for Greenland, it was just the two of us. It felt like a team, like we didn't need anyone else. Now at school, I see my circumstances the way they must appear to the others. My mother's secret, which was mostly a joke or irritation to me before, seems like something much bigger. If I had a father, I think, I would be at home now. If I had a father, there would be someone else to take care of me. If I had a father—and I must have one, right?—if I had a father, Hannah would not be making all the decisions about my life on her own.

"Eloise, I can't believe you're still worried about that," I add, making my voice light. "Really. I didn't take it that way at all."

"Okay, good," she says. She looks relieved and gives my wrist a squeeze. "My family's just so super normal, you know? You'll have to come visit us some weekend. You can meet them."

MOST OF THE CLASSROOMS in Baldwin are small; the teacher and the students, usually ten or twelve of us, sit around a long oval table. That means that no one is sitting at the head, and the idea is that class is a conversation among all of us, that we are teaching one another. Hardwick is very proud of this method of instruction, which I've since learned is called Harkness Teaching. In Ventura, there is no "method." Classrooms are big, about thirty kids, and we sit at old green metal desks with thick, splintering wood tops lined up in rows. At Hardwick, it's much harder to doodle on your sneaker, text friends, chew gum, or skip the reading. Unfortunately, because of my sudden detour into show business last night, today I have not done the reading for American history.

I have two options. The first is to sit quietly, look interested and take notes. Lots of people do this. If you feel like it's been way too long since you said anything, comment on another student's comment. If you look too interested, the teacher will call on you, thinking you have something to contribute. If you are too quiet, the teacher will call on you, thinking you are shy and hoping to draw you out and allow you to enjoy the full potential of your educational experience.

Thankfully I don't have to do either, because Van Rowen Alder has gone with option number two: talking nonstop. I mean, he is so practiced at serious bullshit he'll fill a good thirty of the fifty minutes. I have to question what the teacher has vested in letting it go on so endlessly

(Relaxing break? Comic relief?), but today Van is saving me with his blather. His voice drones on as my attention tunes in and out.

I worry. Will Honor turn me in for being out last night? Is there any way she could find out where Chazzy and I really went? Why is she so mad at me? What did I *do*, anyway?

MY RIDING LESSON IS at noon. Mr. Kelley still has me in private lessons until I can catch up with the advanced beginners. I know it doesn't sound like much, but I'm pretty excited to be considered an advanced anything on a horse.

Chester is busy today, so I'm riding a horse named Stormy. Stormy is a flashy black mare with a jagged blaze like a lightning bolt down her face. Her ears flick and dance a little nervously as Mr. Kelley helps me on, but she's quiet and responsive as we walk in a big circle, sticking to one end of the ring. Her trot is springier than I'm used to, and I have to concentrate on pulling my spine tall and straight—while at the same time relaxing my lower back—when I really want to brace myself and cling to her mane.

"Good," says Mr. Kelley, appreciating my efforts. "Now drop your stirrups and keep everything else the same."

"What?!" I can't help blurting this out, though it's a universal rule of riding that you don't talk back when an instructor tells you to do something.

"Just let your toes slip out, and let your legs and heels hang a little longer."

I do it, though if I were allowed to comment, I would

say it seems a little crazy. To my surprise, the bouncing diminishes, and instead I feel a fluid connection through my back to the horse. It feels like riding a boat through a slight wake. I grin. I can't help it. This is way too much fun to be cool about it.

"Now," says Mr. Kelley, "toes up, and find your stirrups." I look down, fumbling for the stirrups, and start bouncing again. "WITHOUT LOOKING DOWN," he bellows. I pull my head back up and try by feel. It's not easy, but eventually I get my toes wedged back in so that the ball of my foot is back on the metal stirrup. I'm breathing hard from the effort.

"Shorten your reins and organize your trot. Outside leg back. Feel your inside rein. And canter."

I try to follow each step. When Stormy trots faster, I dig my outside heel in a little harder, and the rough bouncing turns to a smooth rocking-horse canter, with an arching lift to the upbeat each time she pushes off her hind legs.

It's all going so well until a bird pecking at something in the grass outside the ring decides to swoop through the fence and right under Stormy's belly. Stormy flings her body sideways in a midstride panic and the saddle vanishes right out from under me. Suddenly I'm sitting on her neck instead of where I should be. I shove myself back and throw both arms around Stormy, trying to stay on.

"Turn her. Sit up! Wren, don't drop your reins!"

It's way too late for that. I look down and see the dirt sweeping by underneath me. That's alarming, so I lift my head and stare into the horse's neck instead, black horse hair and a tangle of mane rubbing roughly against my nose.

Luckily Stormy slows down, and when I can't hang on any longer, I drop with a thud to the ground. It seems to happen in slow motion. I'm surprised it doesn't hurt. My shoulder lands first in the dirt, and I roll onto my back, feeling the wind shoved from my lungs. Stormy, over it at this point, trots to the center and stops right in front of Mr. Kelley, looking bored.

I sit up. Standing along the rail are Eloise, India and, naturally, Honor.

"Ha! You're baptized, my girl!" Mr. Kelley laughs. "You okay?"

"Yeah. I think so," I answer, feeling like a fool. I try to turn away from my suitemates, but I can feel them watching me.

"You okay?" Eloise echoes. Honor looks away, smirking.

"That was pretty, but you should have seen this one eat it last week." Mr. Kelley waves a hand at India, who giggles. "A beauty if I ever saw one. Right. Hop back on."

I don't want to, but I know it's what you're supposed to do. So I do, and then it's all fine again. Part of the experience, right? When I turn back to the rail, the girls are gone.

BEFORE DINNER I GET an email from my mom. She usually emails me windows of time when she'll be at the lab, so we can Skype. It's tricky with the time change. I dial the number, because if I wait until after dinner it will be too late for her.

Last week she sent me a really cool T-shirt with the Greenland flag, a red-and-white rectangle with a red-and-white circle in the middle, split down the center. If Chazzy and I ever brave that open mic again, I think I'll wear it.

We don't get to talk often enough, but when we do, Hannah is full of interesting facts about Greenland—like that it's the largest island in the world. The center will end up underwater, like a donut, if the glacier melts. The ice sheet is the size of Mexico. I think she saves these facts up for our conversations. Not that we have nothing to talk about; we do.

I'm lucky I have a mom like Hannah, I remind myself. But she's far away and I'm in a strange place, so it's different. I can't talk to her about what is really going on because I don't want her worrying about me. I know she feels sort of bad for sending me away, though she says she's convinced it's a great thing for me. I'm afraid if we talk too much about school and home that I'll get mad or say something I don't mean. Or that I do mean.

Anyway, there's no point talking about something when I don't even know what I think about it. And I don't want her to think I'm some miserable, homesick loser, even though the evidence might point to that. So I'm not going to talk to her about Honor.

"Wren, what is on your face?"

It's the very first thing Hannah asks me. Her own face is very pink. She complains about having chapped lips and hands and cheeks.

"My face? Oh, dirt, I guess." I neglected to wash my face or even look in the mirror when I came in.

"Dirt?"

"I fell off during my riding lesson. No big deal, though. I'm fine."

"You fell off? Yikes. What happened? Are you sure you're okay?"

"Yeah, no, the horse spooked at a bird and surprised me. I mean, we were both surprised."

She seems to be squinting at me through the screen, across the ocean. "Be careful. I'm a long way away to come pick up the pieces . . ."

"I don't think Mr. Kelley will let anything happen. He's pretty careful."

"I hope. So everything else good? You're having fun with your roommates? Finding time to play music?"

Having fun with my roommates? I skip to question two.

"Yeah. I met a boy who plays. I'm going to try to get into his music class. You're supposed to audition at the beginning of the year, but since I wasn't here I'm hoping I can convince Gigi—she's this amazing teacher—"

"Gigi? She's still there? She's a legend," says Hannah.

"You took her class?"

"Oh, no way; I wasn't good enough. But she was my advisor, so I got to know her pretty well. You met a boy?" she adds, sounding excited.

"Not like that. Just a boy. Friend-type of boy." I haven't told her about Nick, and I'm not planning to, since at this point there's nothing to tell.

"Friend-types of boys often make the best boyfriends, you know."

"I know. I mean, I know you think so."

"So what's his name?"

"Chazzy."

"Chazzy?"

"Charles Moorehead Robinson the Third."

"Oh, of course it is. Well, I see Hardwick Hall hasn't changed that much since I was there. Where's he from?"

"Chapel Hill, North Carolina. What do you mean, it hasn't changed? Your boyfriends here had names like that?"

"I didn't have boyfriends. I was much too busy studying," she says with a smile.

"Right."

"But yes, lots of people had names like that. I was hoping things had gotten a little more, I don't know, modern?" She throws me a hopeful look.

"Not so much."

"No people of color?"

"Mom, no. I mean, yes, not all the kids are white, but I don't think the ones that aren't really want to be considered 'people of color.' I think they just think of themselves as kids."

"Wren, you know it's really important to embrace people's individuality and differences—"

"Mom, this is high school," I interrupt. "Do you remember high school?"

"A little bit, thank you very much," she says, sounding mock hurt.

"Did you want to be embraced for your differences?"

"Yes."

"Really?" I don't believe her.

"I think I did. Deep down. Yes."

"Well, I guess I would rather mine not stand out so much."

"Wren. I didn't send you there for you to learn to be conventional. You're there to stretch your wings. *Your* wings. Not somebody else's wings."

"Okay. Gotcha. So far today I have stretched my butt by falling on it."

"Well, that's a good start. Have you gotten in touch with Warren?"

"Who?"

"Warren Norwood. My friend. The director I told you about. You should really write him or call. See if you can meet up."

Oh, right. That guy. Meeting up would not be first on my list, but it seems important to her for some reason. "Okay."

"Good." She opens her mouth as if to add something, but decides against it. "We're in the field for the next couple of days, then back in the lab. So I can talk then. Wednesday. Or Thursday, probably."

"Bye, Hannah." I say.

"Bye, Wrendle."

She waits for me to log out first. The window closes, and the screen is filled with that generic, big-blue-marble Earth shot. I look at North America. I am far away from California and far away from Greenland. Somewhere in the middle. Hanging around. I open a new browser and type in the web address for Jonesy's bookstore.

This time, I don't have to search archived photos, because I see that Jonesy has started a blog. Actually, Jonesy has started a blog starring Spite and Malice. He is a nut, but it is fairly hilarious. First he shot them behind the cash register and in the shelves as though they run the store. No idea how he got them to do that because Spite and Malice, as you might guess, follow directions about as well as cats. Next he has given them each their own page for reviews and recommendations. I see that Spite has gotten into cooking and nonfiction, whereas Malice is specializing in current fiction, self-help and children's books. Jonesy's even convinced some poor authors to let the cats "interview" them.

I can see from the flashing counter on the webpage that I am the two hundred and ninety-first person to visit this week. I guess that's pretty good, right? Anyway, I'm glad the cats are earning their keep.

I want to skip dinner, but it's a formal night, so I take a quick shower, put on a skirt and join the later seating.

After first making sure Honor's nowhere in sight, I find a table with a girl from my biology class and some other kids I don't know. We eat quietly. There's some chitchat about lab reports. Another boy from biology joins and asks to borrow notes from last Saturday's class because he had to miss it for an away lacrosse game at the Lyme School. I'm distracted, so I don't respond quickly enough, and someone else offers. I'm replaying the scene with Honor in my head for the hundredth time. Why did she freak out like that so suddenly? What could I have done to her?

It turns out I don't have to wait much longer to find out. Mrs. Baird stops me on the way out of the dining hall. She looks uncomfortable as she gestures toward the coatroom off the entry lobby. "Wren, can I see you for a moment?"

I follow her in, and she closes the door behind us, looking a little pained.

"Wren, I know you haven't been here long enough to know all the rules of conduct at Hardwick," she begins, "and I certainly think you've been an exemplary student thus far."

"Thanks. Is something wrong?" I really don't want her to drag this out longer than absolutely necessary. She must know I was out last night.

"There has been a serious accusation. It's serious enough to call for the disciplinary committee to meet. Do you know what I'm talking about?"

"No," I say, though I think I do. It's about where I was last night.

"A piece of jewelry." Her eyes stray to my neck. "Honor has a charm that is quite valuable and important to her family." She looks up at me, meeting my gaze. "It's missing, and she, uh, believes you may have taken it."

"Are you serious?" I blurt before I can stop myself. I guess that's the answer to why Honor's so mad at me, but I have no idea how she could think I did that. Or that I would ever do that. It makes no sense. She didn't tell Baird I snuck out; instead she made up some lie about how I stole my own necklace?

"I didn't take anything from her," I quickly add, noting Baird's scowl. "My mother gave this necklace to me when I was twelve. I haven't taken it off since. It belonged to my great-grandmother. I wear it every day. You can ask anyone. Honor is . . ." I hesitate, searching for the right word, the right phrase. "Wrong. About this."

"I'm sure we'll resolve it," Baird says, clearly not wanting to hear too many of the details. "I came to tell you that the disciplinary committee meeting is next Wednesday, following chapel. We'll have to bring it to them if you and Honor can't resolve this on your own. It will be held in the headmaster's library. Do you know where that is?"

I nod.

"I will be there as housemother. Honor will also be there as well as the members of the disciplinary committee."

This committee, I already know, is made up of teachers and students: a combo of do-gooders and the power-hungry. All I can think is, I have only been here a month, and I'll end up getting kicked out for a crime I didn't even commit. My mother will be so disappointed in me . . .

"As I said, I'm sure we can resolve this, Wren," Baird says. Then she turns back to the dining hall, giving me a final closed-lipped smile. I'm dismissed.

"Okay," I say. I want to go back to my room before I start crying. On the other hand, I never want to go back to my room.

Next Wednesday. I have to live with Honor with this hanging over me until next Wednesday.

AS THE HEAVY DOUBLE doors of the dining hall clank shut behind me, I can just make out Honor's blonde ponytail and the swish of India's patterned skirt disappearing up ahead on the path. I slow down and let them get far enough ahead to be out of sight.

Under the arched arcade that runs along the chapel, the Madrigals are gathered in the center of a crowd, dressed in their piped navy jackets. Chazzy sees me and gives a quick nod, but his attention quickly turns to the performance. It looks like half the school is here, a big turnout.

The Madrigals move from show tune to jazz standard to a-cappella-adapted rock song to hymn. They stand in a semicircle, switching spots as different boys take the lead. They are all really, really good singers, but Chazzy is great. It's amazing; it feels like this scene could have been pulled from any point in the school's history—this same sound, filling this same arch, reverberating year after year, made by different boys, in a place that never changes.

CHAPTER SIX

Black Anchors

On Monday I wake up feeling terrible, an *oh-no* pit in my stomach as soon as my eyes register daylight. Fortunately there is no one else in the room. I have a few minutes to pull myself together and figure out how to face the day.

When I come back to the room after taking my shower, there is a note under my door. I pick it up, and my stomach lurches into free fall. It's from Nina Taubin. She's the head of the disciplinary committee. Ms. Taubin doesn't even teach any of my classes. I only know who she is from chapel; she usually reads announcements. She purses her bright red lips, raises her eyebrows and stares from behind heavy-rimmed glasses, waiting for absolute silence before she begins.

Wren,
Please stop by to see me at my residence at your convenience.
Thank you.
Nina Taubin

Somehow I doubt she is actually concerned with my convenience. Baird already told me the disciplinary committee isn't meeting until Wednesday. Did Ms. Taubin decide the issue was too important to wait until then? Or is this about open mic night? I flash back to the road and walking with Chazzy in the dark. Any of the cars passing us could have belonged to Ms. Taubin. Not to mention all the other ways I gave myself away: the heavy back door of Selby slamming behind me—which probably alerted the whole house to my lateness—or scurrying through the halls with my guitar instead of my toothbrush or deciding not to find Mrs. Baird and check in late, worried about what Honor would think of me for not knowing what to do.

Stupid. How could I have been so stupid? What is Hannah supposed to do if I get sent home? Quit her job? I can prove I didn't steal Honor's necklace, but I can't prove I didn't sneak off campus.

I decide my "convenience" involves getting this over with as quickly as possible. I am not allowed to skip breakfast, so I go, but I'm too nervous to eat. I also have to go to French, but after that, I plan to stop by Ms. Taubin's house and see if she's there. Many of the teachers at Hardwick who have been here awhile get their own faculty houses, cute little cottages at the edge of campus near the woods—the woods! She could have actually seen me from her house, leaving with Chazzy. I am never doing something like that again.

Eloise and Honor pass me on their way to the dining hall. I am still clutching the note. Honor cranes her neck to read it over my shoulder.

"Taubin, huh? You're in even more trouble?" she asks. She glares at me. I can almost hear her spitting the word: *Thief.* I will not, will not, will not cry. Or even look upset. But from her reaction, I know I do.

"Why do you think Ms. Taubin wants to see me?" I ask Eloise. "Could it be some kind of new student thing?"

"I guess," says Eloise diplomatically, by which she means no.

IN FRENCH, CHAZZY TRIES to get my attention. He is sitting next to me, but I am trying very hard to look like I am a model student in the few remaining hours I may have here. *What's up? Are you okay?* he writes on the palm of his hand.

I shrug and scribble a note on my own hand. *I'm busted.*

He raises his eyebrows. *The other night?* he writes.

Taubin. I reply.

No! he scrawls.

After class he tries to catch up to talk, but I scoot away. I am determined to end the suspense and put myself out of my agony. It's too awful, thinking about how I will explain this to Hannah.

It's a cold day. My breath is steaming behind me as I hurry up the drive that leads to the faculty houses. Ms. Taubin's is on the end. I can see smoke from her fireplace trailing up from her chimney. I guess that means she's there. (There's no Mr. Taubin as far as I know.) I knock, trying to keep my hands from shaking. The door swings open, and warm, slightly smoky air flows out and hits my face.

"Yes," says Ms. Taubin. "Come in." For once, she isn't

wearing her trademark lipstick, and it makes her face look naked. That makes it hard to look at her for some reason.

"Sit down, Wren," she says, walking ahead of me and taking one of the chairs. She doesn't offer to take my jacket, so I keep it on. I sit.

Then it's weird. She just stares at me.

"I got your note," I say. Obviously.

"Good," she says, still staring. "Verlaine? You go by Verlaine?"

"Yes."

"Your semester so far has been . . . ?"

"Good. I mean, I think it's going okay." I think of Honor, of the disciplinary committee. *No*, I should say. *No, it's not really going okay.*

She nods. There's a folder lying open on the table next to her chair, and she closes it before looking at me again very deliberately. "You know your mother was a Hardwick student."

I nod. Of course I know.

"What does she think about you being here?"

I don't know whether Ms. Taubin means here at Hardwick or here meeting with her, so I just say, "I don't know. She's ambivalent, I guess. Although she was the one who sent me here."

Even more strangely, she smiles as if hearing something she's heard before. "Huh. And what do you think? About being here?"

"I'm sorry," I have to confess, since I'm not sure where this is going, "do you mean at school? Or here right now?"

"Hardwick," she says. "How do you feel about being at Hardwick?"

I hesitate again. "I didn't want to come. But now that I'm here, I like it. I think. It still feels new."

"Of course," she says.

I can't stand waiting for her to say it. "Are you going to send me home?"

But she looks surprised, and then suspicious. "Why would I send you home?"

"I don't know," I lie.

"Do you want to go home?"

"No?" Now my mind is racing backward to the note. Did I read it wrong? Wasn't I supposed to come here? Doesn't she know I'm being called before the disciplinary committee in a few days? Has Mrs. Baird not reported it yet for some reason? I can't find a way to ask any of these questions.

"Your mother hasn't mentioned me?" she asks pointedly.

The non sequitur confuses me. I shake my head.

"Well, we were roommates, your mother and I," she says after a long, painful silence. "As First Years. I was curious when I heard you were here. I hadn't thought about her for a long time. Hearing your name took me back. So I invited you out to see what you were like and hear about what Hannah is doing."

"Oh," I say, still confused but relieved. "Right."

Ms. Taubin is looking at me like she wants something. "She's a writer now?"

"A journalist. Yes. For the *LA Times*. She's in Greenland

for six months on an assignment writing about climate research." To my surprise, I feel proud when I say this, not abandoned.

"Huh. Married?" she says.

"No, not married. It's just me and her."

Ms. Taubin presses her lips together as if to resist a smile. "I think you mean, 'she and I.' I remember she wanted to write. But she didn't stick with anything for long. When we were roommates I always tried to get her to sign up for things—yearbook or drama club or whatever—but she liked to hang back and do her own thing."

"I guess I'm kind of like that too," I offer.

She nods.

"Did my mom like it here? Did she do well in school?" Now that Ms. Taubin has opened this door, I feel way too curious not to barge through it.

She turns toward the window. "She did well. People admired her, I think. But I don't know if she liked the school, exactly. She liked to keep a certain distance. She liked to belong if she wanted to, but not need to belong, if that makes sense."

"Yeah," I say, because of course that makes sense. Isn't that what everybody wants?

Ms. Taubin is staring at me again. "Well," she says, "I just wanted to meet you and say hello. I hadn't thought about that period of my life in a long time. It doesn't seem that long ago, and then you realize how long it really is. If you need anything while you're here, please let me know. I remember what it's like, trying to fit in at first. Send Hannah my regards."

That seems to be my cue to go. I am dismissed from this bizarre interview. Outside I run as fast as I can back to search for Chazzy. I think he's in Hale Library because I know he signed up for language lab before lunch.

"I'M NOT KICKED OUT!" I say, barging in on his session of *"Nicholas a trouvé un parapluie."* I want to hug him, but I hold my arms at my side and kind of bounce in place instead.

"Of course not," he says. "That's what I was trying to tell you in French class, but you stopped reading my notes and ran off."

"How did you know?"

"Because if you were being kicked out, I would be getting kicked out too."

"I wouldn't have told," I say, hoping that is true.

"Wren, they don't send you to the D.C. for brushing your teeth five minutes after check-in. If they knew the story, they'd know the whole story." He gives me a once-over, his expression amused. I realize I am panting and quickly pull myself together. "So what did she want?" he asks.

"I have no idea. I thought it was about leaving campus. Then I thought . . ." I'm embarrassed, bringing this up. "Honor accused me of stealing something from her. I didn't, of course. But I'm going to have to go before the disciplinary committee on Wednesday if she won't drop it. But Taubin didn't want to talk to me about that, either. I think she just wanted to see if I was like my mother. They were roommates First Year." I pause, reliving her intense stare. "It was the strangest conversation ever."

Chazzy nods. "What are you going to do about Honor? That sucks."

"I don't know. The only thing I can think of is having her talk to Hannah, but I can't even get in touch with my mom before Wednesday."

Chazzy nods, looking like he'd like to fix it for me, but of course he can't. "Wren, it takes a while to get used to it here. You'll work it out."

"That's what Taubin said, pretty much."

"Yeah. That Taubin." He made a face, squinching up his nose. "She's seriously bizarre."

"I kind of got that impression. Have you had to deal with her much?"

"Last year we had a little run-in. Esme Ritter and I—do you know her? She's an Upper this year. Anyway, we had this idea to . . . well, it was one of the first warm days of spring, and some of us were down at the boathouse after dinner . . . and we thought it would be fun to take a boat out."

For some reason, I'm smiling. "And was it?"

He smiles back. "It turned out it was. But Taubin didn't really see it that way and gave me a warning. I think she wanted to put me on probation, but the rest of the committee convinced her to back off. Speaking of boathouses, what are you wearing?"

My smile fades. I look down at my jeans and sweater, puzzled. Should I have dressed more formally to meet with Ms. Taubin?

"Not right now, dingaling," he says, giving my arm a little shove. "For Halloween. Which is also on Wednesday? Remember?"

Right, I think. Meade House is hosting a Halloween party at the boathouse for Selby and the other two girls' dorms, Porter and Garnet houses. The other two boys' dorms, Lloyd and Garrison, have gotten together to throw a rival party in the gym. Normally we don't get to have parties midweek, of course, but Halloween is traditionally a big day at Hardwick. Wednesday we only have morning classes anyway, so in the afternoon there is a horse show which includes a "gymkhana"—that's British for silly games on horseback—followed by a costume parade, on and off horseback.

Most kids have spent weeks getting ready, or longer. I hadn't given it any thought before now.

WHEN I GET BACK, India and Eloise are standing in the middle of the room. They seem confused. India is holding something in her open palm.

"We just found this." She holds out a tiny black diamond anchor. The ring it hangs from has been pulled into an oblong shape, and there's a gap in it.

I reach for my throat, though I know my necklace is still there, because I was holding onto it practically the whole time I was talking to Taubin. It's just so weird to see it right in front of my eyes, knowing at the same time it's hanging on a chain around my neck, like always. "It's not mine," I say. "Mine is right here."

Perfect timing as Honor walks in, dumping her field hockey stuff without looking around the room. Her eyes go cold as they finally hit me, and she turns to leave again.

"Honor, you goofball," says India, laughter in her voice that sounds to me just a little forced. "I just found your charm. It was right in your dish. In the drawer. I was borrowing a hair elastic."

Honor looks at me instead of India, taking in my necklace. "Oh," she says. Her voice sounds flat, unsurprised. "Thanks."

India holds out the charm to her. She takes it like it's no big deal. I realize suddenly by her lack of reaction that she already knows where her charm was. I don't know if she realized it after she flipped out on me, or if she's known the whole time, but I am seething.

"This one is mine, Honor. I didn't steal yours." I can practically hear my teeth grinding.

"Uh-huh. Well, that charm has been in my family for a hundred years."

"Can I see it?" I ask. She's still icing me out, though it's obvious now that I didn't do anything wrong. Eloise and India stare at her, waiting for a reaction. I feel a surge of relief; at least they know I'm not a liar or crazy or a thief.

Reluctantly Honor hands it over. I gently take the charm and hold it up next to mine. The black anchors are identical, down to the dark glitter and the subtle details on the hooks.

"Maybe that was a popular style back then," offers Eloise. Her cheery tone rings flat. "Like, my mom had those gold knot earrings in the '80s that everyone had?"

"My great-grandmother designed this," says Honor flatly. "It has nothing to do with the style of the times.

She designed most of the jewelry at Gibson's. But this one she made for herself. It was never sold in the store."

I hand the charm back to her. Far from looking happy or relieved to have it back, she looks even more annoyed.

"Well, whatever the story is, could you at least go see Baird and call off the dogs now?" I ask as nicely as I can. *An apology would be even better*, I add silently. But at least she can head off this whole disciplinary committee thing before it's too late. I'm certainly not in a hurry to see my friend Ms. Taubin again so soon. "And next time maybe you could just ask before you go reporting me for stealing?"

Her eyes fall away from mine. "Fine," she says.

And that will be the last thing she says to me for a long time.

CHAPTER SEVEN

Gymkhana

I have secured Chester for the Halloween gymkhana, so I am excited. We are entered in a walk-trot class—that's right: you walk, you trot—as well as the egg-and-spoon contest (just like the regular kind, but on a horse).

After that, I'm riding in the costume parade as a hippie. India, using her expertise as the boarding school version of the above, helped me find a long blonde wig at the pharmacy in Falls Village. We spent Sunday night braiding flowers into it while we watched TV in the Selby common room. It was pretty fun, I have to say.

India said I was lucky they even had any wigs left, I'd dealt with the costume thing so late. Honor is going as Puss in Boots, which I expect means sexy leather thigh-highs and some sort of black kitten ears and tail. Eloise is the headless horsewoman—involving pastel twin sheets and a mannequin head borrowed from the beauty salon in town. India is Lady Godiva. She bought several wigs like mine, but I'm a little nervous to see how it will actually play out. Every time she's asked to sign up on the house list, she tells Baird that her costume is "a surprise." Then again, she's the only one of us who is used to regularly surprising Baird.

THE WALK-TROT CLASS IS first, the most beginner-ish part of the competition. Chester is an angel as usual. I pick up the wrong diagonal once, rising in time with his inside shoulder instead of his outside, and get a yellow third-place ribbon, which I'm still pretty thrilled about.

Kelley gives me a big thumbs-up as we leave the ring.

Lunch is a cookout behind the barn, so they can keep the horse show going without a break. By the time I untack, brush down and return Chester to his stall, it's time for the equitation test for the advanced riders.

I grab a hot dog and take a spot on the bleachers just in time to see Honor cantering a perfect circle on Rainmaker. The advanced challenge consists of a series of jumps that must be completed in a certain order and manner. The whole thing is incredibly difficult and precise. Plus you have to do the whole thing looking like you aren't lifting a finger. Looking like perfection. All the riders in the class are polished, but Honor seems to carry out the whole thing on another level, with ease and a graceful elegance that's impossible not to admire, my personal feelings aside. Rainmaker hits every distance, and Honor sits tall and still. It's like she is communicating with the horse through telepathy.

After that, she has to get off, jump onto someone else's horse that she's probably never ridden—and do the whole thing again, without stirrups.

It's a practice run for the real deal, the ASPCA Maclay Finals in November at the National Horse Show at Madison Square Garden in New York City. Junior riders from all across the country earn points all year competing at the toughest horse shows, and the top hundred or so qualify for the finals.

Honor has already qualified, the only rider from Hardwick to make it this season. Watching her, I think, *I know I'll never ride like that.* But I'm not all that envious. Honor was probably riding before she could walk.

She leaves the ring with the blue ribbon and a small silver cup in her hand, but she doesn't exactly look happy. More like things have turned out as expected. If she hadn't won, would she look upset? Or does it really not matter to her one way or the other?

I sit there alone, looking around, and for the millionth time I try to picture my mom here, watching a horse show. Were her friends the boho set, whatever that meant in the early 1990s? The grunge set? Or was it all just so preppy then that you didn't really have a choice of groups? When she moved to New York to go to college, did she keep in touch with anyone—

Wait.

Out of nowhere, my brain slams on the brakes and takes a sharp detour.

Hannah did keep in touch with someone. Her friend Warren.

Why has she been so anxious for me to meet Warren Norwood?

Warren. Her great friend from Hardwick, who stayed so

close after she left for Barnard. Warren. Wrendle. Wren. I'm aware of my lips moving as I sound it out. It's too close. It must be.

I jump up, trying not to startle the horses standing next to the bleachers, all tacked up and waiting to go into the ring. I toss the rest of my hot dog into a garbage can and run back to my room.

By the time I get to the top of the Selby stairs, my heart feels like it's about to burst, either from the stairs or from my revelation. I grab the canvas schoolbag from under my bed. It's good and dusty, since I haven't needed to use it so far—too big, as it turned out—and dump it onto my bed. It offers up a barrette, half a pack of stale gum, two pennies, a nickel and a pen from Rincon Surf Shop I've been looking for all semester. But no slip of paper.

Damn. My first real lead, and now I'll have to wait until the next time I talk to Hannah to get his number again.

I shove the schoolbag back under the bed where I found it and head back to the gymkhana.

THE EGG-AND-SPOON RACE SURPRISES me; it turns out to be really, really fun. Chester and I end up neck and neck with Amelia Tisdale, a girl who sometimes rides in my lessons. As I urge Chester into a slow jog, balancing my spoon and egg in front of me and bouncing all over the place, Amelia and I both almost fall off laughing.

At the last moment, we are outpaced by Ned Gibson, Honor's little brother. He's not a serious rider like Honor but still has way too much experience from years of summer camp to be matched against pathetic newbies like us.

"Sorry, ladies." He gives us a friendly smile and nod as he takes the cup—in this case plastic and filled with Tootsie Rolls—and leads us from the ring.

"Way to swoop in to victory," I tell him as I hop down.

"Yes, it was all part of my evil plan," he jokes. "Although for a minute there, I thought you or Amelia had it sewn up. Maybe next year."

"You're on. I'm going back to my room to practice right now."

"Baird lets horses into Selby?"

I laugh. "Sure. As long as they're mares. I'd be in major trouble if she caught me with Chester."

"Hey, Honor was telling me you're from Ventura," he calls as I turn away.

"She was?" I can't hide my surprise that Honor would be telling him anything about me at all. "Yeah, I am."

"Do you surf?" he asks, looking hopeful.

I'm used to this question. It's a common misconception that everyone in Southern California surfs and listens to the Beach Boys. "I actually don't," I tell him. He looks kind of devastated, so I add, "I have some friends who do, though."

"Yeah?" Ned's eyes light back up. "Rincon?"

"Sure."

"Pauly Desault? Dean Nesbitt?"

I smile and nod. "Dean was in my class at Ventura High before he dropped out."

Now Ned's eyes are bulging. "When he got his sponsorship with Twister?"

"Right."

"Last May after the Sunset Beach International," he throws in, his voice suddenly much louder.

"I take it you surf," I say dryly.

He looks away, sheepish. "Well, you know, such as it is. In Long Island. You have Rincon. We have the Rockaways and Montauk. Pretty lame compared to SoCal, but my dad has a place in Amagansett." Shyly he turns back. "So, like, so you actually *know* Dean?"

"I do. Not very well, but sure."

"That is so rad." Now the kid is beaming. "So rad. Okay, anyway, I should glide, but . . . awesome. This is awesome." He gives a wave and turns his horse toward the barn.

As I watch him go, I am struck by how much he and his older sister look alike. Because I'm seriously wondering if Ned's adopted. Could they really be from the same family? He's so enthusiastic and funny and unguarded. And Honor's so . . . not any of those things.

AFTER DINNER, I DO a quick search for Warren Norwood on my computer. The only pictures that come up are with whole casts onstage or in big groups, so I can't see his face up close enough to tell if he looks anything like me.

I do spot Hannah in one old Hardwick production, dressed in a bonnet and pilgrim gear as Goody Somebody in *The Crucible*. Norwood stands next to her, gesturing toward something out of frame stage right and looking distraught. His hair is blond, so that's a strike against paternity. But you never know. From what I can determine, he's a medium-successful off-Broadway theater director. Obviously he found his true calling at Hardwick. The bad news is that he doesn't *write* plays, so there are no texts to analyze for clues.

Some of the photos are at benefits for lefty causes: the environment, human rights, the kind of stuff Hannah would be into. But lots of people are into those causes. Nothing concrete.

I'll have to ask Hannah for his address again. I'll have to get in touch with him and figure it out in person.

FOR THE PARTY THAT night, the boathouse has been filled with paper lanterns, and I must say, it looks beautiful. It's warm enough out to keep the big doors open. You can see the sparkles reflected in the river's black ripples. Chazzy and I sit outside with Eloise and India. India's costume is more G-rated than I expected, and I'm secretly relieved. She's got the wigs tied into a long waterfall of hair that reaches her knees, but other than that, she looks dressed for ballet class: pale pink leotard and cutoff tights with bare feet. She would only look naked if her natural skin tone was manicure pink.

"Aren't you cold?" I ask her, looking at her feet.

"Nope. Feeling fine, thank you."

She and Eloise giggle, by which I take it to mean they're stoned.

The party is an official, school-sanctioned one—involving fruit punch and lots of teachers standing around—but even from where I'm sitting I can see some Last and Upper Years over behind the boathouse, tipping silver flasks into their plastic cups.

Nick is among them.

I haven't run into him yet, but I've been aware of him every minute since I got here, like I have some kind of embedded radar or something.

Chazzy groans and stretches his arms toward the starry sky. "I am *jonesing* for a smoke," he complains.

"Oh, come on." I dig my elbow into his ribs. "That's so lame."

India and Eloise look at each other. They are definitely a team tonight.

"He means a cigarette," I explain. "Not pot. Chazzy, why would you do something you know is going to kill you?"

"Wren, no one knows what's going to kill them."

"Yeah, but you can play the odds. Right?"

He gives me a patient smile. "I love it when you get all riled up. It's so un-Californian."

I stare out at the river. "I don't think many people in California think I'm especially Californian."

Near the water, on the edge of the dock, I notice a petite blonde girl, a First Year. She's dressed as Alice in Wonderland, making her seem even younger. Staring at Chazzy with her blue saucer eyes, she pretends to concentrate on sipping her drink. Pretty. I guess Chazzy has an admirer.

"Think we should check out the gig at the gym?" Eloise asks.

"Can't," says Chazzy. "Wouldn't look right for Meade House if I deserted."

I check my Nick radar. He's over behind the boathouse talking to Honor and a couple of Upper guys. "I'm going to stay," I say.

Chazzy smiles at me.

"'Kay," says India. She and Eloise rise, a little unsteady. "Later, then."

When they're gone, Chazzy immediately says, "We need to plot our next escape. But this time we should practice. Maybe some original songs. Do you write?"

I think for a minute, trying to wrest my mind away from Nick and Honor. "Sort of. Nothing I'd play in public, though."

"Can I be the judge of that?"

"I consider you the public."

He pouts, which looks cute. He's such an imp. "That hurts. You know, you're going to have to play something for Gigi to get into her class, and she loves a singer-songwriter."

Since our escape to Falls Village, Chazzy has talked a lot about Gigi. Hannah wasn't kidding when she said she was a legend—a former rock star who left public life in the '80s to teach music at Hardwick. It's rumored she dated Thurston Moore from Sonic Youth before he married Kim Gordon, and that Debra Harry is her godmother, although that rumor I don't believe, because Gigi is about sixty, and Debra Harry's only about ten years older, so it doesn't make sense. I looked it up.

"What about you?" I ask him.

"Oh, no. I'm strictly the sideman of Birdbrain."

"Sucks for me, then. That's kind of a lot of responsibility, don't you think?"

"Oh, I think—"

"Hey," a girl's voice interrupts.

I spin around to see Honor. Nick stands beside her,

smiling at me. Honor is not smiling, of course. "Where did Eloise and India go?" Her gaze flicks across me and lands on Chazzy. I can't really tell which one of us she's asking.

"Gym party," I say.

"Traitors," says Nick, pretending to be shocked. "Hey, Wren. I like the blonde thing. You could almost be Honor's little sister. Look at those blue eyes. Honor, sit next to her."

"Shut up, Nick," Honor says. She looks beyond annoyed.

"We're the same age," I tell Nick, mostly for something to say.

"I'm gonna go find them," Honor says, her eyes off in search of better, more interesting people—anyone but me, I imagine.

"Nah, come on," Nick protests. "Stick around here. We're going to take the boats out later. You too, Birdie. What do you guys say?"

"Are we allowed?" I ask, suddenly turning into Goody Two-shoes. What is wrong with me? "I mean, sure," I add quickly.

"It's a ritual for Last Years. And the captains and strokes of each boat. Coach usually coxes one of the eights," Nick explains.

In case you are wondering what any of this means, I'll digress a moment: The boats for crew hold eight rowers, plus the coxswain (rhymes with "oxen"), who sits in the stern. The "cox" is generally small and light and basically barks orders at everybody. The stroke sits in a key position facing the cox and sets the rhythm for the other rowers. That would be Nick. He is the stroke in the first boat—the fastest one. It's pretty much like being the quarterback of rowing, if that makes any sense.

"Well," says Honor. "I'm freezing. Let's at least hang inside." She starts to walk away, and Nick turns to follow. I'm cold too, but I feel like it will look like I'm following Nick, so I stay put.

Chazzy reclines on his elbows. "Uh-oh," he says.

"What?"

"I think I feel a song coming on after all." He starts singing in a gravelly, deadpan Lou Reed style.

"New York City girl, your ballet flats are so shiny
New York City girl, your pearls are so . . . briny—"

"Briny?" I say. "I should definitely do the songwriting for our band."

"I can't believe you didn't like that."

"No, I did. You're trying out for The Strokes, right? It's too bad The Velvet Underground isn't around anymore. They would have loved you."

"Thank you."

"You bet."

"So who's the blonde?" I ask.

"The blonde?"

"Alice in Wonderland."

A smirk flits across his Peter Pan face. "Gretchen Towne. She's in Gigi's class. First Year."

"Oh," I say. That means she plays. Or sings. And that she's talented.

We sit quietly for a few minutes. Now I'm really cold

and also starting to worry about my American history paper. Just because Halloween is a holiday doesn't mean Thursday isn't coming tomorrow. Besides, lights-out is only pushed an hour later tonight. I glance back into the boathouse a few times, trying not to be too obvious, but it's dark in there, and I can't really make out faces, only silhouettes. Finally the Last Years start gathering on the dock, holding oars and lifting two shells into the water with a gentle splash.

"Yo, Evans!" one of the heavier, super tall guys from Nick's boat calls out. He looks around for Nick. "Where's your stroke when you need one?" he asks the assembled crowd in a raunchy voice—to amused chuckles from his rower buddies.

"He ditched half an hour ago with Honor Gibson," says Bennett Hale. (Yes, like the library, in case you were wondering. I embarrassed myself by asking the same question my first week. He's the cox from Nick's boat, smaller than Chazzy, even.) "Forget him. Let's do this."

I suddenly feel like I have a large stone in my stomach.

Chazzy doesn't seem to notice that I'm even listening to their conversation. "You cold?" he asks.

"I'm worrying about my Federalist Papers paper."

"'Papers paper'?" he teases.

"Don't you have any homework?"

"The difference is, I'm not worried."

"The difference is, you don't care about your grades because you like irritating your father with bad news," I tell him.

"True. Okay, I'm done too. Why don't I walk you to Selby on my way back?"

"Selby's not on the way back to Meade."

"Trying to be a gentleman here. Which, if you were a lady instead of some hippie freak"—he pauses to gesture at my costume—"you would get."

I hold up two fingers in a peace sign. He gives me a thumbs-down in return. Then I follow him up the path to the dorms. It's nice, I realize, having a real friend.

CHAPTER EIGHT

Call Me Gigi

On the way to the arts center the next day, Chazzy helps me strategize about getting into Gigi's class. You're supposed to audition, since it's a practical class, not history or theory, but to do that I would have had to be here in September. I clutch Hummingbird as we walk, trying to mask my nervousness. I can't tell if I want to impress her or him. I don't even know Gigi yet, but what will Chazzy think of me if I don't get it?

"Listen, there are so many people in that class who suck—"

"That's supportive," I interrupt. "I thought you said Gigi liked to keep it about positivity."

"Okay, you're right. There are so many people in that class who just really fucking suck."

"Much better," I say, pretend primly.

What is it with me when I am with Chazzy? Sometimes I feel like we get on a roll talking; it's like we could be in a movie. He says something funny that makes me laugh, and then I say something funny because something about the way he talks to me makes me feel like I'm funny—which I never thought I was—and suddenly we're in a game of witty ping-pong. Back and forth and back and forth.

It's fun, but I get outside myself while it's happening. I watch myself and say, *Who is this girl? How did she have the nerve to say that? Where did it come from?*

Of course, Hannah would say I'm overthinking it.

"If it bothers you, don't watch from a distance." I can hear her saying it now, as though she's walking along the path with us. Ever practical. No nonsense. This is one of the funny things about boarding school. You think you're leaving your family behind, but the relationships you have with them follow you and then play out in your head, wherever you are and whatever you're doing. It's not exactly like hearing voices, but close.

"—that there is no way she is not going to hear you and beg you to be in her class," Chazzy continues.

"Beg?"

"Okay, really, really, really want you in her class."

"How did you get in?" I ask.

"Madrigals. She sat in on auditions last year."

"And then she *begged* you to take her class."

"Pretty much."

"Did she ask anyone else?"

"No," he says and fakes looking at something on his shoe so I won't see him smiling.

"Rock star," I say.

We arrive at class a few minutes early. Chazzy introduces me. "Gigi, this is that new student I was telling you about."

Her hair is dark with thick gray streaks and cropped at her chin. She has on a jean skirt and a billowy shirt with a watercolor-y floral pattern that looks French somehow, black tights and tall leather boots the color of spilled red wine. No boarding-school girl would wear that color. Or cut her hair that short. Not even Honor. Everything about her is sophistication and experience. In a flash I understand the cult of Gigi, and I want in.

"Nice to meet you," she says, admiring Hummingbird. Her clear blue eyes sparkle. "You're a lefty, huh? Like Kurt Cobain. I used to have a J-45."

"Like Aimee Mann! What happened to it?"

"Oh." She laughs. It's a wry laugh. She's the kind of person who does wry well. "It was part of a bad breakup. I still really miss it." She turns those clear eyes to me. "Do you have a free this afternoon?"

"I do."

"So come back at four, and we'll see what we can do. I'm not supposed to add students this late in the term, but Chazzy has really made a case for you."

"That means don't screw it up," he says. But he's smiling.

He stays for class, which sucks, because he can't help me figure what to use as an audition piece. So stupid that we didn't figure that out before.

I'm too nervous to sit still and practice, so I walk the loop past the boathouse and the barn, half hoping to run into Nick (of course). Things are quiet on the dock. Practice doesn't start for a couple of hours. I decide I'll play Gigi an old Glow song. It has enough vocal show-offiness to sound good if I do it right, and the chord changes are simple enough to fumble through on my guitar. I know it backward and forward, thanks to Hannah. She had a record she used to play endlessly when I was a kid.

Back at Selby, I swing by the mailroom. It's a rare event when I get a letter, but I still check every day. You always do, sometimes even more than once a day, even though you know you're much more likely to get an email or a text on the cell phone that you're not supposed to have. Today, amazingly, I am surprised. A letter awaits, addressed to me in a scripty, grown-up hand.

When I turn it over, the return address is in New Haven, a W. H. Norwood.

Look at that. He wrote me first.

TWO HOURS LEFT, AND I'm torn between agonizing about my tryout for Gigi and obsessively wondering about Warren Norwood. If he is my father, does he know about me? Could Hannah have told him at some point, or even this fall before dropping me off at school? If he is my father, is he allowed to tell me? Or if he doesn't know, am I allowed to tell him? *No*, I think. Hannah has made such a big deal about keeping this a secret, she wouldn't have told him. She would explain the decision by saying something about discretion, privacy, or obligation.

For the first time, I'm starting to wonder if it's really her way to protect *herself* from any obligation.

The letter is brief, chatty and friendly. It has that confident, I-know-you'll-like-me, breezy style that very charming people can pull off without seeming obnoxious. Chazzy has it too. Warren—"My friends call me 'Norwood,'" he advises—is in New Haven until Christmas, directing a play he's testing for off-Broadway. It opens in a few weeks, and he would be delighted if I wanted to come up during previews and check it out. Also, he will probably need to go back to New York in early November and would love to stop by Falls Village if they'll spring me for a few hours for tea or something.

I write back right away: yes and yes. I keep it short so that I don't agonize too much about what I say or how I say it.

BY THE TIME I get back to the music room, I'm so nervous my legs are shaking. I sit on the stool, pressing them together to hold them still. I tune up briefly, then start the opening cords. My fingers feel frozen and clumsy. There are a couple of unfortunate squeaks as I move them up and down the frets. But once I open my throat to sing, I think of Hannah's imaginary speech, and I try not to step outside myself.

My voice sounds clear, at least to me. Of course it helps that I've known this song since I was a toddler.

When I finish, Gigi doesn't say anything. She gives me an odd look, as though she's wondering what my intentions are, and says, "Picked one from my era, huh?"

I'm not sure what she means. Maybe she was really into Glow. Or maybe she hates Glow. Damn. Chazzy would have known that kind of thing. I shrug. "I've always loved that song," I say. It's true, after all.

"Fair enough. Well, Wren, I think we can make this work. You don't have another class that conflicts?"

"Nope." I'm smiling so hard I can feel my jaw straining. God, I must look like a total goofball. "Thanks, Ms. Collins."

"Call me Gigi. Nice guitar." She gives Hummingbird another appreciative glance. "Nice open sound," she says again.

There's a hint of a smile on her lips as if she expects me to say something more, but I'm already halfway out the door.

CHAZZY IS WAITING AT dinner, saving me a spot—strictly against the rules, of course. I notice Gretchen has worked up the nerve to sit, not exactly at the same table as him, but at the next one, on the end of the bench, so that she would be sitting next to him if our table was about two feet longer and attached to hers.

"Great," I pretend-huff as I plop down beside him. "There you are. Where were you when I needed you?"

"Uh, in Hale, the most obvious place to look for me."

"Oh." I hadn't thought of looking in the library during the study period before my audition. Dismal.

"So?"

"So it was good. Aside from the embarrassing trembling and almost passing out."

"That's amazing! So you're in?"

"Well, she told me to call her Gigi."

Chazzy jumps up, I'm assuming to hug me. He lurches toward me a sec, then pulls back, like he's reconsidering. He quickly sits.

"She did give me a really weird look when I finished the song, though," I tell him.

"Why? What did you sing?"

"'When It's Over.'"

"Glow? Wren. Really? Are you kidding me?"

"Yes, really. Why?"

"Uh, because she was *in* Glow? Because Elsbeth Collins is her sister? Because they started the band together, and now they don't speak? Do you not listen to any campus gossip? Even the really big, obvious stuff that, like, every other single person here knows?"

I can feel the blood draining from my face. I'd been hungry a second ago; now my appetite has vanished. I shove the tray away from me. "Oh, God. Do you think she thinks I did it on purpose? I had no idea. Really. Jesus, Chazzy! I would never have picked that song."

"Relax," he soothes. "I mean, she must think you're pretty good if she still let you in. Or pretty ballsy."

Ballsy? I am seriously mortified. I know I'm going to be up all night thinking about this. How am I going to face Gigi in class?

Chazzy starts humming the song.

"I really hate you," I tell him.

"Not true," he says.

"Absolutely true. Wait, there's something else. Before the Gigi tryout. I almost forgot, I was so traumatized. So you know about my dad, right?"

"That you have no idea who he is," he says, digging into his mashed potatoes. "That your mom has some drama about it all."

"Right. But I think I have a lead. This guy Warren Norwood, who went to school with Hannah. He invited me to come visit him—"

"I think it's cute that you call your mom by her first name," Chazzy interrupts. "My mom would slap me if I tried as much."

"Whatever." I roll my eyes. "Just listen. I must have been so nervous about school the night Hannah told me, I wasn't even thinking about why she was telling me. Usually I'm pretty alert for any clue. But it makes sense, right? It's someone from her past. They're from different worlds. He's in the theater world. She was in New York a few times for work in the year before I was born. And the name?"

"Norwood?"

"No, *Warren*."

"Warren?"

"Warren. Wren. Get it?"

"I thought you were named after some great-aunt."

"Well, that's what she always *said*. But what if that was just a cover?"

"Seems thin, but I don't know your mother. Why don't you just ask her about him?"

"Because she always ducks the question. My entire life, I was always guessing about old boyfriends, or guys from the newspaper or even people from stories she'd worked on around the time I was born. She said it really didn't matter and that I should become my own person. I guess she doesn't think her own parents contributed much to making her who she is. That always struck me as a super 1970s kind of idea."

Chazzy has stopped eating. "You can't seriously imagine that every man she mentions might be your father."

I just stare at him. Whose side is he on?

"Okay, you *can* imagine, apparently." He looks back at his

tray. "Maybe this time she was giving you a clue. I don't know, Wren. I guess I don't understand the whole shroud of mystery around it. Like, she should either just tell you, or you should accept that she's never going to. In my family, we'd probably just never talk about it. Not that I'm saying that's the right thing to do. I'm not. In fact, I don't really think it's fair of her to keep it from you—or him, for that matter—but since she's decided that's what she wants to do, I don't see that you have any real options. What are you going to do? Go undercover? Ask him for a DNA test? Pull a hair out of his head?"

"Of course not. I'll ask him some questions. Plus I'll just know when I see him."

"I'm not sure I would know. Or want to know," he says darkly.

"Come on, Chazzy. That's not true. Your dad can't be that bad. Is he?"

Chazzy shrugs. "He's not actively bad. He's more of a ghostly presence in our lives. Like he's haunting our house instead of living in it."

"Why? Does he jump out from under the stairs and try to scare you?"

"Are you kidding? That would involve way too much interaction." He laughs as he says it, but for a moment I do wonder whether it might be better to have no father rather than a father who's not really there. But maybe that's just California talking.

RIGHT AFTER DINNER, I dial up the lab on Skype. It's late, but I am hoping Hannah will be back from her trip and be up. I get lucky.

When I tell her Norwood wrote me, she looks happy. As much as a chapped face with purple lips can look happy. She looks older, somehow, or maybe just weathered.

"Is that what you call him? Norwood?" I ask.

"Or Warren. Either one. He wasn't Norwood until after Hardwick."

"How come you've never mentioned him before?"

"I don't know. He's an old friend. I think about him a lot. But it's not like I see much of him. We live on opposite sides of the country. We've met up in New York a few times. He doesn't get out to California much."

"What does he look like?"

"He looks like . . . Why do you want to know what he looks like?"

"So I'll recognize him when I meet him."

"I don't think it will be that hard to figure out. He'll probably spot you first."

"Well, I'm excited to meet him," I say with maybe too much enthusiasm.

"Okay. Good. I'm glad," she replies uncertainly. *Maybe she's not ready for me to find out*, I think. She thinks she's given away too much.

"So I'll let you know how it goes. Bye." I practically hang up on her. It could be more subtle, my undercover investigation. On the other hand, Hannah was the one who started it. Too late, I remember I meant to tell her the thing about Honor having the same anchor charm. Damn. I'll have to mention that next time.

CHAPTER NINE

No Answer

A few days later, in the afternoon, I'm sitting on the floor of the hallway outside our room when Chazzy comes by. During the daytime, boys and girls are free to visit one another's rooms, as long as they adhere to a roster of restrictive, scandal-avoiding rules. The visitor must check in with the dorm parent. The door must remain open. There must be three feet on the floor at all times. (Although to me that one seems designed to inspire Twister-esque makeout sessions. But whatever.)

At home in Ventura, if I ever had a boy in my room—which, granted, was not all that often—I didn't think much about it. At Hardwick, I feel guilty and like I'm about to get busted, even though I'm not doing anything.

"What are you doing out here?" he asks.

"It's Honor. We're locked out for her weekly shrink session. Via cell."

"You can't even use your own room? Let's go down to the common room."

"I left my guitar inside. She locked the door before I had a chance to get it."

"Damn. So we can't practice. What does someone like Honor need therapy for, anyway? Her life is perfect, isn't it?" He flops down on the floor next to me.

"I guess she has her reasons."

"Or therapy just comes with being high maintenance. Like massages, pedicures . . ." Chazzy shakes his head.

I'm not used to hearing anything besides awe in connection with Honor. It's a nice change.

"But would that be fun for her? Like something she'd want to do every week?"

"Talk about herself for an hour?" His voice is getting loud now.

"Shh. It's fifty minutes."

He frowns. "Now you're defending her? She almost got you kicked out for something you didn't even do."

"I know. And I don't like her. But I hate that she doesn't like me. It's hard to explain. I want to be the one to decide we're not friends, not her. I just want to know why she wrote me off without ever giving me a chance. I'd rather do the rejecting."

Now Chazzy's looking at me, really looking, and his regular smile fades. "I'll have to remember that, Birdie."

Birdie. Did he hear Nick call me that? Probably it's just a coincidence.

"Come on," he says. "If there's no guitar, then there's nothing to do but language lab."

"Zut alors." I grab his hand, and he pulls me to my feet.

"Exactly."

As I stand up, my necklace flops outside my shirt. Chazzy reaches out and holds it between his fingers, taking a closer look at the tiny anchor. "This is cool. This is what caused the kerfuffle with Honor?"

"Oh, yeah. From my mom," I tell him. "It was my great-grandmother's. You actually use the word *kerfuffle* in conversation?"

He laughs. "Only with you. It's spooky, that thing. I like it."

"Me too. Although Hannah never did. She's not into family relics. I dug it out of a box in some drawer a few years ago, and she told me I could have it."

With a shrug, he drops it and turns down the hall. "You're lucky you have such a cool mom."

"Yeah." I have to keep reminding myself of this. Pretty often, it seems lately. The thought makes me feel disloyal.

"Your mom sounds fun," I add. "I love all your stories about her, like driving the wrong way up the street because the turn signal was broken and she thought it would be too dangerous to turn left without signaling? Or the chickens in the garage? When she made cabbage ice cream on that cabbage diet? Or painting her shoes for that party?"

Chazzy fiddles with the zipper on his jacket. "Yeah. She's fun. It's more like having a child than a mother. You can't exactly count on her. But that's what siblings are for, right?" he says, sounding disheartened.

"I wouldn't know."

"Poor you, only lonely. Let's go."

This is one thing I've learned about Chazzy: He is always recounting the adventures of his family, but he hates to actually *talk* about them. He's figured out how to turn them into hilarious characters, even his remote father. But it's clear they're not all that funny to him in real life.

AFTER MY RIDING LESSON that afternoon, I spot Nick coming up the path from the boathouse. His hair is damp, and his cheeks are flushed from practice. I'm sure mine are too, plus I have matted hair and smell like a horse, but I try to push those thoughts from my head.

"Hey, Birdie," he says, joining me up the hill.

"Hey. How was practice?"

"Brutal," he says, smiling like that's a good thing. "You look happy."

"I jumped," I tell him, too excited to feel shy. "First time."

"Great. But Chaz tells me you're not really a horsey girl after all."

"Oh." I'm not sure if that's supposed to be good or bad. Or why Nick would be talking to Chazzy about me.

"More of a songbird. Which makes sense, with your name and all. You're in the Gigi club."

"Yeah, I just started that class."

"Awesome. So sing me something. Entertain me on the walk back?"

Now I'm blushing. "I can't," I mumble. "I mean, I don't really sing for people. I just do it on my own."

"What's the point of that?" he asks. "Anyway, you've sung for Chaz. Don't keep it to yourself. You know Tolan, Alder and Hale play, right? Why don't you come over to Meade sometime and jam with them? It'd be fun. We'll hang out."

"Okay." It sounds terrifying, but it also almost sounds like a date, so how can I say no?

He takes my hand, opening my palm and pressing his flat against it. I just stare at our two hands, his covering mine. "Promise?" he says.

"Yeah."

"Cool." He gives me a grin, drops my hand and jogs ahead. "Come on! I'm starving."

I ARRIVE BACK IN our room horsey and dusty and high from the back-to-back thrills of my first jump and Nick's invitation. Open-ended and vague, I know, quite likely never to be mentioned again, but I don't care. It's something. Some hint of yes, something might happen in the future.

Eloise, India and Honor are lounging in our living room: India on the floor, her feet on the window seat, and the other two on the cushions, looking out. They're dressed for dinner, ready to go. The windows are open, and the last warmth of the afternoon breeze blows in.

"Hey. Your boyfriend," says Honor, turning to me. I look out the window. For an insane moment I expect to see Nick, but instead Chazzy gives me a quick salute as he crosses the quad on his way back to Meade House. I wave back at him.

Eloise gives me a significant look. "Right?" she asks.

"He's my friend, not my boyfriend." I tell them. All three are looking at me expectantly.

"We were just wondering. Maybe you could settle the debate," says Honor. "Eloise says straight. India and I say no way."

"Not that we care," clarifies India. "I mean, it's cool whichever way. You know?"

"We've just always been curious," Eloise chimes in.

"We thought you might have, um, insight," Honor says with a half-smile. It's the closest thing to an actual smile she's ever given me. It's also the longest conversation we've ever had that didn't involve an accusation.

"Why do you think he's gay?" I ask. The truth is, I have no idea. Chazzy doesn't talk about girls, at least not to me. He doesn't seem all that interested in boys, either. Chazzy is just Chazzy. When I'm with him, I'm not aware of, "Oh, he's a boy." He just is. We just are. But I don't know how to explain that to my roommates. "I don't know. Honestly."

"Well, then," says Honor, sizing me up, "that'll be your special assignment. To find out."

"By whatever means," says Eloise, giggling.

I laugh too, though I feel a little like it's at Chazzy's expense.

"'Kay," I say, turning toward my bedroom. It shouldn't matter, but I feel included for once, and it's nice.

ON MY BED I find a letter India has dropped there for me. It's a notice from school. Apparently I have not been registered for next year, and the deadline was November first. It's not like Hannah to miss this kind of thing, although we haven't discussed any plans. Maybe she wants to talk to me first about whether I want to come back, in which case I would say the jury is still out, or maybe she's trying to figure out if we can afford it.

It's late in Greenland now, but I figure she might be hanging around the lab writing or something. I pull up Skype on my laptop and dial the lab number. It rings with no answer. Not surprising, but I feel disappointed anyway.

CHAPTER TEN

Deserted

Another quirk of Hardwick Hall is that Corwin Hardwick, the founder, was a big believer in honoring Veterans Day. School is always closed. When he was alive, Corwin instructed the students to spend the day in quiet contemplation, giving thanks to those who had fallen. This still happens at Hardwick, unless November eleventh falls on a Friday or a Monday, like it does this year. When that happens, everyone goes home for a long weekend—a mini fall break—and there's not much reflection.

Of course, I can't go home or go to Greenland, and since it's only one weekend and a day, how bad could it be to stay on campus? Hannah would be back in Ventura for a month starting at Thanksgiving and then returning to the research lab from January until April. Neither Eloise nor India had invited me home for fall break. (Nor Honor, no surprise there.) And even if I had wanted to go home with Chazzy—but that would be weird, right? And not like he had asked me—he lived too far away, and it would have been too expensive to fly. Instead I imagined myself dutifully getting through all my assignments, and maybe even getting ahead. And maybe I could ride.

I also fantasized that Nick might be staying on campus, maybe for some crew reason, but not a reason that would keep him with all the other rowers the whole time. We could take walks down by the lake. We could go to meals together and study in Hale, just the two of us. He would say things like, "Last year when I was a Lower," and give me all kinds of great advice while secretly thinking I was cool and handling my challenging role as new student really well.

Sunday, Norwood would take me out to tea.

This was the only part of the plan that was not just in my imagination. I was finally going to find out what was behind this mystery of my mom's.

BY 4 P.M. ON Thursday, the campus is mostly cleared out. I eat thick, sticky lasagna alone in the dining hall. Formal night is canceled because no one is there, so I don't have to wear a skirt. I put on the jeans I think look good on me just in case Nick is around. He isn't.

I watch TV by myself in the common room and go to bed early after IM-ing a little with Kylie and Erica, my closest friends from home. Not being up on the details of the things they talk about—crashing somebody's party in Montecito, Jimmy Trieste's board snapping on a rock near Rincon, whether the math homework was hard or not—makes me feel even farther away than not talking to them at all.

The next day, I go down to the barn. Chester is lame, so I can't ride him. Mr. Kelley is away but has left instructions that I can take a lesson with an assistant instructor on

Stormy, the horse I fell off, or a different horse I've never ridden. I decide against it. I would ride with Kelley there, but the combination of strange horse (or scary horse) and strange teacher throws me. No pun intended.

That leaves only the studying-and-getting-ahead option. I don't really feel like doing that, either, but I grab a giant stack of books and head for Hale instead of my room. It's still possible Nick is on campus, right? I haven't seen any rowers, but you never know.

Hale is deserted.

I recognize one boy, Philip, the other Californian student, but we're not really friends or anything. I sit by myself in the Founder's Reading Room. This is my favorite place in the library, because it has a fireplace so tall you could walk in (never in use anymore, but still very awe-inspiring) and is filled with all the maps and leather-bound books and Hardwick lore.

Now that I'm here, of course, I don't want to study. I'm wishing instead that I could fast-forward to Sunday, when I'll get to meet Norwood. It's the only excitement I have in store for the whole weekend.

At dinner I just show up in sweatpants, now that I know no one interesting is going to see me. I eat some cold cereal and an apple with peanut butter and call it a night.

WHEN SUNDAY COMES ABOUT a hundred years later, I try to remember the last time I heard my own voice. Yesterday? The day before yesterday? But I can't help feeling excited. Norwood is picking me up and taking me to tea in Salisbury, the closest town to Falls Village. I will not be swabbing the insides of his cheeks. (Chazzy's bad joke.) I *will* be relying on a combination of carefully considered questions and a healthy dose of intuition in determining the identity of my father. I hope I like him, and I hope he likes me back.

As penance for my daydreaming and time-wasting yesterday, I drag myself back to the library and subject myself not only to my biology and French homework, but even to a little math. Though, to be honest, not really that much math.

Norwood is supposed to pick me up at four. At three forty-five, I'm sitting on the curb on the circle at the main entrance. I have signed out and am ready to go.

It's cold. Cold seeps up through my feet, my hands, my coat, my pants and right up my spine. I'm really not used to these temperatures. My ribs ache from pressing my arms into my sides. By four thirty, although still as excited as Hayley Mills (or Lindsay Lohan) in *The Parent Trap* landing at her daddy's ranch in California, I'm just too damn cold and decide to wait inside.

By 5:20, I'm pretty sure he's not coming. I go back to my room. I check my email. There's one from Chazzy.

> *Hey. What's up? Hope it wasn't too beat there all alone. Mom has outdone herself on the daffiness scale. Will tell you when I see you, but it involves a ferret. Dad had to stay in Singapore. Why am I not surprised? Saw coolest old French movie at the old movie place in Chapel Hill.* Irma Vep. *It's awesome. You'd love the music. Luna sings Serge Gainsbourg's "Bonnie and Clyde." Psyched to see you. Later.*
>
> *CMR3*

I get under the covers in all my clothes and lie there in the semidarkness. At six thirty, Mrs. Baird sticks a note under my door.

Mr. Norwood called. Apologizes. Has bronchitis. Will not be able to make it this afternoon.

AT EIGHT, CHAZZY TAPS on my door. "Hey," he says, "are you sleeping? I didn't see you at dinner."

"Oh, hi," I say, stepping out into the hall. "Yeah. Didn't really feel like it." Then out it all comes: I tell him about Norwood.

"That sucks," he says. "Come on. We were supposed to be at Gigi's half an hour ago."

Gigi holds Sunday night singing practices, which you don't have to go to, but everyone does. On the way to the music building, Chazzy tells me that his mom has decided to breed and show ferrets. (Yes, that's a thing, apparently.) His sister Eleanor, who sounds nuts, is planning her wedding. (Even crazy people find other people who want to marry them. Kind of gives you hope.) His twin older brothers, Cross and George, graduated from Hardwick last year and are away at college now. Eleanor went to Duke and stayed home after she graduated, probably because she met her husband there. (Chazzy's theory.)

It's freezing out. Even colder than when I was waiting on the circle. Chazzy gives me his scarf. Ever the Southern gentleman.

We're late for practice, but Gigi's doesn't take it personally if you miss Sunday nights. She kind of treats you like an adult, like if you're not there, you must have a good reason. You're not trying to put something over on her. It's refreshing.

THIS ISN'T MY FIRST time at a Gigi Sunday, but I wasn't planning on coming tonight. I didn't even expect Chazzy would be back until after curfew. The last couple of sessions have focused on vocal exercises and then what she calls "Song-writers' Circle," kind of a workshop for kids to bring in their own songs. Last week Nelson Auerbach, who's a beefy lacrosse player, brought in this really sweet, catchy love song and played it on the mandolin. It was awesome.

I'm not planning to play anything myself, but I have what I would call almost an insatiable curiosity about the other students' songs. Hearing them, especially in their half-finished state, is pretty much like hearing the inner thoughts of people you would never otherwise really get to know. Tonight no one seems to have brought a song in, or maybe we've already missed it.

Gigi's gaze travels the room, looking to draw out the shy performer who has something prepared but is hanging back. She spots me. "Wren. What about you?"

"I just have the exercise from last week. I didn't bring a song."

"You sure you don't have anything you want to share?"

"Yeah. I'm sure."

Chazzy elbows me. I look at the floor and shake my head.

At the end of the class, Gigi calls my name as the students filter out. "Wren. Wait a sec."

I turn back. Chazzy waits by the door.

"You know," Gigi says, "it's a great skill to be able to inhabit someone else's song. But being able to inhabit your own song is something a thousand times that. I know you have it in you."

"I just don't feel comfortable—" I fumble.

"Who said anything about comfortable?" Gigi picks up her bag to go. She looks annoyed. I've disappointed her, which makes me feel awful but mad at the same time. Why is she singling me out? It's not a requirement of the class to write your own music.

"Ready?" asks Chazzy from the doorway. The cold air blows in from the darkness behind him.

"Yeah," I say and follow him outside.

"She hates lurkers," Chazzy says. "Eventually you're going to have to get up there and sing something."

"Eventually," I say, and wrap his scarf more tightly around my throat.

THE NEXT MORNING, MRS. Baird stops me in the hall to apologize for bringing me Norwood's note so late.

"I had just gotten back from the weekend myself. Ellen had left the day's messages in a stack. I didn't realize you were waiting all afternoon, you poor dear."

"It's okay," I lie. I still feel like an idiot for having sat out there all that time like some overenthusiastic puppy. "It wasn't a big deal. Just a friend of my mother's who was passing through town."

"Yes, he called later, and I spoke with him. He explained the situation and has offered you a ticket to his play in New

Haven this Saturday. Would you like to go? I can arrange for you to go and come back on the bus. I'm afraid you'd be back rather late, but Lowers aren't allowed to stay overnight away without a guardian or parent."

"I don't mind coming back late," I answer quickly. A play in New Haven makes up for being stood up, plus it would be nice for once to have something to do on a weekend like the other kids.

"Fine," she says. "The bus is at four forty-five. I will have a teacher take you to the stop in Falls Village Saturday afternoon."

The week crawls by. I am paired with Honor on a project in art history, but she makes excuses for why she and Lauren need to work together, and the teacher allows her to switch. I end up with a bossy First Year named Emily, but frankly it's such a relief to be spared Honor's unhappy company that I am fine with letting Emily run the show.

I keep hoping I'll run into Nick to distract myself from waiting for the weekend and the play, but no matter how slowly I walk back from the barn, even going out of my way and taking the tow-path route past the boathouse or the longer path behind Meade House, I don't.

HONOR WOULD KNOW WHAT to wear.

I try a few combinations before giving up and going with a tweed wool skirt, leggings and a black turtleneck, my most basic fallback. I decide to add a blazer and blow my hair dry because I think that will help make me look less like a runaway and maybe even almost like an adult.

A teacher I don't know, Mr. Simonson, is picking a friend up in town, so he drops me at the bus stop. Mrs. Baird has bought me a round-trip ticket in advance, so I don't even have to take care of that. In my bag I have the address of the theater, money for a taxi to and from the bus station and a copy of *The Catcher in the Rye*. We're reading it for English lit, but it turns out to be so good once you get into it that it's not even like reading a book for class. Especially since it's about boarding school.

The New Haven bus station is hands down the saddest and scariest place I've ever been in my life. I look straight ahead and walk toward the cab stand without making eye contact with anyone. I tell myself Mrs. Baird wouldn't have sent me someplace actually unsafe alone. I feel bad each time I shake my head and mumble that I can't spare any change, because of course I can, but at the same time, I don't think it's wise to stop and chat.

At least the theater is more elegant and less grime-covered than the part of New Haven that surrounds it. Norwood has left me a ticket at the Will Call booth. I settle myself in my seat. It's weird to be at a play alone. Everyone else is here with someone.

The lights dim, and the curtains open, and for the next two hours I am immersed in a strange, jewel-toned, French-Canadian experimental play with a *Peter Pan*–inspired plot. I'm relieved that I won't have to pretend to like it, because I really, really do—but I hope Norwood isn't going to ask too many probing questions. I'm not sure I follow everything that goes on. The basic story is about an Indian guy working in a call center in Bangalore who somehow moves to Montreal and finds a creepy magical world in the subway/sewers under Westmount, the city's fanciest neighborhood.

I don't think I've even been to a movie alone, much less a play. But after the initial awkwardness of feeling like a loser, I find I enjoy it. You can really get inside the story and outside of yourself in a way you can't when you are so aware of the person sitting next to you, wondering what they might be thinking, silently comparing your experiences.

Afterward I walk out in a sea of audience members, scanning faces. I know instantly which one he is. He stands next to an actor from the play, talking distractedly while scanning the crowd for me. Medium height, or even a bit less, hair cut super-short in a style that's in right now in men's fashion magazines. He has on a three-piece suit, a pocket square, perfectly polished shoes. He definitely stands out as Manhattan, not New Haven, where the crowd seems to range from nondescript to fusty and academic, like glossier versions of the teachers at Hardwick Hall.

Norwood sees me at the same time and rushes up. Instantly, I'm swept up in a hug. "Look at you! You are darling!" He turns to the actor. "Anton, look at her!" Anton nods politely.

"Hi," I say to Norwood, feeling shy. "You were amazing," I say to Anton, because he really was.

"Okay," Norwood says, "we're off. Across the street. Richter's." After spending less than ten seconds with Norwood, I see that he is always in motion. We walk quickly—faster than I normally would walk—and enter the old-fashioned Taft Hotel just down the block. He talks the whole time, his voice bright and energetic, occasionally posing a question to me or to Anton, barely leaving a gap for us to answer.

The dark wood tables fill quickly. There's a steady *wheesh* of the taps drawing beer into tall glasses, while dim lights and old photos on the walls tell the lengthy and unchanging story of Yale University. Norwood knows his way around the place, clearly.

I worry that someone will stop me and ask for ID, but once we're in a dark corner booth, I relax. A waiter takes our order. I ask for ginger ale.

"I miss Hannah so much," Norwood announces with a sigh. "But you're a good sub. I made her promise, promise, promise to stop by New York on the way back. But you know how she is. Impossible to influence her, so I hope she just decides on her own to do it."

The way he says "promise, promise, promise" three times like that makes me think of the nanny in the *Eloise* books. That leads me on a brief tangent of wondering if Eloise is named after the character. She's certainly not mischievous like her namesake, if that's the case.

I snap back to Earth when I realize Norwood is laughing.

Anton says, "Give her a break, Warren. You just met the girl."

"There's nothing to be embarrassed about. She's family."

My heart thuds like it's hitting a brick wall, and I wonder if I just missed some vital piece of information. I'm too ashamed to admit I'm not following, so I change the subject. "When's the last time you saw Hannah?"

"Do you hear that?" Norwood asks Anton. "'Hannah.' She's so Californian."

"Very modern," says Anton approvingly.

He's European, but I can't place his accent. Spanish. Italian. Maybe Portuguese. In the play he spoke a little French.

"You know, Hannah saved my life," says Norwood. "Literally. After we left Hardwick, I was at NYU. Tisch. Doing the directing program, and she was at Barnard then. I forget what she was studying. English, right? We were friends at Hardwick, but in New York it was different. So intense. We both were in places where we knew no one, right? Like, there was no one to talk to."

I nod. I guess he's one of those people who says "literally" when they don't actually mean *literally*.

"It was love at first sight," he says.

At this point my heart is racing—but at the same time, something feels off, like he's telling this story to an outsider, not to someone who is a part of the plot. My hands are sweating. Under the table, I wipe them on my skirt.

Anton smiles a little indulgently. "Well, love at first sight?"

"You know what I mean," Norwood tells Anton. "Anton's so jealous."

"Uh-huh," I say, unsure, trying to understand.

"Your mother introduced me to my first serious boyfriend. Anton still hates to hear about it. Even though it was a hundred years ago."

Oh. My brain finally goes *click*. Right.

But at the same time, I don't want to believe I'm at a

dead end quite yet. I jump to other possibilities. Maybe before the first boyfriend? No, that would make me twenty-three. A drunken night seven years later? I watch Norwood and Anton talking like old married people. No way.

"Your mother is wonderful," says Anton. "I don't want to give you the wrong impression. It is just fun for me, teasing Warren. We love to see her; we just wish we could more often. It's great to meet you in person at last."

I sink back into my seat, relieved and embarrassed and unsettled all at once. Hannah really did just want us to meet because she thought we'd get along.

"Thank you so much for inviting me," I tell them. "The play is amazing. What's going to happen if it does well here?"

Norwood provides what must be a ten-minute answer. I don't hear any of it.

IT'S NOT UNTIL I'M sitting on the bus again—same seat, as it happens—on the way back that the disappointment sinks fully into my bones. I was so sure I had it figured out. I'm too tired to read, and too tired to make up stories for myself about the few passengers nearby, so I stare out the window. Finally I close my eyes, bunch up my blazer into a pillow against the seat and try to sleep.

My face pressed against the window makes me think of Hannah's picture in the library under glass, when she was two years older than I am now. I think about Honor's father, two years older in that same picture than Honor is now. And Hannah's father under glass with who? Eloise's grandfather? Will my children years in the future be sitting next to Honor's children? And hating one another? The thought makes the world seem depressingly small.

My necklace is scratching my chest under my shirt, and my blazer is lumpy. But I'm determined to sleep. To sleep and stop thinking about all this.

I COME TO WITH my cheek half-frozen and my neck stiff. There are only a few people getting off in Falls Village, and the bus is almost empty. Mrs. Baird is there to pick me up herself, which is nice of her, because it's really late. She has an overcoat on over a bathrobe, as though she went to bed earlier and then got up again to come get me.

"How was the play? Was it good?" she asks with enthusiasm.

"It was good," I say, but I can hear how deflated my voice sounds.

Mrs. Baird looks disappointed. "Not good?"

"No, good," I say. "It was really good. Thank you for organizing it and for picking me up too."

"My pleasure," she says, and we drive the rest of the way in silence.

Because it's so late, way past check-in, my roommates are asleep. I pause in the living room to send Chazzy a quick update email about the Norwood fiasco, typing by the light of the screen. In my bedroom, I undress and climb into bed in my T-shirt, careful not to wake India up. I don't even brush my teeth.

I lie there, feeling flattened and kind of dumb for convincing myself that Norwood was the one. Chazzy is right. I can't think every man my mother knows or happens to mention is going to turn out to be my father. But I don't understand what makes Hannah so protective of her privacy, what makes her someone who keeps secrets from her own daughter, the only person she's ever really shared her life with. It hurts to think about that, so I push it away.

Hannah would tell me I'm being silly, that it has nothing to do with me. That it's about her. But that's not true.

CHAPTER ELEVEN

Night-Swimming

The next morning, I call Hannah two or three times when I get up, but there's no one at the lab. They must be on some remote overnight trip or something. Usually they don't leave their base for more than a day or two because the weather is so extreme that it's an ordeal to pack and prepare for any longer than that.

I want to tell her about my evening with Norwood, and this time, I resolve to confront her. I'm going to make her tell me who my father really is. Enough with the Nancy Drew crap. I'm sixteen, I'm not even living at home, and I have a right to know.

Eventually I'm forced to give up and go down to the barn for my lesson.

Mr. Kelley helps me tack up Stormy. He assures me that getting dumped last time was a fluke. "She's a good girl, Stormy is," he insists, patting her neck.

She tosses her head, looking imperious, if a horse can look imperious.

"Okay," I say uncertainly.

He's right. The lesson is uneventful. Stormy is obedient, though there's always this edge to her where you feel like the slightest breeze might send her right out of her thin skin. We don't jump, but I manage to canter a few pretty decent circles and stay on the right lead in each direction. It's fun, actually, riding a horse that's so light and quick and sensitive to subtle commands. A little scary, but exhilarating.

When we're done, Mr. Kelley looks quite proud of me and of himself. That's when you know you've really ridden well, when he starts taking credit. I'm happy, and for an hour I've almost forgotten about what's bothering me.

The light is fading, though it's only four o'clock.

BACK IN MY ROOM, I open my laptop and see I've missed two video chats from Hannah. As I'm typing an email to her, another comes through, and I hit ANSWER. She's calling from outside. It's dark where she is, and there are other people sitting behind her, in front of a tent.

Hannah's breath fogs the screen as she hunches over her computer. "Hi," she says. "I don't know if this will work out here. The signal's lousy, and it's really cold. The computer's battery is probably going to drain in a sec."

"Well, thanks for getting back to me." I don't know why I waste time being sarcastic.

"I saw you called a few times. I was worried. Is everything okay?"

Is everything okay? I don't know how to explain it to her, that nothing's wrong, but everything's wrong; that there are so many questions here that I need her help with; that I can't go on not really knowing who I am.

"It's just been really hard—" I start to say. I can hear my voice shake. I stop when I realize I'm also telling ten other people who are shivering in the subzero weather, waiting for Hannah to be done with her needy daughter. "It's nothing," I continue. "Everything's fine. I met Norwood finally. I saw his play. I just wanted to tell you about it."

Hannah smiles, and her face seems to warm. "Norwood," she says. "I'm *so* glad—"

And the screen goes black. I call back about seventeen times. Nothing. I sit there, staring at the computer, willing the connection to return, tears of frustration running down my face that I barely feel, even as I wipe them away.

Coward, I tell myself. *Coward, coward, coward.*

LATER THAT NIGHT, CHAZZY and I stand outside Selby. The wind whisks dead leaves off the ground. The hairs inside my nostrils tickle with frost each time I breathe in. Not an unpleasant feeling, exactly, but weirdly unfamiliar.

Chazzy looks up at the night sky. The clouds are low and blowing, heavy gray streaks through ink. If this were one of those vampire stories, the setting would be perfect. He sniffs the air. "I wish it would snow already. I hate all this waiting."

"Me too." Mostly for the novelty. Snow's not something I've experienced many times in my life. I'm still thinking about Hannah, out on that arctic ice sheet, snow as far as she can see in every direction.

Chazzy turns and grabs my arm. "Wait, you know what I found out? You know how Gigi was in such a bad mood at practice this week?"

"I didn't think she was in a bad mood," I say, defending her automatically and for no reason. I did notice that she was in a bad mood.

"Wren, come on. She ended early. She barely said anything about the song we did."

"Maybe she thought it sucked. *I* kind of thought it sucked."

"Oh, stop it. Anyway, I read something online about how Elsbeth Collins is starting Glow again—with someone else. Touring and putting out a record this winter."

"Oh, wow," I say, imagining myself in Gigi's skin for a moment. "That must feel just awful."

"I know. I wonder what she'll do."

"Do? What *can* she do?"

"I don't know," he says. "Fight back. Or get out there and play on her own. Something."

I try to imagine what I would do. Sit on the sidelines, mope, lick my wounds. But then, Gigi is much tougher than I am, as well as much cooler. Maybe she *will* fight back somehow.

"Wren, you should play that song you're working on in class."

Chazzy's talking about what he heard me fiddling with in the common room before we met to practice. As usual, he convinced me to play it for him, or as much as there is of it. I'm having trouble with the ending. It's not like Birdbrain is a real band or anything, but it does give me a sense of purpose. We have almost three-quarters of a set together now. A short set, but nonetheless, a set.

"It's good, you know, and it might help you finish it to have a deadline," he adds.

"It's not ready," I say. I think about my non-call with Hannah. I feel too raw and messy to get up and do something like that in front of Gigi and the whole class.

Chazzy won't let it go. "Most of the songs people bring in aren't finished. You mean, *you're* not ready."

"Okay, fine. *I'm* not ready."

"So what are you going to do when we play the Bantam next month?"

Chazzy and I have this joke that we're going to play a show at the Bantam Theatre, this big, run-down local place where the old folks go in the summer to see revivals of Broadway shows performed by Falls Village residents. Chazzy calls the old folks the Blue Hairs; he wants to work on an encore of show tunes for the imaginary occasion. For a moment I flash to Honor, Eloise and India asking me whether Chazzy is gay.

"I'm not exactly writing the next *Oklahoma*, my friend." I counter.

"You never know," he says, grinning.

He's not gay, I think. I wonder about past girlfriends. Are there any? Esme Ritter? That story he told me about taking the boat out with her? For a second I think, I could just kiss him and find out. Crazy idea. I immediately shake it off.

A second later, Mrs. Baird pokes her head out the door. "Wren," she calls, "sign-in is in ten minutes. You must be freezing out there."

"Good evening, Mrs. Baird," says Chazzy, the Southern gentleman again.

"Okay, check you later." I give him a quick hug and

hurry up the steps to the dorm. When I get to our room, everyone is already dressed for bed. India's propped on pillows on the floor doing the history reading she didn't finish over the weekend. Eloise is painting her toenails. Honor is lying in bed, talking quietly on her cell phone. I can tell by the tone of her voice she's talking to a boy, and I strain a moment to hear if it's Nick on the other end.

We all say hi, except Honor who doesn't bother to look up. I get my toothbrush and bath pail.

"Jesus, Eloise," India complains, "that stuff reeks. Do you know how toxic nail polish is? Those chemicals are going to seep into your toes."

"Giving me, what, toe cancer? Wren, what do you think? Too dark?" Eloise is applying a preppy fuchsia color barely a shade darker than the innocent bubblegum pink she usually uses.

"I don't think so. It looks nice."

"For winter, right? I think it's okay." Eloise nods, convincing herself. "How was last weekend, anyway? Pretty chill with no one here?"

"Yeah, a little too chill. How about you guys?" I ask.

"Can you open a window or something, Eloise?" asks India.

"It's freezing out. Look at Wren's cheeks. What were you doing out there anyway, Wren?"

"A little reconnaissance?" asks India, suddenly interested. "What happened?"

"Or maybe someone else walked you home?" Eloise gives me a cryptic look. Then her gaze darts to Honor, still on the phone.

"Who's she talking to?" I can't resist asking, now that I have an opening.

"Nick." Eloise says it in a flat, final way. I'm not sure if it means "I can see right through you" or "hands off" or "good luck." Maybe all three.

And I feel very uncomfortable all of a sudden. "'Kay, so, I'm going to brush my teeth and go to bed, I guess."

"Me too," says India. "I'm so done." She slaps her book closed.

"Same," says Eloise, hobbling with her painted toes splayed out.

India is right. That stuff *is* toxic.

I'M THE LAST ONE out of the suite and the last one to the table at breakfast the next day. They always make pancakes on Mondays to try to get us psyched for the week. After chapel, all four of us head for art history. I sit in the dark and look at paintings of those wan, beautiful ladies with long necks and rich, jewel-toned robes. Mannerism again. Those ladies with the necks.

Mr. Winchester tells us the term describes a late period of Renaissance painting that stressed an intellectual, aloof and exaggerated approach to its subject. I can't help glancing at Honor as he says this. She pretends not to notice.

RIGHT BEFORE DINNER, I grab my towel and bath pail from my room. I'm horsey and sweaty from my lesson, but really, the shower is a good place to think. There are so few places at Hardwick where you can be alone.

I am furious with Hannah, who has not called or emailed me since we got cut off on Skype. I get that she has no problem moving three thousand miles away from her parents and grandparents and barely talking to them, but I can't believe she's ducking *me*. It feels like she's punishing me, but for what?

I suppose it's possible that there is some technical problem—my computer, the Greenland Internet, her computer at the lab—that is keeping her from getting in touch.

With wet hair, in jeans and a sweatshirt, I head down the stairs that lead to Baird's room. Mrs. Baird opens the door, her expression friendly but professional. "Wren? What can I do for you?"

I can hear what smells like chicken soup bubbling on the tiny stove in her kitchen. I'm interrupting her.

"I'm sorry," I say. "I know we're only supposed to use the phone in an emergency, but I haven't been able to reach my mom for a while, and I was just worried maybe it was my computer? Or has she been trying to reach me here?"

Mrs. Baird gestures me inside and shows me where the phone is. "Do you have the country code? Do you need help dialing?"

"No, it's okay." I hold up my hand to show her that I have the number written in pen across my palm. She gives me a look that says, *Every year I am amazed at how consistently idiotic teenagers can be*—but it's not without sympathy.

"Go ahead," she says, and turns back to the kitchen.

I dial the long sequence of numbers, wondering how much per second this call will cost, and then stand listening to the foreign ring, which is really more a repetitive cat purr/smothered alarm clock buzz than a ring. There's no answer.

Finally I give up.

"Thanks," I tell Mrs. Baird. My voice quavers. "I don't think she's there."

I wonder why I feel like crying. It's something that happens to me sometimes in front of teachers, even when there's nothing wrong, so I shove it aside.

AFTER DINNER I GO back to my room, finish the rest of my homework and change for bed early, still seething at my mother, wondering if I've studied enough for my American history test tomorrow. I am just climbing under the covers when I hear the dull *plonk* against the window of our shared living room.

A stone covered in a gym sock catches on the iron handle of the window. India's up first, always game for adventure. I follow, opening the casement window, retrieving the sock and squinting down into the quad. Nick, Bennett Hale and Van Rowen Alder are grinning up at us. Honor and Eloise come to the window.

"What's up?" asks Honor, not all that quietly.

"Excursion," whispers Nick. "You'll need bathing suits. Or not. Your call."

"But it's freezing," I whisper back.

"We have an American history test in the morning," says Eloise.

Five minutes later, of course, we're all in the quad, bathing suits under our nightgowns and snow boots on our feet—having snuck down the service stairs to the fire exit. Shivering, we follow the boys to the back of the pump and mechanical building behind the athletic center. Bennett feels his way in the dark, running his hands along the top of some pipes that run across the back wall. I hear a little *clink, clink* as he withdraws a very old, rusted key.

"Wow," gasps India. "There really *is* a key."

Apparently this is Hardwick lore, but I still have no idea where we are going.

"Yeah. If you donate a library, they tell you where it's hidden," jokes Van.

Bennett manages to look proud and sheepish at the same time. He opens the back door in a confident, practiced way, then replaces the key. We follow him into a corridor with metal steps leading down, and Nick pulls out a flashlight.

I am never doing something like this again, I remember telling myself very recently. Too late now.

"Ladies," Nick says, gesturing with faux chivalry.

Eloise giggles. We descend the steps, which lead to a tunnel—cold, drippy, smelly—and finally come to a door. I'm not scared, exactly, but when Nick pushes open the door at the end of the tunnel, and the damp, overheated, chlorine-infused air rushes in, I feel relief. Now I know where we are. We just took an underground steam tunnel to the indoor pool. Van flips a switch, and the blue water is lit from underneath.

"Awesome," declares India, immediately shedding her pajamas. The rest of us follow. I'm wearing my old, stretched-out navy-blue eighth-grade swim-team suit. Eloise is in a pink Lilly Pulitzer bikini with a flippy little skirt. India's suit is all complicated macramé with beads on the straps. And Honor is in a petal pink, expensive-looking silk slip that has no business anywhere near chlorine or even water. She dives in first, not hesitating.

The boys wear baggy swim trunks, probably exactly like the ones their dads wore and still wear. They plunge in after her.

I slide in slowly from the edge of the pool, letting the water climb my legs to the point where it reaches my belly. The cold makes me inhale sharply.

"Eek!" I say to nobody.

Nick swims up. "What are you waiting for, Birdie-Bird?"

"It's cold."

"Come on. It feels great once you get in." He reaches a hand out to me. I can't resist, of course, so I take it and slide in the rest of the way.

"I'm still freezing," I say, and then, looking around, add, "This is amazing, though."

"Isn't it?"

Nick is not looking around. He's looking right at me, still holding my hand. My heart gives a double thump, and I struggle to think of something to say.

"I could stay here all night. Couldn't you?" he asks.

"Yeah," I say stupidly. We tread water like that for a while silently. From across the pool I hear India's laughter, splashing, Van teasing Eloise about something, Bennett saying, "Guys, watch this!"

The moments tick by. Nick gives me a quizzical look. His eyes go soft, and he swims a little closer. Our mouths are just above the waterline. For a second, I think he will kiss me. Right here, right now, and right in front of everyone.

Van kicks water at Nick, splashing his face, and yells, "Yeah, Evans, show her your Hardwick!"

Nick turns, laughing, and splashes him back, while I feel crimson spread across my face. In my peripheral vision, I catch a dark streak come toward me under the water, but I'm not really aware of what it is until Honor emerges right next to me, her honey hair perfectly sleek across her shoulders, her slip clinging to her peachy skin. For the first time ever, I think, she looks me right in the eye. "You. Bitch," she says, not loudly, but emphatically.

Then she flips underwater in an expert turns and swims away fast. Nick is behind her in a second, but Honor's already out of the pool and exiting through the main door as though she doesn't care who sees her.

"Shit," says Bennett.

"Yeah," says Nick.

The party seems to be officially over. One by one, we climb out the pool, all of us realizing at the same time that no one brought towels.

"Dudes," says Van, "this sucks."

We dry off as best we can with paper towels from the bathroom and an old, questionable towel Bennett digs out of the lost and found. It's much colder on the way back, with wet skin and wet hair. The three of us sneak back into Selby without talking.

When we get to our room, Honor is either in her room with the light off, or not back at all.

THE FOLLOWING NIGHT AFTER dinner, Chazzy agrees to come over to the Selby common room to practice with me. I tell him the story of the night swim caper, mostly because I think it's a good story and partly because I think it makes me look cool—or at least like I have friends other than him. But when I get to the Nick part where Honor snaps at me, I stumble and skip the details. I'm not sure why.

"I don't get why she suddenly lost it, though," Chazzy says.

"I don't know. It was out of nowhere," I say, though of course I have a pretty good idea why.

"Freaky chick."

"Really."

"We should keep working on our song about her. *New York City girl, your pearls are so briny,*" he sings cheerfully. He grabs for Hummingbird, and I grab her back. I swing the guitar at him mock-threateningly, pretending I'll break her over his head. Chazzy laughs and tickles me in self-defense. "Oh, yeah? Bring it, Wren! You're not rock and roll enough to—"

And then, for some reason I can't explain, I lean forward and kiss him.

His lips are warm, soft and dry, in a nice way.

Chazzy pulls back, looks into my eyes with a startled smile, and then kisses me back.

WHAT YOU HAVE TO understand about this kiss is up to this point I have kissed exactly three boys:

1. Gavin Renfrew, the boy I kissed when I was fourteen and starting to get nervous that if I didn't get

this milestone over with soon, I would be labeled a complete loser. It was more slobbery than I expected.

2. Dave Saperstein, who kissed me at a ninth-grade party. We were officially "together" for a week, until I figured out that I didn't have to like him back just because he liked me.

3. Jason (I never got his last name), the UC Santa Barbara freshman I kissed last summer when Kylie and I went to a Vampire Weekend show at the Bowl and pretended we were in college. That was fun, but I decided to get out of there before things got too crazy. Kylie, on the other hand, stuck around and had a somewhat wilder adventure with her new college "friend."

In no situation (of the grand total of three) have I or would I have considered being the kisser rather than the kissee. I mean, never.

THIS REALIZATION COMES RUSHING in, and I pull away. Chazzy and I look at each other and don't know what to say. So we don't say anything for a while. Eventually I decide to go with, "Do you want to work on that duet from last week?" while really thinking, *WHAT JUST HAPPENED!?*

"Sure," he says, while really thinking I can't imagine what.

If Honor was on speaking terms with me, I realize, I actually *could* report back to her on Chazzy. Oh, well.

My next ridiculous thought is that I feel disloyal to Nick.

Disloyal only in my crush, not because he would care at all about what just happened. I know that. Halfway through our song, Mrs. Baird interrupts, looking for me.

It's about Hannah, and it's not good news.

CHAPTER TWELVE

A Change of Plans

My lips are numb. My tongue is numb. This is what I'm thinking as Mrs. Baird's voice comes at me from a cloudy distance.

We are in the infirmary. Why are we in the infirmary? I'm not the one who's sick. But I can see from her perspective: it's a quiet place, a private place, a place with no personal attachments.

I try to refocus, pressing my tongue against the back of my teeth, trying to feel something concrete. Trying to ground myself to the scratchy orange tweed fabric covering the chair.

"She looks really pale, Mrs. Baird," says Chazzy. He asked to come with me, and they let him for some reason.

"Shock," says the nurse, standing by. Where did she come from? I didn't notice her come in. I try to clear my head.

"Take a deep breath. Now out all the way. Wait, I'm going to get you a paper bag to breathe into." The nurse walks out, her sensible nurse shoes squeaking against the clean floor.

Hannah is not dead. She's not dead, but they can't wake her up. She and part of the research team fell through a snowbridge hiding a crevasse. They were only found because their sled dogs barked all night; the rest of the team tracked the sound and pulled them out.

Hannah hasn't been avoiding me. She's been freezing to death under fifteen feet of snow.

One of the scientists died, and the others are in a hospital in Greenland in hypothermic comas. Their bodies were frozen for so long that they have to be brought back to normal very slowly. They can't be moved.

I piece this information together in bits, but that's the gist.

"I need to go there," is the first thing I blurt out when I finally can speak.

Mrs. Baird and the nurse look at each other. There must be something they are not telling me. Chazzy squeezes my hand.

"Why don't we wait a few days and see when things stabilize?" asks Mrs. Baird. "We couldn't send you over there alone, anyway. We would have to arrange for a staff member to accompany you. Do you have a passport?"

I shake my head. I haven't needed one until now. Everyone should have a passport, I think, just in case. If I ever have kids, I will get them passports right away, even if I have no plans to take them anywhere.

All this time, I was so angry with Hannah, thinking she was too busy or too inconsiderate to call me back. I'm a terrible, terrible daughter.

"It would take at least a week or ten days to get you one,

even if we have it expedited," Mrs. Baird says, ever organized, ever practical.

"Is my mom going to be okay?" My voice sounds tiny.

"The research team leader says the clinic there is very
good and practiced at this technique. But it's a slow pro-
cedure. Fairly nuanced. It could take a while before she's
back to feeling herself," says Mrs. Baird carefully.

Meaning what? Before she can walk? Talk? See? Does
hypothermia cause blindness? I have an almost uncontrol-
lable urge to run back to my dorm room and start madly
scouring the Internet, looking up symptoms and prog-
noses. Then I realize I will have five days all by myself to
do so. The prospect of staying alone at school for Thanksgiving, especially having just experienced it for a weekend,
and now feeling even more—what, orphaned? That's not
right . . .

I can feel my brain tilting into full soap opera territory.
Okay, I tell myself, *get a grip*.

She's not dead. They know what to do. I just need to sit
tight, be patient and wait to hear that she's okay. Then I
will somehow get a passport and go over there and see her.

CHAZZY WALKS ME BACK to Selby, talking quickly in his reassuring
voice. The kiss is a hundred miles behind us, like it never
happened. I half-listen as he talks about breaking things
down, step-by-step this, day-by-day that. I know he's saying
all the right things, and I'm so glad he's there, but honestly I don't think there's anyone who could make me feel
better right now.

Mrs. Baird has managed to get back to the dorm before

me, so Chazzy leaves me at the door. She escorts me upstairs. (Why? Where does she think I'm going to go? That I'll hop a plane with no passport and no money?) When I walk into the room, Eloise, India and Honor are all there. They look expectant, like they know something bad has happened, but they don't know what. Honor's cold glance swings to meet me, but then I see something shift in her eyes.

Wow, I must really look like hell to get any sympathy from her.

"Wren? Are you okay?" India stands up and takes a step toward me.

"Do you want to, uh, talk about it?" Eloise asks uncertainly.

"Not really," I say. "I think I'm going to go to bed."

"'Kay," says India, looking a little relieved. "If you need us . . ."

"Thanks," I say, and head for my room.

Without bothering to change into pajamas or brush my teeth, I climb into bed. I should have insomnia, but instead I feel like I could sleep for days.

Which is what I do, just about.

THE NEXT MORNING, MY roommates, Mrs. Baird, everyone leaves me alone. No one seems to expect me to go to class today, so after waking up at noon, I go for a long walk around the lake.

I stop in at the barn. It's early enough in the day that lessons haven't begun yet. The horses and I pretty much have the place to ourselves. I stand in Chester's stall, letting him snuffle my hair and breathe hot horse breath in my face. Another revelation about riding is that when you feel like you want to be alone and feel like you want a bear hug both at the same time, your horse's stall is the perfect place to go.

I spend the rest of the afternoon alone in our suite on my computer, obsessively researching recovery and/or death from hypothermia. After more than too much time at this, I decide it might be a good idea for me to eat something, even though I'm not hungry. I take a shower, make a peanut butter and jelly sandwich in the common room kitchen, and wrap it in a paper towel to take back upstairs.

On the way, I stop by Mrs. Baird's to see if there's any news. She tells me she's been on the phone twice with the clinic already today, and things are unchanged. Stable, she emphasizes. They won't know for a while how much rehabilitation Hannah will need once she's awake, but she's responding and they're optimistic.

I try not to picture Hannah going through all this. I know too much about it after spending the afternoon combing over every freaky, outlandish detail of the thawing process. It sounds impossible, but you can bring a frozen person back to life.

One story I read was about a three-year-old girl who fell into a pond in Austria. She was brain-dead for an hour and a half before the surgeons managed to bypass her heart with a machine that circulated her blood. They opened her chest and lungs and covered them in foil to get oxygen directly into her from the outside. Amazingly, after a few weeks, the girl revived. She was partly paralyzed at first.

She couldn't talk. And two years later she was fine. Like it never happened.

The lungs, though. I can't think about Hannah in the same situation as that little girl. In my head I see this crazy animated film, *Street of Crocodiles*, they showed us in an art class earlier this fall. The creatures work in a strange factory, full of buttons, doll heads, scissors and screws. At one point, they are smoothing tissue paper over raw meat. The tissue sticks to the meat, turning transparent. The way they do it seems affectionate, almost loving. I picture Hannah, Hannah's lungs—meat under tissue paper—and my mind goes blank.

"Wren?" Mrs. Baird smiles at me, but I haven't heard anything she's said.

"I'm sorry?"

"It's going to be a slow road," she repeats. "We can look into getting a passport for you if you really feel you need to go over there before your mother is recovered enough to travel."

Mrs. Baird seems like she's almost as relieved as I am at the news Hannah is stable. I can't help it, I give her a hug, just because she's there and she does give me the feeling she's going to take care of me. I suddenly get the "house-mother" concept. It's not just an old-fashioned, holdover title.

"The more immediate concern with you is Thanksgiving," she says, stepping back. "Usually we have a few foreign students who plan to stay on campus during the holidays, but this time everybody seems to be accounted for. We can't keep the dining hall open for one student, as I'm sure you understand. I'll be in Salisbury with my family, and you are very welcome to join us."

I try to swallow the lump in my throat away. "Thanks, Mrs. Baird. That's really, really generous." I am touched, but at the same time, I'd much rather hide out in my dorm room for five days. How awkward would I feel staying at a teacher's house? Even a teacher like Gigi, which would be nerve-racking for sure in its own way, but still easier to picture.

I scramble for an alternative plan. Go back to Ventura and stay with Kylie? But that would be awful without Hannah, not to mention expensive.

Thinking about Gigi reminds me of her sister. I wonder what she and her sister do for Thanksgiving. Do they visit their parents? Did Elsbeth tell Gigi before she decided to start the band up again? Maybe she asked Gigi to be in it, and Gigi said no. Maybe Gigi doesn't even care if Elsbeth is in Glow without her. Do they really never talk?

"It'll be just me, Mother and my sister. Her children are visiting their father in California," Mrs. Baird adds in the silence. "Quiet, but Linda's a good cook."

"Thanks," I say again, trying to keep the dread out of my voice. I gesture with my paper-towel-wrapped sandwich and look upward. I really am grateful. Really. "Okay, so . . ."

"There's one more thing. Administrative. It can wait a few days." She brushes it off. "Ms. Taubin will talk to you about it. And I should hear more from the clinic first thing tomorrow. Stop by on your way to chapel."

I head upstairs with my sandwich. Everyone else must be at dinner, which is nice. More time alone where I don't need to answer questions or act like everything is okay. I sit on the window seat and open my biology textbook—because it's mostly memorization, not a ton of thinking. I let my brain wander, forcing it away from Hannah, from what Ms. Taubin could possibly want. Of course, it drifts straight to Chazzy and the kiss.

I wonder briefly if the whole thing even happened. What was I doing? I could never have imagined myself making a move like that, even with Nick. Especially with Nick. Never.

Do I like Chazzy? I mean, of course, I love him; he's my best friend—but why did I do that? Was that even me? I try to imagine what he's doing right now. Maybe he's at dinner, or back in his room, thinking the same things.

I sit like this for a long time, my thoughts circling. Needless to say, I get no biology studying done.

CHAPEL, CHAPEL, CHAPEL. I overslept, and now I'm late. I contemplate just wearing the same clothes I pulled off last night and never bothered to put away, then decide I'd better try to keep it together just a little bit. I throw on tights, a jean skirt and one of those sweaters bought in Ventura so long ago—or at least that's what it feels like, another lifetime. I gather up the books I need and hurry down the stairs, completely forgetting to brush my hair.

We're not allowed to skip breakfast, so that means I'm going to have maybe three seconds to talk to Mrs. Baird before I head for the dining hall. What I'd really like to do is sit in her room by the phone all day. But I think a day or two of lying around feeling sorry for myself is about all Hardwick is going to let me get away with. That goes against its stoic New England values.

Mrs. Baird invites me in and offers me some tea, even though we both know I have to be at chapel in ten minutes. Her voice is even as she gives me the update. Hannah's body temperature is rising slowly. She's still unconscious. She's on a respirator and they have drilled a small hole into her brain and installed a monitor in there so they can keep the pressure perfect. The next thing to do is just to wait for her to wake up.

I nod, trying not to picture that probe thing, and get up to go.

IN MUSIC, I HAVE to will myself back to class, to the drafty room with its whitewashed pegboard walls. Normally this is the easiest place—aside from the riding ring—for me to keep my mind where it's supposed to be, but today I can't. Gigi looks around the room, eyes flashing, challenging us.

Next to me, Chazzy is fighting laughter. His body shakes as he looks at the ground, trying to contain it. He's laughing at me, and it is seriously irritating.

I elbow him, so Gigi doesn't notice. "Shut up," I whisper.

He bites his lip and shakes his head. I don't know what he finds so funny. Besides, I'm not the only one who doesn't bring original songs into class on a regular basis, but almost.

Even shy little Gretchen, aka Alice in Wonderland, has gotten up there. Most people, it seems to me, talented or not, are dashing off epic ballads about trimming their toenails or whatever else comes to mind. Which is fine. I admire them for being able to put it out there. I just feel like if I'm going to sing something, it needs to feel finished, and it needs to feel important, at least to me.

Gigi leans on the edge of a table, arms crossed, eyes intense. She has assigned us the task of writing a song to perform in class, whether completed or a work in progress. Before it was optional, but now it's a requirement.

"I'm not going to tell you what to write about," she says, "just like I would never tell you what to feel. But I will tell you that if you're faking it, if you're posing as someone else, if you're not showing the class something authentic that really comes from you, I will know. And I will not be happy."

"But no pressure," whispers Chazzy to me.

Some of us—or specifically me, because it's obvious she is talking about me—are relying on technique and vicarious emotion in our performance, she goes on, rather than letting the audience in.

Letting the audience in. Doesn't that sound like it would hurt? I can't help picturing a *Night of the Living Dead* scenario in which the zombie audience staggers onto the stage, rips open the guts of the last surviving singer-songwriter, and tries to climb inside. Eww.

"So I'll look forward to hearing what you bring in next time. *All* of you. No excuses. Remember, it's not a recital. I'm not expecting anyone to be perfect."

Gigi turns and erases the blackboard. She does this at the end of every class, though I've never seen her write anything on it. I have no idea why. On the way out, she gives me a funny look, like she wants to say something, but doesn't. Maybe she's heard about Hannah and can't figure out what to say.

"You're scared," Chazzy says as we walk back to Hale after class for another language lab session. "You should put all your freaking out to use. You may as well get something out of having to go through this. Look what it did for Neko Case on her last album. She was depressed as hell, and those are some of the best songs she ever wrote. *Tu . . . as . . . peur.*" He exaggerates the French translation, putting too much emphasis on and space between each word.

"I'm not scared. I just don't need people to hear my songs."

"Well, if you don't care, then what's the issue with people hearing them?"

"That's not what I mean, and you know it," I say.

He starts making clucking sounds, like a chicken, and then like a chicken *en français,* and that pretty much wraps up the conversation. I'm not going to argue with a chicken in any language.

I DO HAVE ONE song. It's about the letters I used to write to my dad as a child, complete with snapshots, now faded in a box. I've been looking through them lately—yes, pathetically, I did bring them to school—wondering what I was so dying to tell him about myself and why. And wondering what I would say now if I actually had the opportunity.

If I am going to let the audience in—"bring something personal to the performance"—this is the topic that's on my mind these days. This, and unconscious Hannah. But I can't write a song about that. Chazzy's heard the one

I'm working on, the one about the letters. Parts he thinks are good. Parts he thinks could be better. Anyway, it's not finished.

A COUPLE OF DAYS later, though I sense Mrs. Baird has put it off for as long as possible, I do have to go see Nina Taubin. She is quite honestly the last person I feel like seeing. I would rather have a meeting scheduled with Honor.

At the appointed time, I pull my coat on, trot down the path toward the woods and knock on the little cottage with the smoke coming out of the chimney. Ms. Taubin looks surprised. Her mouth purses. This time she has lipstick on.

"Oh, hello," she says.

She looks around, like someone else might be there, but then she opens the door wider and nods toward the living room. I take off my coat, because whatever it is she's about to say, I have the feeling it's going to be a fairly long conversation.

"Wren, I'll get right to the point. It's unfortunate timing, but I need to inform you that your enrollment contract has not been signed for next year, and your tuition for the second half of this year has not been paid. Do you know your mother's intentions in regards to next year?"

"No," I say truthfully, because Hannah and I were just focused on getting through this year. We hadn't talked about next year.

"Normally under circumstances like these, it would be possible to make some efforts toward emergency aid for next semester, but without a signed contract and deposit toward next year, it's impossible for the school to extend any financial assistance. Which I'm sure you can understand."

I just blink at her. *I'm sure you can understand* is a phrase reserved for use only in the case of the not understandable. If Hannah has not said I will come back next year, no one can or will help me *this* year.

"I know it's a tough situation," she continues. "If there was another responsible party? A relative?"

I realize I don't even know if Hannah has ever chosen an official guardian in case of a catastrophe. Like being in a coma, for example. There are no relatives she keeps in touch with. So who does that leave? Jonesy? Her yoga teacher? Friends from the paper? There's no one.

"I have a great-aunt," I hear myself say as if listening to someone else, a stranger. "Helen Chisholm. Hannah's— my mother's aunt. But they're not really in touch."

Ms. Taubin nods. "We can look into that. Wren, I really am very sorry about your mother. She's been on my mind so often lately, and then this . . ."

I think about my mother in limbo, oblivious to all that's going on around her. *I have to stay*, I think. This is where she wants me, where she thinks I'm safe. I have to stay, at least long enough for her to wake up and be herself and decide what to do next.

"Now what are your plans for Thanksgiving?" Ms. Taubin asks brightly.

"I don't know yet," I say. "I might go to Mrs. Baird's house."

"What about your roommates? Couldn't you visit one of them? What are their plans?"

I find myself staring at my shoes. "India's family is going to the Bahamas. And Eloise is going to New York with Honor." My face is hot. I don't want to go to Honor's, of course, and I wouldn't expect to, but it still feels awful to say it out loud.

Ms. Taubin stiffens. "Huh. And Hannah and Honor's father were so close. I would have thought—Well, never mind."

I glance up with a start. She puts the brakes on just as she seems to realize she's making it worse. "They were?" I ask.

"We three were in the same class," she says. "Of course. Didn't you know that? Hannah's never talked about Gibby? Or me?" She laughs, and her laugh sounds bitter. Meaning Taubin and Edward Gibson weren't so close? Meaning Taubin had a thing for Honor's dad?

I can't help smiling, imagining how much *that* would bug Honor. Ms. Taubin is not smiling. I suddenly have the impression she's mad at my mother. Or that my mother hurt her feelings somehow. It has never occurred to me before now that a grown-up could feel left out or injured by a friend, especially by a friend from high school, just like she is a girl my age. But I can see on her face it's true.

"Well, it was funny that she ended up . . . in that whole group. Because that really went against all her ideals. They were so different." *Popular* is what she means. Ms. Taubin hesitates, as if she's said way more than she intended. "Anyway, that's eons ago, worlds away. Well, figuratively worlds away. Let me look into the matter of getting in touch with your aunt, and we'll hope for Hannah's rapid recovery."

I move toward the door, but she's not finished with me.

"There's something about friendships in First Year, Wren, before everyone settles in and decides who to be. I understood Hannah like a lot of people didn't. We shared a lot of the same ideals: wanting to lead independent lives, wanting to get out of the shadow of our families' expectations. She wasn't really part of that preppy set deep down. That's not what she wanted. And she proved that. She didn't stay on the East Coast. She didn't let other people choose her career or lifestyle for her. Right?"

The way she says "right," it's like a wish.

"Right," I say. "She thinks it's great you're still here." I'm making this up, of course. Hannah's never mentioned Ms. Taubin or any of her roommates.

"She does?" Ms. Taubin looks startled.

"Yes." I flounder. For some reason I want to make her feel better. "Because you are—you can help students find their independence and—she says it's a real sacrifice. Because of what you wanted to do." I have no idea what she wanted to do.

Ms. Taubin nods, retreating inside herself for a moment. I need to get out of here before I dig myself a hole I can't get out of.

"I know at boarding school, social life can take on a disproportionate relevance," she continues. "Always remember though, what's important is your education. Once you leave here, that's the only thing that will matter. Don't get caught up in the superficial details. Come and talk to me again if you need anything. We'll keep working on the tuition problem. Perhaps we'll hear something from your mother soon, and we can resolve it."

"Thanks," I say.

I walk back to Selby in the cold, feeling like I know a lot more about Ms. Taubin now than I want to. As I reach the top of the stairs on the floor below ours, I pass the room that was my mother's her first year. Two Lowers, Betsy McBride and Sabrina Cantwell, live there now. I picture Hannah and Nina Taubin in that room, sharing notes for history class, gossiping about the boys in their class—does Ms. Taubin know how to gossip, even if she wanted to?—or maybe not sharing, not talking, having nothing in common. Ms. Taubin, hoping for a smile or an invitation. My mother, the Honor of her Selby days. Could that have been the way it was?

I have an art history paper to write. I should focus on that. Although who knows whether I will be here to hand it in.

CHAPTER THIRTEEN

Stone Cove Island

When Mrs. Baird comes to get me from dinner and tells me I have a long-distance call on the house phone, I have this wild hope that it's Hannah—awake, alive, intact—but it is not. Unbeknownst to me, I *do* have an official guardian, the same person whose name popped out of my mouth to Ms. Taubin. If this weren't my actual life, it might be funny.

This guardian comes in the form of my ancient, icy great-aunt, Helen Chisholm. The one my mother never talks to. Great-Aunt Helen has always disapproved of Hannah's "inappropriate life choices." Those are her words, at least her words according to Hannah. Hannah has a special squinched face and Yankee accent she does when she imitates Great-Aunt Helen. It goes without saying that Hannah has always despised her aunt's puritanical, closed-minded, miserly ways. Yet this is the woman she has chosen to take care of me in case something happens to her.

As it turns out, Great-Aunt Helen really *does* talk that way, with the Yankee accent and, I will see later, the squinched face. Charles Dickens apparently drafted her character while on some New England vacation, because they just do not make them like this anymore. Great-Aunt Helen is no more delighted with her fate than I am. The duty only falls to her as my closest living relative. Her voice on the phone is stony, as though I have interrupted her at the most inconvenient moment possible, when really she is the one who called me. Maybe it is the fact of my existence that is the real inconvenience.

"I have been apprised of the situation," she says after a negligible hello and zero beating around the bush. "And I believe the best course of action is for you to come here so we can discuss matters. My groundskeeper Bernard will call for you in my car and bring you to me." Great-Aunt Helen does not ask how Hannah is or how I am. I don't think I say a single word after, "Hi, Aunt Helen." Then she spends a minute or two on the phone with Mrs. Baird, who hangs up with a sympathetic shrug for me.

"It will be okay," says Mrs. Baird. "Your mother will get better, and it will all get sorted out."

My mother remains in the same medically induced coma, carefully thawing. Or at least I hope that's what's happening. I haven't been able to talk to the doctors in Greenland myself, so I am going by Mrs. Baird's reports. I hope they are not sugarcoated. According to her, the doctors say that Hannah will eventually be fine. But how can they know that for sure? And how long can a body be held like that in limbo, not dead and not living?

BACK IN THE SUITE, I fill Eloise and India in on what's happening. Honor is there too, but I don't count her as present.

She's clearly not interested. I try to describe Great-Aunt Helen, but really I don't have much to go on. I stick to the facts: she used to live in Boston, but about fifteen years ago she moved full-time to the family beach house on Stone Cove Island, an island off the northern coast of Massachusetts and the place my mother spent every summer growing up. It's where my grandfather tried to teach me too many sailing knots in the cold, the time my mom got so mad.

"We used to have a place there when I was little," says Honor from her bed. She's on her cell phone, reading something. She doesn't look up.

"Really?" I ask, mostly shocked that she's decided to join the conversation.

"Before we got our place in Amagansett. We sold it when I was a baby, though. My father never really liked it. Plus it's way too hard to get there from New York." She finally looks at me. "Nobody goes there in the winter, you know."

I stare back. "My aunt does, apparently. She lives there year-round."

Honor turns back to her phone. "You'll see."

India and Eloise look at each other but say nothing.

IT'S A VERY LONG drive, with the silent Bernard—another character from Dickens. He and Great-Aunt Helen are perfect for each other—in my great-aunt's huge, unstylish Lincoln. Lucky for me, I have a good book (*The Secret History*) and can read in the car without getting sick.

About three and a half hours later, we arrive in the small port town of Gloucester and load ourselves onto the car ferry. It takes another forty minutes from here to Stone Cove Island.

The island is clearly a place for people who like their privacy. The ferry docks in the harbor of what seems like the downtown. A row of neatly painted Victorian storefronts sits hibernating, their perfect facades closed up, awaiting summer's throngs. I see no one. The sun is setting, and the wind kicks up icy spray off the water.

Bernard swings left onto the main street and then along a winding road that hugs the bluffs. Dark shingled houses nestle into the cliff side, surrounded by evergreen hedges and windblown pines. It's already snowed here at least once. A few of the houses have lights on, but most sit dark, shut up tight for the season.

Great-Aunt Helen's house is a pristine Victorian, at the top of the hill near the end of the road. It's tall and angular and seems prim compared to its beachy shingled neighbors. White clapboard. Black shutters. From a distance, the house is pretty. Close up, it is austere. Maybe in the summer there are some flowers to cheer things up. Bernard stops the Lincoln in front of the house and nods to indicate this is it. I can count on one hand the number of words he's spoken on the way here.

GREAT-AUNT HELEN GREETS ME at the door without a smile, looking exactly the way I expected. Her white hair is pulled into a low, neat bun. She is wearing a gray wool dress and a darker gray cardigan: monochromatic hostess wear. Her eyes are blue ice cubes. Immediately, it seems, we are sitting in what she calls the drawing room, what I would call her den. She is drinking tea, and I am perched with my hands folded in my lap, drinking nothing. She doesn't offer me a cup of tea or even a glass of water. So maybe not that much of a hostess. Really, more all business. She launches straight into the topic at hand. The school has called and asked her about my plans for next year and my tuition for this year.

"I find it rather offensive," she says. She squints at me distrustfully, as though I am trying to work some scam.

Here's what I know from Hannah: Great-Aunt Helen had two sons, both of whom went to Hardwick Hall. One left college early to come back and now lives as a "gentleman farmer" in New Hampshire. (Again, Hannah quoting Great-Aunt Helen.) The other was killed in an embassy bombing in Kenya in the late 1990s. This personal history—combined with the fact that when Great-Aunt Helen was a girl, her father thought it was pointless to educate girls seriously and would never have let her attend a coed school—meant Hardwick was not an option. That probably contributes to her point of view that Hardwick is a waste of both time and money for me and possibly for anyone.

"Especially as you live in California," she finishes, pronouncing *California* in an unfamiliar, suspicious way as though it's a benighted foreign land or an unsavory food. "What could it possibly mean to anyone there?"

I clear my throat. "Well, people do come east for school. I'm not the only student from California at Hardwick."

This is almost not true, but her argument is ridiculous. I think of Philip Han (computer 1), and then am surprised to hear myself defending the school, listing the variety of courses I can take there, the many sports I can try, the wonderful teachers, the riding, the tradition and history, the independence I'm gaining being on my own, the excellent preparation for college . . . I swear I sound like a robot programmed to recite the Hardwick Hall catalog.

I guess I must believe some of it, though I've never verbalized any of it. I think part of it must be a pure gut reaction to Great-Aunt Helen, the kind of person who makes you want to disagree with everything she says just to deny having anything in common.

The gloom of this house and the austerity of its furnishings reminds me of the Salem witch trials in *The Crucible*, something we've been studying at Hardwick. The real Salem isn't far from here, and it's easy to picture Great-Aunt Helen right at home at the stake with her torch. What will happen to me if I have to leave school at the end of the semester? They won't let me go home. I will have to live here—if Great-Aunt Helen will even have me—and I can't do that.

"It would be quite another thing," she insists, "if your mother had made any *arrangements*. Then I would be prepared to consider allowing you to continue, though it would be a real hardship for me to take on that responsibility from this distance."

The word *arrangements* rolls uncomfortably from her mouth like it's something dirty. She is talking about money, obviously. Great-Aunt Helen is from that old-money New England world that finds the discussion of anything financial to be utterly distasteful. There are lots of students like that at Hardwick, wearing worn khakis fraying at the cuffs and moth-eaten cashmere sweaters that belonged to their grandfathers, driving beat-up old Mercedes and Volvos with Haverford Lacrosse stickers on the bumpers and an assortment of old ropes and sails stuffed into the trunks. And yet every one of them has a trust fund guaranteeing they'll never have to work. I don't know if this is exactly true of Great-Aunt Helen, but Hannah always gave me the impression she was rich.

BY THE TIME DINNER is finished—Great-Aunt Helen eats a very plain and very early dinner; lots of boiled things and no spices at all, not even pepper—the matter is settled. She is not prepared to keep sending me to Hardwick, and there will be no further discussion.

All I want to do is go back to school and sleep in my own bed for what little time I'll have left in it. If it weren't three hours and a ferry ride away, I would call a cab.

The room Great-Aunt Helen puts me in—*my* room, I guess, in the event that things don't go well for Hannah—is tiny and dark, full of creaking, ancient furniture too tall for the narrow space. The effect is kind of Haunted Mansion at Disneyland, where the room stretches vertically while you stand still, and the paintings have eyes that seem to move. The paintings here don't actually have eyes that move, of course, but just about. Above the bed is the portrait of a dour Puritan lady holding a very pale baby in white lace. Is it dead? The plaque in the frame reads, "MRS. GRIMES AND HER INFANT."

The pipes in the old bathroom sink screech when I

turn the water on—separate hot and cold faucets. The hot water never gets hot, no matter how long I run it. I huddle under the cold, thin quilt and wish for a nightlight for the first time in about ten years.

I THINK I SLEEP for a few hours and then wake up, feeling the cold air stir above my face like someone is standing over me, breathing. I spend the rest of the night staring at the tongue-and-groove ceiling, my eyes unwilling to close. When the sun starts to come up, I fall back to sleep uneasily, only to be awakened at seven fifteen. Helen wordlessly shakes me into consciousness, then turns away once she's convinced my eyes are open.

By daylight, I realize the room is not scary, just bleak. Despite knowing what Great-Aunt Helen will think, I put on the same clothes from the day before—the warmest things I have with me—and go downstairs, where she has half a grapefruit and some black coffee waiting for me. I sit across from her in the kitchen at the plain farm table while she stares over her coffee cup at me. She raises her pointy silver grapefruit spoon. It has tiny, sharp teeth.

"As a girl," she says, stabbing the air just above her plate with the implement, "I was raised not to laze abed and inconvenience my hosts. But I suppose one cannot fault you when there has been no one to teach you any manners."

With that, she consumes her grapefruit in silence, section by section, and pours herself another cup of black coffee. *The Boston Globe* lies folded on the table to her left, but Great-Aunt Helen doesn't allow herself the luxury of reading while she eats. I'm too afraid to ask for milk or sugar, and I'm even more afraid to tell her I don't like coffee. Instead I take tiny, bitter sips. I feel like a little girl at a tea party, pretending to drink from her miniature china cup, except this scalding sludge is real.

AFTER BREAKFAST, I AM turned out into the yard like a pony or a dog. I'm supposed to be here for two days, but it's obvious Great-Aunt Helen a) thinks that's two days too long and b) expects me to entertain myself. That's okay, I realize. Roaming the island alone, even in the cold, is preferable to spending hours with her.

I follow the footpath around the side of the house to the back, curious about the view. It's incredible. So different from California, where the coast is wide and sweeping. Here it's rocky and craggy, with little coves and inlets. Where California is open, the terrain here seems full of secrets. The houses sit close to the edge of the island for maximum exposure to sky and water. But in a few places, the earth has buckled in narrow slides. It's a little unnerving. I make sure not to stand too close to them. It must be beautiful here in the summer, I think. At the same time, Honor's skepticism also makes sense: it's frigid and lonely right now. No one would come here in the winter.

From the shingled cottage next door I hear a gentle jingle of wind chimes, and a fat black Lab comes loping over to me, pink tongue extended.

"Sparkler!" I hear a man's voice shout. "Don't worry. He's friendly."

The man is middle-aged, maybe fifty, maybe older. He

has on a parka and round glasses with wire frames, and his graying hair is about as windswept as the bluff. He strides over, his right arm extended just like Sparkler's tongue. When he reaches me, his handshake is dry and firm. He looks me right in the eye. Great-Aunt Helen has friendly neighbors. Much friendlier than she is.

"Jay Northsworthy," he says. "You staying with Mrs. Chisholm?"

"Yes, she's my great-aunt," I say. Sparkler is standing on my foot, staring up at me imploringly. "I don't have any treats," I say with a laugh. Great-Aunt Helen has no pets, of course: another strike against her. I never trust people who don't like animals. Jay steps away and tilts his head, as if sizing me up. He shuffles his mental Rolodex briefly and smiles when he comes up with the answer. "I'm going to say Hannah's daughter, but I'm going out on a limb. Am I right?"

"Yes. You're right."

"You don't look *exactly* like her, but there's something there."

My eyes tear up a little. It feels funny to talk to a stranger about Hannah when I don't know when I'll see her again. Funny in a bad way. I take a deep breath and recover. "I'm Wren. I'm her daughter. It's nice to meet you."

Behind his glasses, his own eyes are rheumy from the wind. "Great to see you. Is she on the island too?"

I shake my head. "No, she's . . . working. In Europe. I'm here on my own." I can't quite bear to tell the whole story.

"Too bad. I'd have loved to see her. I run the newspaper here, the *Gazette*. Hannah wrote for me a bit during her summer breaks from Barnard. Then, of course, she went on to bigger things. The *LA Times* . . . We're so proud of her here." He's older than Hannah, but only by maybe ten years. He must have been young then to be the newspaper editor.

I nod and turn away, worried that if I talk, I'll start crying. I focus on Sparkler, reaching down to scratch his head. He pants in gratitude.

"But don't you live in California?" he asks. "Or did she move to an East Coast paper?"

"We still live in California," I manage. I look up. "This was just a long assignment. And I started boarding school."

"Ah. Of course. A Hardwick family. She caved at last, eh?" Jay smiles. "She's an incredible girl, Hannah. Woman, I mean." He shakes his head ruefully, loosening a memory. "I was her boss, but you know what? She had me twisted around her finger." He laughs awkwardly. "Don't tell her I said that. Anyway, long time ago." He backs away from me toward his house and snaps his fingers; Sparkler bounds over to him. "You know what? Why don't you come by the paper later, if you're not busy? I've got something to show you. I think it's something you'll want to see."

"I'm not busy," I tell him. I'm the opposite of busy.

"Great. Sparkler and I will be there. I'm usually there by now, in fact. Getting a late start today."

I watch this man—yet another stranger from my mother's past—disappear back into his house with his dog. I don't ask where the *Gazette* is. It's a pretty small island. Besides, I'm too busy wondering what he wants to show me.

As I come back around to the front of Great-Aunt

Helen's house, I catch the taillights of the Lincoln turning out of the driveway. I wave, hoping Bernard will give me a ride. Either he doesn't see me, or he doesn't want to see me. At any rate, he doesn't stop. Thanks, Bernard. I have to walk down into town.

BY THE TIME I get to the main street, I'm too cold and hungry to find the *Gazette* office without something to eat besides sour grapefruit. The freezing wind keeps reminding me of Hannah. However bad this is, it must be nothing compared to what she suffered in that crevasse that night. I try not to think about it, keeping my head down as I walk. The grapefruit is searing my stomach, making me more hungry rather than less.

There's a diner that looks open, so I decide to stop there.

The waitress is young, but no nonsense, like my great-aunt. Her plastic red nametag reads KELLY. She gives me a quick appraisal, then dumps me and a menu into a booth. I order hot chocolate and a blueberry muffin. The diner is warm, but I can still feel the cold air from outside seep through the glass.

I sit there, thinking about Jay and how much he and my mother have in common. Both work at newspapers. He lives next door to the family house. Has he lived there a long time? If she were writing for the paper here when she was in college, he would have been about thirty. Could she have been attracted to him? Is he attractive? It's impossible for me to judge if a fifty-year-old man is attractive, but it's conceivable.

Someone from Hannah's long-ago past: check.

They live in different worlds: if this island isn't another world, I don't know what is, so double check.

Would she have had a reason to come back here, though, closer to the time I was born?

Waitress Kelly interrupts my thoughts, slipping my order onto the table with an efficient *clunk-swish.*

"Got everything?" she asks, but she's already walking away.

When I look up to answer, I'm facing a girl my age, who's sitting two booths away. Now I wish I had my book, because I'll have to eat staring at her. I look out the window again. Maybe I can look like I'm taking in the sights.

"Muffins are better at the Picnic Basket," she says in a loud voice.

There's no one else in the diner, so I would have known she was talking to me even if she'd whispered.

"Excuse me?" I ask.

"The Picnic Basket has really good blueberry muffins," she repeats with a friendly smile. "I usually stick to toast here."

"Thanks," I say. Too bad; that advice would have been more useful before I ordered. I smile back. "You're right." I put down the muffin. "Too sweet."

"And too dry. Who're you visiting?"

"How do you know I'm visiting?" I ask.

"Because I know everyone on the island. Especially this time of year," she says. "Especially any kids my age."

I have to laugh. "Right. Makes sense." I want to tell her she can come sit with me if she wants. It seems silly to yell across the empty room. She has a notebook, though, so maybe she's working on something. And it seems too weird to invite her to sit with me. She's pretty in a low-key way, the kind of girl who, in a movie, the guy doesn't notice until the end. Her hair is straight, dirty blonde, shoulder-length, and her full smile seems a little big for her face, but it's a friendly smile that softens her sharp cheekbones.

"I'm Eliza," she says.

"Wren," I say. "I'm here for a couple of days visiting my great-aunt. Helen Chisholm? You probably know her."

Eliza almost makes a face but stops herself in time. I grin, though. It seems like we're on the same page. "Where do you live?" she asks.

"Right now at boarding school, in Connecticut. But normally I live in California. Kind of north of LA."

Eliza nods. "Never been. What grade are you in?"

"Lower Year," I answer automatically. "I mean, I'm a sophomore."

"Me too," she says. "Our school's teeny. It's all the same kids since kindergarten. It's like having forty brothers and sisters."

I nod, even though I have no idea what that would be like. It would be hard to grow up on a tiny island like this. But even as I think it, I realize I've pretty much grown up on the tiny island of Hannah and Wren.

"So you know my aunt?" I ask Eliza.

"I do. I know all the year-rounders. Your aunt, your whole family, are old-timers. They've had that house forever. They might have even built it."

"This is the first time I've met her," I admit. "I don't have that much family. Just me and my mom, but she's away."

Eliza brightens. "Oh, you should come back in the summer. There's a lot more to do. The beaches are great. And the sailing. Do you like to sail?"

I shrug. "I've never really done it. Hey, listen do you know Jay Northsworthy? Of course you must, right? He's my aunt's neighbor, and he invited me to stop by and see the paper. I don't know where it is, though."

"Sure, I know Jay," says Eliza. "You know where the high school is?" I shake my head. "You just keep going down Water Street past the village green, and then it's just another block. You'll see."

"Thanks," I tell her. I sip my hot chocolate and wonder: If I really did have to come live here with Great-Aunt Helen, would this girl be my friend?

THE OFFICE OF THE *Stone Cove Island Gazette* is tiny, not very high-tech and jammed full of file boxes and stacks of old editions. It makes the Ventura bureau of the *LA Times*—home base to three reporters—look like command central. But I kind of like it for that. Jay and Sparkler seem to be the only employees, other than one high school boy struggling with a printer that looks as old as some of the furniture in Great-Aunt Helen's house.

"You made it," calls Jay, his welcoming voice booming. I've met three people on this island so far (not counting Bernard), and the two who aren't members of my family are infinitely friendlier than the one who is. "Come in.

Come in. I was just going through some files. Wait until you see what I managed to find."

I think, *Just like this? Without me even having to dig? In front of his son, or the intern, or whoever that boy is?*

Jay beckons me over to his desk. "Not what I was looking for, though." He hands me a blue bandanna, an assortment of kitschy postcards, still blank, and a lobster claw key chain. "I tend to keep stuff. Not what I was looking for, exactly, but this stuff is your mom's, I think. The bandanna, definitely. The key chain, I'm not sure, but—"

"That's why they call it the *Packrat Gazette*," the boy chimes in from under the printer.

Jay rolls his eyes good-naturedly. "It's more organized than it looks," he explains. "Most things I can put my hand to, despite Charlie's wisecracks. Maybe it's at home, though. We need to close the issue pretty soon, but what do you say I take a look tonight? You'll still be here in the morning?"

I nod. But again I wonder: *Why doesn't he just come out and say what it is he wants to show me?*

I HAVE HOURS IN front of me, a whole, unscheduled day stretching out. Wren, hanging around. It feels strange after Hardwick, where there's always somewhere you need to be.

First I wander to the end of the ferry dock. From there I can take in the wide crescent of the harbor. Above the town, an old hotel rises up like a giant dollhouse on the top of a hill. To my right, as I face the main street, I can see a lighthouse, painted in wide stripes of black and white. I can't tell how far away it is, but I decide to walk there. I've got all day.

I walk and walk, out of town, then down a big hill, along the road that looks like it should take me to the lighthouse. I can see it in the distance, but I never seem to get any closer. The wind off the water blows sand across the road and stings my face. Dampness creeps into my shoes. On a warmer day, this would probably be a nice walk. I am just considering giving up when I see a weathered sign: BEACH ACCESS.

I follow it down a sandy path that weaves between two enormous, sprawling summer houses: "Summersweet" on my right and "Beach Glass" on my left, both closed up tight for winter. *Pretentious*, I think. No one in Ventura names their house. Though it's hard to argue with the beauty of the houses themselves.

The path cuts through brambles before leading me to a rocky drop and onto the beach. The sand isn't wide here, but the turn in the cove forms a barrier, causing the waves to break far offshore. The water is very still and clear. It would be a great place for little kids to swim. There's a ring of blackened stones where people have built fires before, and I wish I had one now.

I could have been a kid swimming here, if my father is Jay, I think, *if Hannah hadn't run away from this life.* On the other hand, I could see how Great-Aunt Helen might make anyone feel like running was the only reasonable option.

But what if it *is* Jay? Will that mean summers here? Sunbathing at this beach? Sitting around this fire at night?

There are initials carved all over the giant logs, old ones and new ones. I don't see an "HV + JN" or even just an "HV." I search until I'm too cold, and the sun has sunk down too far to warm my little patch of sand. I give up on the lighthouse expedition.

I'M HUNGRY AGAIN, SO I decide to stop in at the place Eliza recommended, the Picnic Basket. It's a cozy, wood-paneled cottage that looks warm even from the outside. The door shuts behind me with a cheerful jangle. It almost feels hot after wandering around the island for so long.

"Welcome," says a lady in a denim shirtdress and apron. "Boy, your cheeks are pink. Wind blowin' out there?"

"Yes," I say, rubbing my hands together. My mouth waters at the list of delicious sandwiches. They all have names like Irene, Hugo and Gloria. "Are those famous people from the island?" I ask.

"No, they're named after storms. The Ida's my favorite. Roast turkey with cranberry chutney. She was an almost Thanksgiving hurricane." She eyes me curiously, as Jay and Eliza did. "This your first visit?"

"It's that obvious, huh?" I answer with a laugh. I contemplate ordering the Ida until I realize I only have five dollars left from breakfast. I didn't think to bring much money from school, so I go with Eliza's recommendation. It looks like a muffin-only diet today. "Do you have any blueberry muffins?"

She smiles back. "You're in luck. Three left. Usually they're gone by ten, but this time of year, weekends are slow. It's the best season to see the island, though, in my opinion. You're a little late for the foliage, but you got the place to yourself. Just the rocks and the ocean and the salt air and the sky."

And all the stuff nobody wants to talk about, like money, I think. But I let her talk on, which she seems to enjoy, as I spend two of my last five dollars on my muffin.

BACK OUTSIDE, I START the climb to Great-Aunt Helen's house. On the bluff road, two girls whiz past me on bikes, and one waves. Eliza. This island really is small. I already feel like I know half the people who live here.

OVER DINNER, I TRY asking Great-Aunt Helen about Hannah's island friends, about who she hung out with the summers she came here. I mention Jay a few times, and Hannah's summer job writing for the newspaper. Great-Aunt Helen has nothing to say, other than that Hannah "did not always comport herself like a Verlaine." She gives me a pointed look, making it clear that for all she knows, the other side of my family is made up of South American chinchillas. She's not going to provide any clues to my father's identity, but at the same time, if she has no idea who he is, maybe I can rule out Stone Cove Islanders or any old family friends in Boston.

"I don't know what your mother was thinking," concludes Great-Aunt Helen at the end of the dinner, apropos of nothing but another long silence.

"Having me, you mean?" I can't help it.

"Of course not," she snaps, but has enough grace to look a little embarrassed. "What I mean is, she could have had a lovely life here. She had her family, she had nice friends and she knew everyone . . ."

Everyone, meaning everyone worth knowing.

"Maybe she was looking for an adventure. Somewhere she could make her own rules."

"She certainly did that," says Great-Aunt Helen, pursing her lips. "She certainly did."

IN THE MORNING, IT takes about three minutes to pack the few items I brought with me. When I hear the wind chimes next door, I go out back and find Jay crossing the yard in my direction. I'm so jittery, wondering what he wants to show me. I've been thinking about it ever since I woke up. An old baby photo? A letter? A page torn from my mother's old diary? A copy of my birth certificate?

He hands me a typed sheet. "Here it is."

It's a yellowed sheet of newspaper. I read the headline: "The Future of the Piping Plover."

Piping Plovers have made their home on Stone Cove Island for hundreds of years. But their nesting habits make them vulnerable to predators as well as humans . . .

"What do you think of that?" asks Jay. I glance up, baffled. He is beaming. "Your mom's first story in the *Gazette*. She wrote that when the Migratory Birds Convention Act Amendment was passed in 1994."

Yes. That's my mom. Once the environmentalist, always the environmentalist. "And you've kept it all this time," I say. That could mean something, couldn't it? I picture Chazzy, snickering at me for being a fool again.

"I keep everything. Charlie is half right about that. The *Gazette* has an incredible archive, should anyone ever be interested. Which I highly doubt, of course. I've got no illusions. There were a few patchy years there while I was on leave—"

"On leave?" I ask. *To California? Or New York? About seventeen years ago?*

"I took a little sabbatical. I was in the Peace Corps in Mali for about five years. Then I came back, and no one else seemed to want to step in at the *Gazette*, so I took up right where I left off. And here I am today. Not what I expected from life, but I've had a good run. No complaints."

"Wow," I say. He and Hannah definitely have a lot of things in common, but geography is not one of them. "That must have been amazing. When were you there?"

"Oh, let's see. Ninety-eight to two thousand three or four. It was quite an experience. But it was also nice to come home."

"Uh-huh. I bet," I say, watching my hunch flame out.

WHEN IT'S TIME FOR me to go, my great-aunt does not say goodbye. Instead she leaves a note. (As a kid, my mother taught me to say goodbye to people in person, but whatever.) Her penmanship is excellent. Apparently Great-Aunt Helen had errands to run. She's got to be the busiest lady on this almost-deserted island.

I don't understand why she had me come all the way here if she'd already decided not to help me—unless it was to make the point that it was her decision. Sparkler gives me a lick before I take off though, so that's nice.

As I climb into the Lincoln, I almost feel like asking Bernard what it's like working for my great-aunt. But there's no point. He'd never tell me.

CHAPTER FOURTEEN

Yearbook

It's almost check-in by the time Bernard finally pulls the car up to Hardwick Hall. When we crunch onto the long gravel drive, I don't think I have ever been so relieved to arrive anywhere in my life. Two days on Stone Cove Island have made me see Hannah's world through her eyes, at least more than I think I did before. It's both beautiful and ugly, tiny and frozen in time—frozen so as not to let anyone in or anyone out. I can see how hard it was for her to leave and how impossible it was to stay. I wish so much I could talk to her about summers there, about writing for the *Gazette*, exploring those craggy coves, and whether Great-Aunt Helen's house creeped her out the way it did me.

I picture her as she appears in her Last Year class portrait, poised and self-assured, looking like she belongs. She spent a lifetime saying how different she was from her parents, how she never felt at ease in their world, how she couldn't wait to get away once she was old enough. But in that photo, at least, she looks completely at home. Hardwick wasn't uncomfortable for her the way it is for me.

I wonder what Stone Cove Island was like for her. Was she at home there? What I am pretty sure of is, if she'd stayed, that island would have been pretty uncomfortable with some of her choices.

LATER THAT NIGHT, IN bed, I can't sleep. From the moment I shamble into the suite, I make it clear that I don't want to talk about the weekend. Eloise and India leave me alone, thankfully. Honor, of course, is no issue. She barely notices I've returned.

I see my mother, frozen in some hospital in Greenland, and my heart races. She can't die. She can't just die. Especially now. We've always been so close; now she's like some stranger. Not like my actual mother. I need to understand her, who she is now and who she used to be. I can't let her go, not knowing.

I take out the blue bandanna Jay gave me and spread it across my pillow. It doesn't smell like Hannah. It doesn't smell like anything.

I shift onto my stomach. Dwelling on this is only taking me down a spiral to nowhere. Even if I could get answers from Hannah about any of this in theory, I can't do it in reality.

Then I remember I have her yearbook. I haven't looked at it since I unpacked the day I got here. As quietly as I can, I hop down to grab it from my bookshelf and get back under the covers with the little reading light I use when I don't want to wake India up—not that I'm in any danger of doing so. She's snoring just as loudly as always.

I open the book and search for Hannah's page. Each

Last Year gets a page with a black-and-white portrait and a smaller collage with pictures of their friends, quotes, interests, summer houses, horses, cryptic lists of past accomplishments, predictions, inside jokes. I pass Nina Taubin's picture as I page through to my mother's. She wears the same pinched mouth and unhappy smile she does now. Her collage is minimal: all achievements and no fun. Hannah's page, on the other hand, is packed—mostly with things other people wrote about her. The first line reads, "Prettiest girl not to care about that kind of thing." Her prediction is, "Go west, young girl (but we think the Man on the Moon might not let you go)." She's salutatorian, with an honor medal in English. There are scribbled notes from friends and admirers—lots of boys, judging from the terrible handwriting. "Man on the Moon"—I know that song; it's by R.E.M., one of my mother's favorite bands. Another song I'd heard over and over growing up.

I flip to Warren Norwood. Not surprisingly, his page is theater top to bottom: Norwood in Shakespearean bloomers in one shot, an abstracted horse costume in another, a tuxedo with rouged cheeks in a third. A quote from Oscar Wilde: "Always forgive your enemies; nothing annoys them so much."

Nearer the front, Honor's father's page boasts an impressive list of accolades: "Most likely to succeed without even trying"—as well as favorite quotations and inside jokes with friends: "Gibbous! Never say never!" (The only reason I know the word *gibbous* is because it's in the Aimee Mann song "Ghost World," and I looked it up. It means a waxing moon.) And several quotes from *The Catcher in the Rye*.

I turn back to Hannah's page. In cramped boy-freehand is a little drawing that fills the left margin: a gnarled tree, a heart carved into its trunk with the words "Holden loves Franny," and below the drawing, the initials EG. Initials, like the clue I was looking for in the driftwood on Stone Cove Island.

I just finished reading *The Catcher in the Rye*, so I know who Holden is. "Franny" must be my mom. I picture Hannah's bookshelf at home, *The Catcher in the Rye* filed next to *Franny and Zooey*. It's obvious who EG is. Edward Gibson was obsessed with J. D. Salinger, Edward Gibson was in love with my mom. *Gibbous. Gibby.* The Man in the Moon. My horrible roommate's dad loved my mom. I sit straight up in bed. My hands feel clammy. The facts tip slowly against each other: *tip, tip, tip.* And then in a terrible rush of dominoes, they clatter down inside my head.

1. Honor and I have matching anchor charms, though she swears the design is one of a kind.
2. Honor's dad and my mom were close at school, according to Ms. Taubin.
3. Both spent time on Stone Cove Island.
4. Before I left for boarding school, Hannah, in a grand gesture, bought me a Gibson guitar. Hannah doesn't know what kind of guitar Aimee Mann plays. Of course she doesn't. She was thinking about the *name* of the guitar. Gibson. Her old love. Her secret.

I drop the yearbook, recalling what Honor said about their house on Stone Cove Island, how her father had sold it when Honor was a baby because he "didn't like it there anymore."

Was that because Hannah had moved to California and was never coming back?

Someone from Hannah's long-ago past. Check.

They live in different worlds. Not *from* different worlds. Double check.

"Holy shit, Hannah." I say the words out loud. I feel like I'm dreaming, but I know I'm not. India's jackhammer snoring reassures me that I am firmly here, now, in reality.

I'm sure I know who my father is. Not Norwood. Not Jay. Edward Gibson. Honor's father. I confront this idea full-on. It seems both obvious and impossible. Honor is my half-sister. I have a half-sister. And a half-brother! I almost laugh. Ned is good news, at least.

I know how Honor's going to feel about this. But what about her father? My father, I mean. What's his reaction likely to be?

In the Disney version of this, Honor and I become best friends and scheme to get our parents back together. In the real-life version, the news of me being her (half-)sister is likely to be the single stain on Honor's platinum-plated life. Yes, I'm pretty confident that no one involved is going to be all that happy about this messy revelation. Hannah isn't going to hop on a plane, thrilled that the secret is finally out, all set for a tasteful wedding ceremony in a cream-colored suit and minimalist bouquet, coma notwithstanding. That leaves me alone with the good news.

I stare up at the underside of India's bed, and the whole room spins.

THE NEXT MORNING I go to breakfast early, when I'm sure almost no one will be there. I need to think, and I need to be by myself to do it. I also need to get out of our room before Honor is up. I dread seeing her, even though of course for her, nothing has changed. But somehow knowing and being in the same room with her not knowing seems intolerable. How can I say anything? Or not say anything? Thoughts are pounding so loudly in my head it seems strange that people around me—walking by on the path, the few early birds lining up to check in, the kitchen staff spooning out oatmeal—can't hear them.

I sit at the farthest table and stare into my plate. I don't know what to do next. I don't even know what to want to do next. I want to meet my father. I want to understand why my mother did this, because it makes no sense. Of course, only two people can answer those questions—the what and the why—so for now, it's still a riddle.

I'M SO HAPPY WHEN I see Chazzy in the Hale stacks after English that I can barely keep myself to library-level volume. We spend half an hour in the language lab working on the *plus-que-parfait* and *conditionnel passé*. I've already resolved not to tell him or anyone else about this crazy business until the dust settles internally and I can talk to Hannah. Eventually she'll wake up, and I need to hear her say I'm right.

She has to wake up. She *will* wake up. The doctors say she will.

But on the way back to class, Chazzy asks, "So what's new, Wren?"

It's a joke we have since we see each other multiple times a day, pretty much every day. Usually we'll ask it after we've already spent hours together. And I suspect it's also a sort of unspoken joke about the kiss. Because that is something we still haven't discussed or repeated. But miraculously, nothing has really changed between us. He's still my best friend. I cling to that. I wonder if he does too.

"What's new?" I say. "Oh, you know. The usual . . ."

Then I stop in the middle of the path and start to bawl. It is ugly, snotty, and loud. Definitely not the answer he was expecting.

"Okay," Chazzy says, a little stunned, but putting on a brave face. To his credit, he doesn't even glance around in embarrassment to see if people are watching, which I know they are. "Okay. Why don't we just sit for a minute?"

We plunk ourselves down on some icy logs to the side of the path, since there's no bench handy. I'm cold, but it feels good to just stop and let myself fall apart.

Chazzy rests his hand on my back, between my shoulders. "You don't have to tell me, Wren. But if you want to, you can tell me. Okay?"

"Thank you. I want to. You are the one person I can talk to."

"Right back at you," he says, his Southern drawl pronounced.

"Okay," I begin, leaning into him. "Over fall break, while I was hanging around here by myself, I got on this

Nancy Drew kick and started looking into my mother's past. When she was here in school."

"Yeah?" Chazzy encourages, his hand still on my back, steady.

"Anyway, when I got back yesterday, I remembered I had her old yearbook. I don't know why I even packed it. But you know how kids write those secret messages to each other about what they'll always remember from school? It turns out my mom and Honor's dad were together. Like, in a big romance. In love. You know, I was so convinced Norwood was my father . . ."

"Right." Chazzy chuckles lightly. "'Wren Has Two Daddies.'"

"Anyway, when I thought about it, when I put everything together, it makes total sense. Which makes Honor my sister."

Chazzy is silent. His hand falls from my back. "You're kidding, right?"

I sniffle and shake my head, looking up at him.

"Wait, no way," he says. "First of all, you said you were going to stop with the random speculation. Second, how do you get from Honor's father and your mother knew each other in high school to he's your dad? I mean, it's definitely a weird coincidence—"

"There's more, obviously," I interrupt, a little indignant.

"Like, because Nick noticed you and Honor both have big blue eyes, you must be sisters?" He says this in a way that sounds not entirely friendly.

"No! Can I just finish? It clicked because Honor and I got into that whole thing where she thought I'd stolen her charm, and then it turned out we each had one, the identical anchors. Her great-grandmother had them made, designed them herself . . ." I pause.

"Uh-huh." Chazzy is not convinced.

"And mine came from my great-grandmother too. I always assumed Hannah meant *her* grandmother, not my father's."

"That doesn't make sense. Why would your mother have one, then?"

"I don't know. Maybe Honor's dad—my dad, whatever—gave her one too. But there's another thing: right before I came here, Hannah gave me my guitar as a going-away present. She told me it was a 'remember-who-you-are present.' It's a *Gibson*."

Chazzy looks away, up the path, toward the music building—either processing all this, or trying to think of a way to ditch me. "I don't know, Wren."

"It's the only thing that makes sense. Because of the anchor. Because of Hummingbird. Because I just know." I sit still a moment, letting the cold seep into my thighs. "I need to talk to Hannah."

"Or Honor's dad." Chazzy looks me in the eye. For a second, I almost feel like kissing him again. He's not going to ditch me. He never would.

"Honor's dad might not know anything about it," I say.

"But he might."

I think about that. He might. But if he does, he hasn't made any attempt to get in touch with me.

"Are you going to say something to Honor?" Chazzy presses.

"I am never telling Honor," I blurt.

"That's one approach. No, but seriously. Listen, if you're so convinced it's him, why don't you find out for sure? There is no way to talk to your mom right now. And you might have to leave school in January. There isn't a lot of time here."

"I can't talk to Honor. I do want to meet him, but I can't tell her. I don't know," I say. "It's an impossible situation."

Chazzy pulls me in for a quick hug, then stands. "We'll figure something out. By the way, congratulations. Assuming, you know, everything."

"On what?"

"On having a dad."

"Oh. Right. Yeah. Thanks." I laugh and blush.

"Kind of a famous, fairy-tale dad at that."

"Kind of," I say.

He gives my hand a quick squeeze. "So how was your trip, anyway? What is Stone Cove Island like?"

I take a deep breath. "It's like a Victorian orphanage. And that's where they're going to send me. I'm going to have to run away, hitchhike back to California or something. You should have seen my great-aunt Helen. She wouldn't listen to anything I said. She hates me. God, I wish there was something I could do. If I could get my passport and some money, I would go to Greenland. But you know what? If Great-Aunt Helen's my legal guardian, she would have to sign my passport application, and she never would. She doesn't want me to stay at Hardwick. I don't think she even cares if I finish high school . . ."

I suddenly realize I am ranting. He's staring at me like I'm a crazy person.

"Wren, there is something you can do," he says finally.

"What?"

His eyes narrow; he's incredulous. "Could talking to Honor really be worse than everything you just told me? Maybe you're right, and maybe her dad does know something. Maybe *she* even knows something, and that's why she's so weird with you. I don't get why you're so intimidated by her. What could she possibly do to you?"

"I'm not intimidated," I lie. "But I can't talk to her without talking to my mom first."

What could she do to me? I think about what she's done to me so far, and I haven't really done anything to upset her. Yet.

I KNOW CHAZZY'S WRONG about this, that I should wait to talk to my mom, but once the idea of telling Honor is in my head, there's a sense of inevitability. I'm afraid I will walk into our suite and just blurt it out. Or it will happen one morning, on the way to breakfast. Or after my riding lesson, standing around in the tack room. I know I can't say anything, but at the same time, Ms. Taubin's deadline of "no money, no school" looms closer and closer until I can't think about anything else.

It finally happens in the bathroom. We are the last ones up, brushing our teeth. I take a good, close look at Honor, trying to imagine how we could possibly share any DNA. Then, before I can stop myself, I say, "Honor, can I talk to you for a sec?"

Honor looks at me coldly, blankly.

We're standing there together at the row of sinks alone,

holding toothbrushes. Why on earth am I asking permission to talk to her?

"I guess," she says. "Why?"

Now that I've gotten this far, I'm really not sure where to start. I decide to focus on the facts she'll recognize. That seems easiest. "Well, you know my necklace? The pair of anchors we have?"

That doesn't make sense, even to me. But she nods and looks a little defensive. "What about it?" she asks.

"Okay, well, I guess I just keep thinking about what a strange coincidence that is. The story about your great-grandmother designing it and my great-grandmother . . ."

Honor gives me a look that says, *Not strange, and not interesting.* She returns to brushing her teeth.

"Did you know my mom and your dad dated when they were here? At Hardwick?"

"No," she says, not bothering to look at me. She finishes with her toothbrush and starts packing up her pail. "But I'm sure my dad had all kinds of girlfriends in high school." She wipes a towel across her face, then stares at me like she can't believe I have such nerve. "What do you want, Wren? Everyone is talking about how you can't afford to stay here. Do you really think my dad is going to help you out? Because he knew your mom in high school? Don't be ridiculous."

I stare right back. "I don't care about your family's money. It's not that." My voice is trembling, and my fists are clenched at my sides. I'm honestly worried I'll punch her. "That's not what I'm asking. I'm asking if your dad ever talked about my mom."

Honor's jaw twitches. She looks like she's on the verge of punching *me*. "This is pathetic. You're pathetic. Don't talk to me, Wren. Don't talk to anyone in my family. I'm requesting a room change."

With that, she walks out, not looking back. I feel awful. Of course I do. But it would be worse to find out that she knows—that she and Edward Gibson both know—and haven't said anything to me. Until now, that possibility hadn't really occurred to me.

CHAPTER FIFTEEN

Thanksgiving

I must admit one of Honor's strengths is her resolve. Not only can no one tell her anything she doesn't want to hear or make her do something she doesn't want to do, but once she's decided on something, it's done. The school doesn't have a room available to make the switch she requests, but they offer a resident counselor to meet with the four of us. This is "to explore" whether we are having "significant issues" living together. They also strongly recommended we seek guidance from Mrs. Baird.

So now we sit in Mrs. Baird's living room, not drinking the tea she has made us, not explaining what's going on between us.

I feel bad for Mrs. Baird. She tries various tactics to get us to speak up, ranging from encouragement to disapproval, all to no avail. Honor is not going to say one more word about this to me or anyone else. Mrs. Baird has been pretty nice to me the last few weeks, but if Honor's not talking, how can I?

IT MAY BE COINCIDENCE on Honor's side, but it seems to work out that when Honor gets up early for breakfast, I get up late. When I study in the library, she studies in our room. It is like we have some radar for where the other will be. I am, if I'm being honest, relieved Honor is avoiding me—I don't really know what else to say to her at this point, and I'm embarrassed that she assumed I was trying to hit her dad up for money. I hope she hasn't told Eloise or India, but I'm sure she has.

As the days draw closer to Thanksgiving break, I find myself in an unrelenting, news-less pattern. I go to class. I check in with Mrs. Baird. Mrs. Baird tells me that Hannah's condition is progressing as expected. Mrs. Baird hands me a now-overdue tuition bill and contract, but tells me not to worry about it until Hannah is better. Unless that is later than December first, at which point—well, we'll just have to see.

Hannah remains unconscious. Honor ignores me. Eloise and India act nice, pretending Honor isn't ignoring me.

And Chazzy. At some point I am going to have to talk to Chazzy about that kiss. But I can't. Because if I lose Chazzy right now, I will really, really be alone.

RIDING IS THE ONLY thing that distracts me, if only because when I'm concentrating on staying on the horse, there is no room in my head for any other thoughts.

Mr. Kelley decides I'm together enough to learn the next level of sophistication on the flat—that is, beyond turn, stop and go. I'm riding Stormy again. Mr. Kelley explains how the engine of the horse comes from the hindquarters. The idea is to build up a contained energy, bundled and ready to go. What I have to do is keep the power bottled up by compressing the horse between my legs (which makes her go) and holding with my hands (which keeps her from going).

When he explains it, it seems contradictory and like what it might do is just piss her off, but after forty minutes or so of practicing this at the walk and trot, she rewards me with a couple of strides where I actually get it. I feel her back round up underneath me, like she's coiling her haunches under like a spring. Her neck arches, her nose dips and her jaw softens. I suddenly feel this amazing, fluid, elastic energy, and her trot goes kind of floaty. It feels unbelievable, kind of like riding a Slinky.

"That's it! That's it!" booms Mr. Kelley from the center of the ring. And as he says it, Stormy pins her ears, sets her jaw, tugs me forward in the saddle and goes back to being her regular, crabby self. But she can't take it away from me. I got it. I should remember this feeling, I tell myself, next time I think I can't do something.

My legs are like wrung-out sponges. I probably won't be able to walk tomorrow.

"You see?" asks Mr. Kelley. "You understand what we're trying for here?"

"Yes," I say, walking to the middle of the ring. "It felt amazing. But it's so hard."

"The goal is to have the horse in that frame, listening like that the whole ride."

"Oh my God, I'll never be able to do that."

"First rule of riding, Wren," says Kelley. His voice has an edge of disapproval. "Never say 'I can't.'"

"Okay," I say, feeling chastened. "Am I allowed to think it?"

"No. Now back on the rail, and let's see your canter."

AS I HEAD FOR breakfast the Monday before Thanksgiving, Mrs. Baird stops me in the hall. "Mr. Gibson, Honor's father, would like you to call him. I have his telephone number if you would like to come back this afternoon and call from here."

She gives me the studied neutral look that I have gotten to know so well. I can't figure out if she understands my suspicions or is wondering what the hell could be going on. At this point it must seem like every time her phone rings, it's another call for me, each crazier than the last.

"Okay," I say. I smile politely, covering my shock. I feel bad that my life is taking up so much of her time these days. But she's my housemother. Somehow she never looks like she minds. "I can come after music."

Mr. Gibson wants to talk to me. Wants. To. Talk. To. Me.

THE REST OF MY day inches on, hour by hour. To get through it, I make a list and check off the classes I have to survive to get to the phone call:

Chapel: Why does he want me to call him? Maybe there's a simple explanation, like he is planning a surprise party for Honor and thinks we're friends? Why? Does he know? Also, Nick is sitting with Lauren Benaceraf. Rumor is, she likes him. Look at her. Obviously she likes him. I don't see Chazzy.

American history: What if my mom never wakes up? Have to copy Eloise's notes when I realize I have missed the last fifteen minutes lost in my own thoughts.

Classical lit: She has to wake up. She's going to wake up. I can't wait until this class is over. Why does he want me to call him? Nick and Honor, sitting together.

Biology: Should have studied. Pop quiz. Seriously, should have studied! Run into Gretchen on the way to music. She asks me if Chazzy and I are "together." I turn red, mumble something about needing to go get my guitar and basically flee.

FINALLY THE INTERMINABLE AFTERNOON is over. Music is usually the class I don't want to end, but today I book out the second I can, barely saying bye to Chazzy. I probably look like a freak sprinting across the quad to Selby, but I can't help that.

The harsh, winter air feels good in my lungs, but I'm boiling after two minutes of running. When I arrive at Mrs. Baird's, I hesitate before dialing the number she hands me. My hands are shaking, and not from the cold.

Mr. Gibson's assistant puts me on hold.

Mrs. Baird tries to look busy so I won't feel like she's listening. There's nowhere for her to go; I'm using her phone, but it's better than the common room phone, especially at this time of day, with everyone coming back from class to change for sports.

Finally I hear a click and then a voice. "Wren? It's Edward Gibson."

His voice is smooth and confident, like his picture behind the glass. Deep, professional. There's too long a silence before I realize I need to answer, or he's going to think I hung up.

"Oh. Yes. Hello." *Sir?* I don't know what to call him.

"I realize you may be surprised to hear from me."

"A little," I admit.

He chuckles. "I hope you don't mind my getting in touch like this. Honor told me what's been going on—"

"Excuse me?" I can't stop myself from cutting him off. Honor told him what? Why would Honor tell him anything?

"She told me about Hannah's accident."

"Oh," I say quietly.

"Wren, this is such distressing news. I can only imagine what you are going through. Your mother and I were very close when we were younger, and . . . I'm concerned about Hannah, and I'm concerned about you." He is obviously used to being direct, but his voice sounds sympathetic.

"Thanks. They say she's going to be okay. It's just hard waiting." I try to say this like I'm sure it's true, that she'll be okay.

"That's good. But what about you? Do you need anything? Is there anything Honor and I can do? Do you have somewhere to go for Thanksgiving?"

"No, I do. Mrs. Baird . . ." It feels funny to explain this with Mrs. Baird right in the room. "Mrs. Baird invited me to her house."

There's a silence as though he's deciding what to say next. "Why don't you come to New York with Honor?" he asks.

"Excuse me?" I say again.

"For Thanksgiving," he clarifies, as if it requires clarification. "It will give us a chance to meet. Honor can show you around New York, and if Hannah needs anything . . ."

"Thank you," I say, accepting before I even consider whether I want to. "Are you sure you don't mind? Honor won't mind? I really don't want to intrude—"

"Why would Honor mind? You're roommates." He says "roommates" like he means "friends," but there's an edge of impatience in his voice. I don't know if it's meant for my question or Honor's objections. "It will be fun to have a big group. Eloise will be there."

Of course I know already that Eloise is invited to the Gibsons'. Maybe she and Ned could provide something of a buffer. But now that I've said yes, I'm worried. I'm ninety percent sure I'm right about Edward Gibson, but I've been wrong before.

"Thank you," I say again nervously before we both hang up.

If Mrs. Baird is curious about all this, she doesn't show it. "Everything okay?" she asks.

"He invited me to New York for Thanksgiving. But Mrs. Baird, it was really nice of you to ask me too." I don't want her to think I don't appreciate her offer, but I have to admit, at least to myself, that I've been dreading the idea of gray afternoons drinking tea with the Madames Baird. I've already done a lot of that with my great-aunt Helen on Stone Cove Island. I almost laugh; this is the way my mother must have felt visiting there.

"You'll have more fun," Mrs. Baird says as if reading

my mind. "Go on." She walks to the door with me. "It's too quiet at our place. No kids around. And I must say, I am relieved that you and Honor have patched things up. That's good news. If I hear anything about your mother, I'll let you know, but I've already made sure they have your email address."

"Thanks," I say again, for what feels like the hundredth time in ten minutes.

I'm not so sure that it will be fun, exactly, but I do want to go. I want to meet him. I *have* to meet him. I don't have a choice, even if I'm just imagining the history between Edward and my mother.

THE WEEK CREEPS BY. Honor is still cold, still ignoring me. Now that I know she's talked to her father, I can't help feeling like it would be better to just have it out, whatever "it" is. All I get out of her is, "My dad said we had to invite you for Thanksgiving, so you're invited. We're done."

AT DINNER, I FORCE myself to sit with my roommates. It feels too weird to show up at Honor's house in two days after hardly having spoken. Eloise and India smile as I put my tray down. Honor barely looks up.

Nick walks into the dining hall with Lauren. They laugh together as he pretends to steal something from her tray. I guess maybe those rumors are true. Nick leads Lauren to our table. She sits first, but instead of joining her, Nick swings around the end of the table to sit next to me at the end of the bench.

I'm momentarily surprised, and instinctively I look at

Honor. Her eyes are on Nick. She gives him a pretty smile and says, "Hey there."

Lauren looks flummoxed. She's blown her chance to sit near Nick, and short of getting up and moving—way too obvious—she's stuck.

"Are you going to DC for Thanksgiving?" Honor asks Lauren.

"Vail," she says. "With my family. They have snow already, and my brother's at Colorado College, so he can come meet us."

"Oh," says Honor, winking slightly at Nick, like they're both in on some joke. "How lucky you're both going to be there."

"I know, right?" says Nick.

So I guess that means they're together. Or will be together by the time Thanksgiving break is over. Instead of appearing to be jealous, Honor seems to be giving Nick and Lauren her stamp of approval. Or maybe she just has her mind on something—or someone—else.

"What are you doing this year?" asks Lauren.

"I have to be in New York," says Honor, like it's a mild inconvenience. "It's the Maclay Finals and the Assemblies Ball."

Lauren gasps. "You're *in* the Assemblies Ball?"

"No, just going to it. You have to be eighteen to be presented. Eloise is coming too."

I keep quiet. I don't know what this ball is they're talking about, and it certainly doesn't seem like the ideal time to remind them that I'm going to be around for it.

"Don't worry, Lauren," Nick says. "I promise you'll have

a great time. Vail is killer." He leans toward Lauren as he says this, away from me, but as he does, he reaches his right arm behind him, along the bench, until it rests on my leg. I'm confused. He's talking to Lauren, his back is to me, but his hand is on my leg. Not accidentally brushing against my leg. His hand is *resting on my leg*. It makes so little sense that I almost want to look down and check that it's really happening. I can't breathe.

The conversation continues around me in fragments: the back bowls, bars in Vail where you can get served and that amazing barbecue place mid-mountain. What Honor's wearing (vintage Valentino) and is she nervous about the horse show (no) and isn't it crazy, the idea of horses in Madison Square Garden (yeah, I guess). Nick leaves his hand on my leg the whole time. Finally Eloise, diligent student that she is, breaks it up.

"Art history time," she says, rising with her tray and gathering her reading.

"Ugh," say India and Honor together. "I'm too tired for the library. I could go to bed now," India adds.

I say nothing.

Nick turns to me. "You have a good break too, Birdie."

He doesn't ask me what I'm doing, but he gives me this smile like we have a secret. Then he follows Honor, Eloise and India out of the dining hall. Lauren hurries on his trail, not about to miss her moment for the second time in one night. That leaves me sitting there alone with no idea what just happened.

CHAPTER SIXTEEN

New York

Wednesday afternoon, I pack. Chazzy attempts to help me—yeah, yeah. Door open. Three feet on the floor. The problem is, I have no idea what I'm going to need.

At least Honor has finally acknowledged I'm coming by telling me to meet her and Eloise on the circle at five, when the car will pick us up. I don't know if I'm expected to go to this ball with them—not a packing problem in itself, since I don't own anything I could wear to a ball—or parties, or how dressy for Thanksgiving, or anything that might help prepare me. I fall back on a thin selection of semi-proper items, mostly chosen by Hannah over the years.

"Hey, bring a little Wren wear, will you?" Chazzy teases.

"What do you care?" I ask.

"Well, for one thing, I don't want your new family to get the wrong idea about you. And for another—"

"For another what?"

"Nope. Can't say. It's a surprise. But you can't wear any of that prissy stuff."

"If you won't tell me what it is, how do I know what I can wear?"

"Um, I don't know. I didn't think you would undergo a personality change before the weekend, so I didn't think it would be an issue."

"Chazzy. What the hell—"

"Okay, I guess I have to tell you. It's a show."

"What's a show?"

"I booked us a show. At the Sidewalk. In the East Village. Saturday night."

"No way. Are you kidding?" A tingling of fear and excitement merge in my belly. We're going to play? In New York?

"I'm not kidding. I'm going to drive down on Saturday with my sister."

Apparently, he's not kidding; Chazzy's family has plans to meet in the Berkshires at some idyllic inn so that his mother won't have to cook.

"Why would they want us? And on a Saturday night?"

"Because we're awesome."

"Chazzy, come on."

He sighs. "Because they have a little upstairs room where you can sign up to play. It's basically like the open mic we went to. And we're on at one A.M. No one will even be there," he admits.

I smile, half delighted, half petrified. I wonder briefly if I'm going to be allowed to stay out that late. I don't know the rules at the Gibsons' house. But if Honor's stories are anything to go by, it shouldn't be much of a problem. "That's just . . . wow."

"I know," says Chazzy. He can't stop grinning. "I know!"

I dig back into my closet for more clothes, trying to avoid anything Chazzy might deem prissy.

LATER, I DRAG HUMMINGBIRD and my clunky old suitcase downstairs, stopping in at Mrs. Baird's room. The clinic in Greenland was finally willing to set up a Skype call, so I could at least see Hannah. After about as much time as it would take to read the rest of that six-hundred-page Saul Bellow book I still haven't finished for lit class, they get the connection working.

Hannah is lying on a bed under heat lamps and high-tech layers of foil that must serve as blankets. She's very pale and seems tiny. She looks like Snow White or Sleeping Beauty in one of those Disney movies where the heroine is stretched out waiting for the prince to wake her up. Except she's missing the pink cheeks, and her hair looks kind of greasy, if I'm being honest.

That is not my mother, I think.

I don't know why I'm expecting her to talk, since they told me she wouldn't be able to, but just watching her lie there silently feels scary. After a minute or two, I say I'm hanging up. The doctors tell me they shouldn't tire her, anyway. I wonder how having someone stare at you while you lie there could be tiring, but the doctors assure me she can register a lot of what's going on, and knowing I was on the phone will help her.

Does she even know? I wonder.

"YOU'RE BRINGING YOUR GUITAR?" Honor comments in disbelief as we get into the limo. She settles in to ignore me for the rest of the drive. I've never ridden in a limousine before so I decide to savor the experience and ignore her right back. I sink into the cushions as far as possible from Honor (me on one side, Honor on the other, Eloise in the middle, the buffer) and focus out the window at the bare trees rushing by in the fading light. *Away we go,* I think. Away from Ms. Taubin, tuition bills, Great-Aunt Helen and whatever awaits my return.

After an impressively long silence, Honor allows herself to show some excitement about the ball and the after-party to Eloise, her captive audience. Her dress is beautiful, she boasts: thick cream fabric under a stiff crust of black lace. She thinks it's okay to wear black and white even though it's not a black and white ball. Amelia Apthorpe did last year and it was fine; she looked fantastic. Amelia is actually having the after-party this year. Francesco, the guy she met earlier in the fall, is coming to that. Honor couldn't invite him to the ball. He's older, not even in school. He owns a restaurant in Tribeca. Her escort, Tim Mabley, won't care. They're just friends. Actually, he would be *so* cute for Eloise. Why didn't she think of that before? She's *totally* going to set them up . . .

Eloise's escort to the ball is a second cousin who lives in New York, and not the object of any romantic interest. Fun, they agree, but no one you'd want to hook up with, even without the shared DNA.

As Honor drones on I think, *This is better, being invisible.* It's certainly more comfortable than her overt hatred.

On Sunday, Honor will be competing in the Maclay Finals at Madison Square Garden. Rainmaker arrives at the arena by trailer Friday night. They'll use a special entrance with a ramp to get him up to the temporary stalls they build for the horses. Honor will have a scheduled time Saturday night—in the middle of the night, the only time other show events aren't occupying the arena—to ride in the ring and acclimate him. She'll compete Sunday morning. She has a 6:35 A.M. slot. I know, because I heard Mr. Kelley going over the schedule with her, though he won't be there. She'll be riding with the fancy Long Island trainer she shows with during the summer, when her family spends most of its time in Amagansett.

It's funny; I'm thinking about Honor's horse show, but she and Eloise don't talk about it at all. It strikes me again as amazing to have that kind of talent, plus an opportunity to compete at the Garden—and just not care. Of course, three months ago, I didn't know what the Maclay Finals were.

As we near New York, Eloise tells me about Honor's neighborhood, Beekman Place. It's on the river, kind of next to the UN, so there are all these embassies around. You see African diplomats in dashikis going in and out of these grand marble buildings, and Katherine Hepburn used to live nearby.

Honor's street is so quiet and pretty. It's only two blocks long. Walking there, you feel like it's, like, a hundred years ago. People still have those old-fashioned gas lanterns over their doors. And it's not that far uptown, so you can get to the East Village or the Lower East Side or even Brooklyn super quick.

In any other situation, it would be weird that someone's

friend was describing her house instead of that someone herself—but that's Honor and Eloise for you. Anyway, I am barely listening. My stomach contracts as the silhouettes of skyscrapers loom larger out the window. I am about to meet my father.

Possibly.

Probably. I'm pretty sure.

BEEKMAN PLACE IS JUST as Eloise described: lined with redbrick apartment buildings and townhouses, their fronts neatly painted and their lawns perfectly planted. Streetlights are dim, and lanterns glow above each door, made to look as they must have two hundred years ago. It *is* beautiful. Not to mention entirely different from anything I've ever seen in California.

It's cold outside the car, but not as cold as at Hardwick. I feel funny letting the driver carry my stuff, especially since he's so loaded down with Honor's and Eloise's things, so I take my suitcase and guitar from the trunk myself. When the doorman in the building sees Honor, he rushes out to take my bag from me. I keep hold of Hummingbird.

Inside, the lobby is gleaming, warm and quiet. The marble floor is highly polished, with blood-red runners lining the path. The doorman leads us to the elevator, where another man in a dark uniform trimmed with braid rattles open the old-fashioned, crisscrossing brass elevator gates.

"Thank you, Carlos," Honor calls to the driver.

The elevator man gives a quick nod as we get in and then stares straight ahead, pulling the lever and setting the car in motion with a shudder. He stops it on a high floor. The door rattles open, and we step off into a small hallway.

There's an antique table, an umbrella stand and tiny-print wallpaper. Like the rest of the place, it seems to be from an earlier time. I almost feel like I'm in a movie set or a museum. There are two doors, each to an apartment occupying half the building's floor. Honor pushes one open—it's not locked, which surprises me. That's not what I would expect in New York City, but I guess with all those guys downstairs guarding the lobby and the elevator, nobody is likely to sneak in.

There's a wide gilt mirror above the hall table. Honor glances at herself as she passes by. Her hair is messy from the drive; she smooths it in a practiced, automatic way.

I don't bother looking at my own reflection. My heart feels as if it's about to thump right out of my rib cage. *You can do this,* I tell myself. *You got Stormy to trot around the ring twice in a frame; you can do this.*

"Daddy?" Honor calls out.

Eloise and I follow her inside.

Ned's already here. He opted for a morning train since two of his classes were canceled. He pokes his head into the hall. I have to admit, it's really nice to see a friendly face.

"You brought your guitar!" he says to me. "Very cool."

"Yeah. I'm actually supposed to play a show on Saturday. With Chazzy Robinson. From school?"

"You are?" Honor and Eloise say, looking at each other in surprise. It feels great that for once I have something of my own going on.

"Awesome," says Ned. "Where? Can I come?"

"The Sidewalk. Yeah, I guess, if you want. But it's pretty late. Are you—are we—allowed to stay out?"

"Sure, why not?" says Ned. "Hey, too bad I don't still have my drum set."

Honor rolls her eyes.

"What happened to it?" I ask.

"The co-op board happened to it," says Honor, smirking at her brother.

"Honor, it was not that loud. You were already at school, so you barely even heard it."

"Okay, so great," I tell Ned. "At least we'll have someone in the audience."

"I have to help get Rainmaker ready," Eloise says apologetically. "I said I would braid. For good luck. Otherwise . . ."

"That's okay," I tell her. "Honestly I think I'll be less nervous if I don't know that many people. You know what I mean?"

She starts to answer, but suddenly her attention swivels from me down the hallway.

Edward Gibson makes his way toward us. I'm holding my breath. He is tall, with a warm, movie-star smile. His hair is darker now than in his Hardwick picture, and a late-in-the-day shadow of whiskers is starting along his jaw. He is dressed in a super-soft, expensive-looking camel-colored sweater. His eyes are lively and friendly. He's not at all stiff and formal, the important man in a suit I'd pictured—although I'd pictured so many things over the years that the images of imaginary fathers got very jumbled.

Of course, I realize, he owns a family business, one he grew up in and has always known, one where he can work at home or not work at all. He can do what he wants, really. Why wouldn't he be at ease?

He holds his arms out, his voice booming, "Girls! Girls! You're here. Come in!"

Honor reaches up and flings her arms around his neck in a little-girl hug. Eloise blushes and looks away as she offers her cheek to be kissed. Ned gets a pat on the shoulder, even though he's been here all day.

"And Wren," he says. "Great to meet you!" He shakes my hand enthusiastically.

He doesn't know.

I can tell by the way he approaches me, friendly, but without curiosity. I can feel the chill rising off Honor. I force my thoughts away from her.

I try to visualize him young, at Hardwick Hall, walking the path along the lake with my mother, or standing under one of the Gothic archways at an arch sing. He was a Madrigal like Chazzy—I remember from Hannah's yearbook. It makes sense that Ned would be a musician.

It makes sense I would be too, I realize.

He doesn't look like me. At first glance, it doesn't seem like we could be related. He is warm, expansive, sociable, comfortable in his skin. But as I watch him welcome and question and chat, sometimes a gesture gives me a jolt like catching myself in a mirror. It makes it hard to follow the conversation.

"Wren, you brought a guitar," he says, pleased. "You'll have to play for us."

"Uh, okay," I stutter, but I see from his expression that he's not going to hold me to it.

Honor stands very still, looking at the pale pink of her fingernail. Not moving. I feel her listening to every word and every movement her father makes. After a minute she takes out her phone and pretends she's checking for messages.

"Should we unpack?" Eloise asks her.

Edward jumps in. "Look, all of you, come with me, and let's get your things put away. Eloise, you okay in Honor's room? And Wren, this is the guest room. We'll stick you in here, okay? What do you guys want to do for dinner? The Waverly Inn?" Even I know this is a famous New York City restaurant owned by the editor of *Vanity Fair*.

Honor rolls her eyes, but in a more good-natured way than I'm used to. "Daddy, seriously?"

"Just because it's not as cool as it used to be doesn't mean it's not as good, Ho-Ho." I almost laugh out loud at the nickname.

While Honor and Ned begin a debate over dinner plans, I put my guitar down against the bed in the guest room. I wouldn't mind being stuck here forever. The bed is dark wood with four posts; simple, thin posts, not swirly and complicated like at a bed-and-breakfast, and not stark and unfriendly like the bed at Great-Aunt Helen's. There's a low bench along one window. It looks out to a courtyard garden behind the building. The bedspread is a silvery, quilted satin with rows of tiny stitches. Maybe it's Indian. Everything about the room—the tall armoire, the sheepskins draped across the chrome-legged chairs—is elegant and cozy all at once. It's going to be hard to drag myself out of here for dinner, I think, suddenly exhausted and wishing I could lie down right now and go to sleep. I stare longingly at the fuzzy mohair blanket folded at the end of the bed.

As far as dinner goes, Honor decides for us: takeout. Dozens of black cartons of Thai food arrive from a fancy nearby restaurant called Ting. I help Honor and Eloise distribute the food onto china plates with blue-and-gold flowers and dragons. Ned sets the table with real silver chopsticks (and a little block to rest them on) and pours water for us, wine for Edward.

When I ask Honor where the closest bathroom is so that I can wash my hands, she pretends not to hear me. Eloise has to answer for her. Ned and Edward seem oblivious to her rudeness, and I'm not really sure what that means.

OVER DINNER, HONOR STEPS into her accustomed spot at center stage, but tonight the performance is solely for her father. First she tells a couple of funny stories about Hardwick, almost as if designed to be something he'll relate to from his own days there. She says, "Your favorite teacher Gigi is still there, and boys still crush on her." She makes fun of Ms. Taubin's little fairy-tale cottage with the chimney, and Edward laughs wistfully, saying he's not surprised she ended up "squirreled away in there." Apparently in his day, it belonged to Mr. Pengrove, another Hardwick eccentric who taught an AP ancient history class that involved the mandatory wearing of togas to the last class of the semester.

Next she asks her father all kinds of questions, drawing him out like a socially adept grown-up at a cocktail party, or like I would imagine a socially adept grown-up might, if I even knew any adults with her talent. What is he reading? Did he have a chance to see the new show at the Musée du quai Branly when he went to Paris in October? Did he see that interesting piece in Buzzfeed about election predicting? Should she still plan to come in one weekend in December so they can go to a hockey game together?

He pauses over Honor's last question. "Maybe Wren would like to come," he says. "Have you been to a hockey game before?"

Maybe he's just trying to include me to be polite. "No, I haven't," I say.

Honor handles this intrusion by changing the subject. She turns to Ned, alternately quizzing him and giving him advice in an interested, sisterly manner—again, a performance for her dad's benefit. Ned should really take Spanish as well as French next year because it's so much more practical for travel. Interning in LA looks much more serious to colleges than interning in Hawaii and he could still surf. They still need to figure out with Mom about Christmas, and should they go to Paris for part of it or just go straight to Chamonix to ski?

It's hard to know if Honor puts all this on, or if performance is all she knows. Maybe it's an automatic response to her surroundings, just like it would be automatic for me to hole up in my room and listen to music. Only this seems much more exhausting. It's not fake, exactly, but it's definitely a show.

To Honor's takeout-ordering credit, everything is delicious. The food is in some realm way beyond normal food. I forget that I'm nervous and eat a ridiculous amount. Luckily, so does everyone else.

WHEN WE'RE DONE, HONOR and Eloise decide to go out. They invite me, probably because Honor feels like she has to with her dad standing right there, but I'm so tired all I can think of is that mohair blanket. When I fall into bed a few minutes later, after brushing my teeth and not even bothering to wash my face, I sleep a perfect, dreamless sleep.

CHAPTER SEVENTEEN

Thanksgiving

The holiday arrives. Honor and Ned's mother is remarried and lives in France, so they usually go there at Christmas as well as part of the summer but always spend Thanksgiving in New York. (I learn this all from Eloise, Honor's official translator.) The Gibsons are planning to have about twenty people for dinner this afternoon. I'll admit that when we got here, I was surprised to find zero preparations underway.

Hannah and I usually spend the day before Thanksgiving gathering, then lugging, bags of ingredients from the farmers' market—including the giant turkey she always orders way in advance. We load up our old Prius with everything else we need from the big supermarket on Ocean. Everyone else is there, shopping for *their* Thanksgiving dinners, so the lines are insane. Hannah collects all the strays she can: reporters for the *LA Times* who have nowhere to go; Jonesy from the bookstore; Paloma, who teaches my mom's yoga class—and one or two of my friends come over. I love it. It's definitely my favorite holiday.

It doesn't work like that at the Gibsons'. At all. By 9 A.M., the doorman is buzzing every two minutes for another delivery from the catering company. Trays of hors d'oeuvres line the kitchen counters: little round and square tartlets and toasts, perfectly decorated with leaf-shaped pastry or fluted edges, waiting to go in the oven. The Gibsons' housekeeper, Nadia, is polishing, ironing, setting, and organizing.

While I'm laying out clothes to wear to Thanksgiving dinner—I decide on a black kilt and some ballet flats I ended up borrowing from Eloise—I hear a gentle rap on the door.

"Come in," I say, expecting Nadia, who was in here a few minutes ago, unearthing holiday linens.

The door opens. It's Ed on the threshold, looking sort of breathless. I've been calling him Ed since dinner last night, even inside my head, because he doesn't want me to call him Mr. Gibson. Anyway, "Ed" works for me. I call my own mother "Hannah," as everyone on the East Coast can't stop pointing out.

"Wren, I have great news. Your mother is awake. I just spoke to her."

"Really?" My heart leaps into my throat, if a heart can do that. Everything else vanishes. *She's awake. She's actually awake. They said she would wake up, and now she has.* "Can I talk to her?"

Ed blinks rapidly at me. His smile is as broad and easygoing as ever, but his eyes are unsettled. He rushes forward, and the next thing I know, he's hugging me. "There's something else you should know. When we talked . . . I'm not sure how—"

"I know." I cut him off. "I already know." I could kick myself. I wanted to hear him say it. My whole life I've been waiting to hear someone say, *Wren, I'm your father. It's me.* Now I've blown my chance. But when I step back, I see relief in his face.

He takes a deep breath. Maybe he wants me to say more.

"Do Honor and Ned know?" I ask. My throat is tight. I want to hug him again, but I'm not sure that would be the right thing. I can't tell. I wish I knew him better.

"No. Ned doesn't. I don't think Honor does," he manages, regaining composure.

I wonder about that, about how much Honor has thought over our bathroom conversation. She could have figured it out.

I absently twist the black anchor at my throat and think back to that day in our room, when she first hurled that accusation at me. Maybe she was hoping I *had* stolen her necklace. Maybe she figured it out long before I did.

MY FATHER'S EXPLANATION (my father!) is a bit of a blur, but I retain all of the vital information. As soon as the school got in touch with the now-conscious Hannah, and as soon as the now-conscious Hannah found out I was in New York and staying with the Gibsons, she demanded to use her first lucid moments to speak to Ed. He says they almost had to hold her down. I can't tell if those were the doctor's words or if Ed is embellishing. Hannah told him everything. I guess she realized her secret was blown. Or maybe it hit her that she'd almost just left me an orphan.

"It's funny," he says, looking me up and down and

smiling. "When Hannah wrote and asked if I thought I could help her daughter get a spot at Hardwick this fall, I wasn't imagining it was for *my* daughter."

"I bet," I tell him. The words just sort of tumble out, though I'm afraid they sound rude.

Ed pats my shoulder, just the way I saw him pat Ned's, then lingers in the doorway uncertain, maybe wondering if he should hug me again. It's not a state he's used to, I can tell. "I'm sorry I missed so many years, Wren," he says. "I'm not mad at Hannah, though. I understand why she didn't tell anyone, including me. I would have wanted her to stay, and they would have made her stay."

"Who's 'they'?" I ask.

"Oh, her family. Her . . . all the people we knew. At Hardwick. On Stone Cove Island. They have a lot of rules. And the rules always drove your mother crazy. She was not on board with people making decisions for her." He looks straight at me, and a smile flickers on his face. "And she was well aware that unmarried couples and single mothers and globetrotting journalists were not in the rulebook."

I can't help but smile back. *It's true,* I tell myself again. *It's really true.*

"I like surprises," he says. "They keep life interesting."

It's nice of him to say that. I hope he means it. "I have a feeling Honor may not feel that way."

Ed's face darkens for just a second. "Don't worry about that. I'll talk to her. It might take her a little time. Ned's the easygoing one. Honor's so sensitive."

Sensitive as Teflon. I keep that thought to myself.

"Are you okay, Wren?"

"Oh, yeah. I'm good. Everything is good." *I'm happy,* I want to tell him, but maybe that's too much to say out loud.

"I'll let you finish getting dressed."

"Thanks. I . . . Thanks," I say.

Ed leaves and shuts the door quietly behind him.

How will he introduce me to his family and friends this afternoon? What will their reaction be? I would prefer to fade into the background, observe without being observed, let Honor keep the spotlight.

I realize that my palm is still pressed against my necklace. Normally, I never take it off, but wearing it somehow feels like flaunting the . . . situation.

I decide not to wear it. Today it feels like too much of a statement. It's Thanksgiving. I should be thankful for what I've got, right?

I wish Chazzy were here. Then I wouldn't have to do this alone. And really, I *am* thankful. Hannah is awake and alive, and I finally know the truth. Ed can tell the truth in his own way, in his own time. Anyway, it's not my decision to make for him. My mother decided for both of us, a long time ago.

WHEN I DO GET to talk to Hannah, early that afternoon, I remind myself I can't be angry, not when I've come this close to losing her, the sum of my family until today.

The doctors give us five minutes because of her fragile state. I need to spend those five minutes being positive. But at the same time, I don't understand how she could keep a secret like this, only to dump me on that secret's doorstep.

At home in Ventura, when it was just us, we had to be on the same side. I didn't have a separate point of view.

"I'm happy you know," she says, her voice paper thin. "It's a good thing."

"Me too." I bite my lip. "But I really don't understand. Why didn't you tell me before I went to Hardwick? It's like some kind of cruel joke, sticking me here." My voice sputters, sticking on the words.

"I didn't know about Honor," she says. "I'm sorry. I never would have put you in that situation if I had known you'd be in the same class. Or the same room." She laughs, and I wonder if it's the drugs she's on. There's nothing remotely funny about this.

"Mom, Honor and I are the *same age.*"

"I realize that," she says.

"I don't even get how that can be possible," I say. Then I rephrase. "No, yeah, I *get* how that can be. But how did that even happen?"

She hesitates. "I know. It's insane. It was just bad luck," she says. "I had to go to Stone Cove Island for Carter Chisholm's funeral—Aunt Helen's son—and Ed happened to be there. He and Annabelle had broken up. She was going to move to London for a job. It was a moment. Too many Dark 'n' Stormy's at the Anchor Inn. We had a lot of memories and had been together for a long time when we were younger . . . I knew it was a mistake to go back there."

"A mistake?" I spit, my positivity out the window.

"Not a mistake, Wren. Obviously. I didn't mean you were a mistake."

"So you just never told him."

"I didn't tell him. And when Annabelle found out she was pregnant with Honor, she decided not to go to London. They got married, and that's about all I know."

I open my mouth to respond and nothing comes out, so I just hang on the line in silence.

"Fate," she says. "Can you believe it? 'Of all the gin joints in all the'—how does that go? It's from *Casablanca.* You've seen that movie, right? If you haven't, I'm really a terrible mother."

She isn't making any sense. "I can think of some other reasons you're a terrible mother." It's mean. I know. I'm so happy to have her back. I shouldn't be mean.

"He wasn't married then, if that makes any difference to you. He wasn't seeing Annabelle. I didn't think that—" She catches herself, coughs. Her voice gets a gurgle, like she has water in her throat. "Of course it's up to you, Wrendle. I just want . . ." Her voice cracks. I can hear the doctors hovering near her bed, conferring in Danish. There's fumbling on the other end.

"She's sleeping," one of them tells me in a thick accent. "She will rest more, and you can talk again. Goodbye." He hangs up before I can say anything else.

RIGHT BEFORE THE MEAL is served, I see Honor and Ned emerge from Ed's study, looking dazed. They stare at me like I'm a ghost that has just materialized in their hallway. Then Honor looks away and sweeps by, making a show of not seeing me.

Ned steps forward, his lips parted like he's going to

speak, but he doesn't. Instead, he touches my arm. To say it's okay or to see if I'm real, I can't tell. He looks really young, I think for the first time, and there's a lot swirling under that mellow, summery surface.

Before either of us can say anything, the doorman buzzes from downstairs, and we hear the *clang* of the elevator gate as the guests start to arrive. There's no time for the long conversation we need to have.

Ed does not try to cover up by introducing me as Honor's roommate, though I wouldn't blame him if he did. Instead he treats me like a wonderful surprise, like I fell out of the sky and he couldn't be more delighted.

He introduces me as "my new daughter—can you believe it?" He takes me around, arm across my shoulder, as if he just won the lottery. People laugh at his joke and smile welcomingly at me. No one, other than Honor, looks outraged or even disapproving. Or even terribly curious. Ned trails us, listening, but doesn't join the conversations. Since I know that Ed hasn't had time to fill in all the attendees in advance on my backstory, I have to assume that with their good manners, they must be impervious to shock, sort of the way Great-Aunt Helen is. *Oh, your mother is dying? That's terrible, but it doesn't mitigate your inconveniencing me.* Here the unspoken sentiment seems to be, *Another daughter! How lovely, especially as she's at Hardwick.*

I feel like Cinderella, but at the same time I feel how hard it must be for Honor. I don't know why I keep seeing her side, but I do. She's not short of attention at this event, though. Her younger cousins crowd around her in obvious worship. The older ones tell her to come visit at college; I can see they fancy her a cool, younger version of themselves. But Honor's distracted. All afternoon I catch her watching me. She looks like she would like to dissolve me in a vat of acid.

Eloise has been to lots of Gibson family gatherings, so she knows a fair percentage of the crowd. Occasionally she shoots me a questioning look, but I know she won't cross Honor by asking me what's going on. So I decide to lose myself in what I can't control. The food is delicious. The meal marches along in a smoothly orchestrated fashion.

It's not like our Thanksgivings, where a few people straggle in late, then somebody realizes we forgot the mashed potatoes, so we end up eating them with dessert. The Gibson holiday is not ragtag like that. Departures are smooth and polite. Ned, and the younger cousins get dressed in coats and hats for their annual touch football game in Carl Shurz Park. Honor and Eloise exchange looks and sneak out to get dressed for something else. I imagine it involves Francesco, but I'm not in on it. The football game sounds more fun to me anyway.

I change into jeans and a woolly sweater. Ned lends me a hat and scarf because, despite my New England shopping trip with Hannah before I left home, I still never have the right clothes for the weather here. We leave the lobby together and fracture into small groups headed in different directions. I look up at the tall buildings of the Upper East Side kaleidoscoping above me, the sun sinking behind them, and feel like it has all been too much to fit into one day.

CHAPTER EIGHTEEN

Black Friday

Personally, I've never gotten Black Friday. I understand that it's supposed to be the biggest shopping day of the year, the day shoppers are trampled outside malls, and fistfights ensue over the "it" item of the season that's trending on Instagram.

But when you own a department store, it turns out it's a really big deal.

Because Gibson's Department Store belongs to Honor's father, that makes Honor the Gibson Girl (the modern-day version, at least), and thus she is charged with ceremonially unlocking the doors as the stores open on this very special day. I go along with Eloise and Ned to watch Princess Black Friday greet her public.

The six-story, white-marble department store is like the tallest, most glamorous wedding cake you ever saw. A long line of customers stretches out the door and along Fifth Avenue, waiting to be let in. The portico above the door is carved in the old Roman style, where *U*s look like *V*s: LAWRENCE WARING GIBSON & SONS. Technically, Ed is the only son, so I guess the plural is just tradition. So *W* for "Waring," not for "Wren."

But wait a minute—now that I see the letters spelled out like this, with so much space between them, and after hearing the way the Gibson family draws out their names ("Honor" sounds like it has about four syllables)—it's so obvious. Lawrence, Ed's middle name, is "La-Wren-ce." How did I not realize that before? Of course I wasn't named for a suffragette. Or maybe I was named for her too. I kick myself, at least metaphorically. A little late to the party there, Nancy Drew.

I expect Honor to put on a very professional show at this event, but for the first time she looks really uncomfortable. Standing at her father's side, dressed perfectly in elegant layers of camel and cream, her job is to pass out gifts to the first fifty shoppers. They are wrapped in Gibson's signature apple green with matching bows. Perfume for women, key fobs for men. Kids who are tagging along with their parents get a swirly green lollipop.

Ed is super at ease in this situation, chatting just the right amount without getting stuck in a real conversation, keeping the line moving. Honor smiles at everyone, but ignores the strangers she's not interested in talking to. Most people lining up this early to shop, who care about being one of the first fifty, don't overlap much with her world. There's the exhausted dad with overweight, twin boys, both in Rangers jerseys and flammable-looking sweatpants; the elderly lady searching through her purse for her Christmas list; a woman on her cell phone, her hair in a rounded, shellacked mound, loudly complaining about how she has to be at work in fifteen minutes and why can't André pick their kid up? Three giggling Japanese girls about our age in knee-high socks clutch little plastic manga-themed purses and jump up and down with excitement.

Honor fumbles as she tells them, "Hi. Welcome. Here you go." Her brief smile holds no promise of further chit-chat. I've seen that before, but the way she keeps glancing at Eloise beseechingly as the next shopper steps up? I have never seen this Honor, this beleaguered, out-of-her-element Honor. When you think about it, how many sixteen-year-olds could do this well, other than professional actors?

When it's all over, Honor snaps at Ned. "I can't believe you didn't have to do it," she mutters, brushing past him toward the exit. "Dad will make you next year. I had to do it when I was a First Year."

Ned shrugs. "Whatever, Ho-Ho." If he does have to do it next year, easygoing Ned will be good at it and probably won't even mind.

"You were great," insists Eloise, in her supportive best friend voice, but it falls a little flat. Honor remains in a funk—until she spots a beguiling leather bag. Honor and Ned get fifty-percent discounts, but their charge card bills go to Mr. Gibson anyway, which effectively makes anything they buy one hundred percent off.

"Do you want anything?" Ned asks me, holding his card out.

"Uh . . ." Oh my God, of course. Where to start? The store is like a six-floor luxury universe. *I wish I could get something for Hannah*, I think. "That's okay. Thanks, though."

Ned gives me a look like I am crazy, or else he doesn't believe me. "Really? You sure?"

"Well, maybe I could get a sweater or blanket or something for my mom?"

"Absolutely." He shoots a glance at Honor.

She rolls her eyes but turns back toward us, bringing the leather bag.

ALL FOUR OF US head for the bedding department, where there are stacked piles of dreamy soft throws in every color and texture: cashmere, cotton, alpaca, mohair. I pick up a fuzzy, deep coral one and wish I could roll myself up like a sausage in it and never come out. I feel a tap on my arm and turn. Honor is holding up a pale linen throw with tiny dark brown flecks in it.

"What about this one," she says, not like it's a question. At first I think she's picking the drabbest one to make fun of me, but when I study it up close, I see that she's actually picked something beautiful. The texture is like silk and water, but instead of being shiny, its surface has a subtle glow, like the moon. The rich coffee color specks add a landscape, like a map. Also, it costs as much money as Hannah gave me for the whole semester.

But I know she is not suggesting I pay for it. Well, I'll give Honor credit where it's due. She's got an eye.

"Are you sure?" I ask. Honor nods impatiently, like it's no big deal.

Ned is already walking to the register.

"How are you today, Mr. Gibson?" the salesgirl chirps politely to Ned.

"Thank you," I whisper to him, feeling grateful and kind of like an idiot at the same time. "This is really nice of you."

He shrugs. The salesgirl folds and refolds the blanket on the dark wood counter and wraps it in crisp tissue. She hands it to me in an apple-green bag.

I'm in a daze as we head back to Beekman Place, but not an unhappy daze.

Back in my dove-gray room, I unwrap my luxurious gift, lay it out on the bed, and miss my mother.

BY FRIDAY AFTERNOON, THE Gibson way of life seems almost familiar in a weird way. Here are the rules:

Keep almost no food in the refrigerator, but always have a chilled bottle of very good champagne just in case something comes up.

If you are hungry, order in.

If you need something, it can be delivered or walked to, no matter what time of day, no matter what it is.

You won't need your own shampoo, because the guest bathroom will be stocked like a fancy hotel.

No need to bring keys, because someone else will open the door for you, and another someone else will drive.

Easy, right? Right?

Then there's a flurry of getting ready for the Assemblies Ball. Ned isn't going, and I kind of wish I were staying home with him to watch TV or whatever. But Ed wants me to go, and Honor is willing to (i.e., being forced to) lend me something to wear. It revs up at about three o'clock. Nadia has pressed and hung Eloise's dress, running the shower in the bathroom to steam out any lingering wrinkles. Honor's dress has been delivered from the cleaners, professionally blocked and pressed to perfection. Even before she puts it on, you can see how perfect she will look in it. Its tapered waist and stiff, arching skirt and ballerina straps make you think of an Audrey Hepburn movie. Eloise's is straight and elegant, silky and regal. Too serious a dress for me; I would feel like someone's mother. But she looks great.

Honor is a few inches taller than me, but if I wear something that isn't floor-length on her, one of her dresses should be okay.

With a lot of reluctant sighing to emphasize that she has many more important things to do, she leads me into her walk-in closet. It is about the size of my bedroom in Ventura, jammed with every imaginable texture: gauze to satin to suede in pearly, sophisticated grays, subtle taupes and of course blacks, punctuated by the occasional hot pink or lime green. (Is that what they call resort wear?) And a thousand shoes. No old, paint-splattered T-shirts or ratty shorts, though she probably has those stashed away somewhere too, for the right occasion. But no time to dawdle. She's doing this because she has to, not because she wants to.

Honor frowns as she pulls out a rich, satiny Prada dress. It's clear she loathes the idea of my wearing it, but has resigned herself to getting this clothes-lending thing over with. "From last fall," she clarifies, so I won't get too excited. She holds it out to me, standing as far away as she can, making me step forward as if I'm a pet asking permission for a treat. It is a midnight purple-black with a big skirt that swirls and a fitted waist with a big open neck where the extra material kind of folds over and drapes. ("The *cowl*," she corrects me after I tell her I love the "neck part.") I hold it in front of me, sizing myself up in her full-length mirror. It is seriously gorgeous, last year's model or not.

I wonder how many times she's worn it. I'm guessing once. Honor and Eloise want to do some elaborate Grecian thing to their hair, where it's pulled back into a dancer's knot but then spills down your neck in a jumble of curls. A stylist named Melody from Honor's salon arrives, and before I know it Honor and Eloise are whisked into Honor's bathroom, where Melody rolls and unrolls their curls, paints on their lips, spritzes and dries and re-spritzes them from top to bottom.

This movie-star treatment apparently is routine for them. Honor can sit still for this like I've never seen her in class or even on a horse. When Melody catches me peeking in at them, she offers to do mine too. I feel embarrassed and say, "Oh, that's okay," but Honor tells me to let her do it. Another command, not a question. I guess she thinks I'll embarrass them if I go as myself.

My hair is too short to pull off the Grecian look, so Melody instead bends and tucks it into an elegant bob with a swoop in front of one eye. She parts the hair into sections, flopping them back and forth across my head, spraying cool, seawater-scented hair stuff. With just her fingers, not even a brush, she pulls the ends back and under, and suddenly I am a new person.

Simple, but the kind of thing you could never recreate yourself. Then she pulls out a bunch of eye makeup— powders, creams, brushes and sponges—and goes to work implementing the "smoky eye." I've seen it in magazines. It's not the kind of thing I would try at home.

"Eyes closed," she says, brushing powders and cream across my lids and brow bones. "Look up," she says, as the mascara coats my lashes. "Don't blink."

Again, a look I will never be able to copy myself, even if I did wear makeup, but when she's done, it really does look damn good. I peer in the mirror, trying to recognize myself somewhere under all this and think of Chazzy telling me to pack some Wren wear. If he saw me now, I wonder, what would he think? That I was a sellout? A fake? I emailed him right before Thanksgiving dinner, a short message: *I was right. Advantage, Nancy Drew.*

And what would Nick think? That I actually belonged here? Or Hannah? Watching me do everything she turned her back on?

No, I admit to myself, this is all strictly Cinderella. Although I do really like the dress.

THE CARS PULL UP with our escorts, and there is a lot of complicated negotiation about who is sitting where. Honor works it out so that Tim Mabley sits with Eloise, even though he's officially Honor's date. Eloise's other cousin, Griffin, who's a year younger than her escort, Coleman, is taking me. Or whatever—sitting next to me so it isn't as obvious that I'm alone and don't know anyone there. Ned said he would go if I really needed him to, but I could tell he felt ill just thinking about it. Besides, there was a new surf documentary he really wanted to see.

So I end up in a black car (that's what Honor and Eloise call them. Never *limousine*, because that is "so tacky") with Eloise, Tim and Griffin, while Honor rides with Coleman. Eloise and Tim chitchat about kids they know at other boarding schools, squash (which Tim is good at) and the summer finance program Tim is applying to in Hong Kong. Griffin is mostly quiet and looks intimidated, while I sit there and think, *Sheesh, these people live like they are forty.* I mean, squash? Finance in Hong Kong? The kids I know in Ventura work at the pizza place and surf in the summers and maybe go to movies.

I stare out the window at the lamp-lit cityscape and drift off on my own tangent about the summer. What life will I be living by then? One where I help out in Jonesy's bookstore? Locked up in Great-Aunt Helen's spare room like some gothic ingenue? Or a *Gossip Girl* summer, where Ed—"Daddy" for sure in this scenario—gets me an internship at *Teen Vogue* or the Tribeca Film Festival?

Mostly I wonder if Hannah will be there next summer. Walking and talking? If she's better, maybe she'll take me back to Greenland with her or on her next trip, wherever that is. Is she going to become one of those nomadic journalists who can't turn down the next assignment, who doesn't even have a home? Is she going to have a choice?

Whoa there. I force myself back to the conversation in the car before all this speculation spins out of control and I end up needing Griffin to run out and find a paper bag for me to breathe into. When I tune back in, we're onto the details of why Tim chose Deerfield over Exeter, even though the squash program at Exeter is *really, really excellent*, and why Hong Kong is *so interesting* right now. He hopes it won't be overrated, like Shanghai.

"Oh, wow. When did you go to Shanghai?" I jump in, trying to sound like I've been following attentively all along.

"Oh, no, no," says Tim. "My parents just came back from Shanghai. My father has some business there. It's supposed to be the fastest-growing cultural center, but it's, you know, really screwed up how they're doing things. Like there's no control, and the pollution is really bad."

I turn to Griffin. "What are you doing for the summer?" I ask, changing the subject away from something neither of us seems to know anything about.

"Camp Tenakama. In Maine. My dad went there."

"That sounds fun. What do you do there?" I'm hoping for a less monosyllabic evening than what this promises.

"You know, canoe, swim, campfires, sneak out at night. It's all boys."

"Sounds a lot like boarding school," I offer.

"Yeah. Kind of."

Oh, boy.

I can't tell if Eloise likes Tim, though she's listening attentively and laughing in the right places. She's so very good at hiding her feelings. So good, in fact, I wonder if even Honor really knows her.

When we get out at the Pierre Hotel, where the ball is being held, Coleman and Honor are already on the sidewalk, waiting. Coleman looks sort of light-headed and giddy, the way guys often are after direct exposure to Honor. From this distance, she does look perfect.

I WON'T MAKE YOU sit through the whole evening, because you get the idea from the conversation in the car how much fun it was. In one way, it was amazing. Like, if I had watched it happening in a movie without having to feel so nervous and out of it and could fast-forward through the boring parts, I would have enjoyed it. The ballroom was a wintry white and filled with tons of tall candles and low bowls of gardenias and southern magnolias and other sweet-smelling flowers that don't grow in the winter and never grow in New York.

The food was beautiful, not actually that good to eat, but gorgeous to look at. The music was beautiful too, supplied by a real, live full orchestra. And when it was time for the debutantes to be introduced—to "society," I guess was the idea originally, though in New York kids Honor's age, and even Ned's, have been out and about plenty, way before turning eighteen—they walked in one at a time, very slowly like a line of brides. They wore white dresses and carried bouquets made of flowers like the ones on the table. When they got to the center of the ballroom, their names were announced, and they did a deep curtsy before being joined by their escort and father, who walked them away to the dance floor.

As I sat there, I tried to imagine what this was like back in the days when these girls had this one season to land a husband or they were over, tossed out while the next batch stepped up. I could not believe this still went on and girls signed up to do it. What was the point?

Honor and Eloise giggled with Tim about a debutante last year who got so drunk before she came down to the ballroom that she slipped and slid all the way down the stairs on the skirt of her poof-ball dress, then staggered up, walked in and made a perfect curtsy. She spent the rest of the night in the ladies' lounge throwing up.

DURING DESSERT, THERE'S A lot of back and forth between the table and the dance floor and surreptitious champagne drinking. I'm half tempted to swipe someone's cell phone to text Chazzy a picture of this lunacy. My eyes are on Honor's purse when suddenly she wobbles towards me on her expensive heels and gazelle legs. She laughs loudly, a happy, expansive drunk. She beams a dazzling smile and says, "Come dance. You have to. It's so fun." For a second, I think she's talking to me, and I'm sucked inside her circle, and I understand the pull of her orbit, what it must be like in there.

Then I realize she's looking past me to Griffin, my hapless escort.

She's really drunk, I realize. I've never seen her so off-balance. There's a wildness in her eyes behind the regular prettiness, something unhinged that makes me nervous.

At a certain point, I'm just ready for the whole thing to be over. I stop saying yes when Griffin or Coleman asks me to dance. Eloise and Tim dance a lot. I guess Honor has the setup eye as well as the shopping eye. Not surprising, although I can't quite squelch the thought that

Eloise might like Tim because Honor thinks she should. I end up sitting at the table by myself, in a sea of white napkins and tablecloths and heady, over-scented flowers and glowy candlelight, and I think, *Okay, that's enough.* I have a twenty-dollar bill in my bag, which I use to take a cab back to Beekman Place.

Ned greets me at the door, all smiles, just to make sure I get back in okay. But it's clear he wants to get back to his room. He's binge-watching *John from Cincinnati*—the HBO show about surfing that might count Ned as its only fan—and he's in the middle of an episode.

Once I'm alone in the tranquil guest room, I change into sweatpants and curl up with Hummingbird on the dreamy gray duvet, practicing songs for tomorrow quietly enough, I hope, not to rile the co-op board.

CHAPTER NINETEEN

The Show

Saturday morning, Honor and Eloise are nowhere to be seen. Sleeping off their hangovers, I think. Ed presents me with his first official gift: an iPhone.

"I should have given this to you last night," he says in his easygoing way. "Ned told me you took a cab home with your own money. I apologize for that."

Then he hands me two hundred dollars.

I am surprised and overwhelmed by all of it. But what mostly overwhelms me is the fact that he says "took a cab *home.*"

I thank him, set up my new iPhone, and email Chazzy.

CHAZZY CAN'T MAKE IT down from the Berkshires until the afternoon, so I'm a little nervous that we won't have enough time to rehearse. At the last minute, his sister decides not to drive down. He's taking the bus.

There's a sound check at six at the club, but each band only gets fifteen minutes. I tell Chazzy I will meet him at the bus station and bring him back here. I feel funny bringing him to the Gibsons' to practice, but I don't know what else to do. It's too cold to play outside.

When I get to Port Authority, I regret this plan, because I'm fifteen minutes early, which means I have to sit in the waiting room, my feet sticking to the floor, the smells of cold fast food and diesel fumes wafting around me. Homeless people sleep against the walls. Several couples fight loudly. A skinny, dirt-streaked man in a shredded raincoat who smells like urine wanders in a circle, hassling the poor guy at the newsstand. I stare at the gate until Chazzy's bus finally pulls in from Great Barrington.

I break into a grin when I spot him from far away, before I can see his face. He has a loping walk that sways side to side; over his shoulder he's slung a little cowboy guitar. He sees me, waves, and smiles. I smile back and hop to my feet. We lean together as if we're going to hug but then just stand there instead.

"Soooo," I say. I can't stop smiling.

"Soooo," he says, looking around. "Have you been pretty much hanging out here the whole time?"

"Yeah. Wait till you see Honor and Ned's place. It's just like this."

"Uh-huh. That's how I pictured it. Can't wait."

"Luckily, you don't have to, because it's doubling as our rehearsal space."

"Awesome," Chazzy says. He pauses, dropping the witty banter routine, and looks at me. "How's your mom?"

I look up at him. He's not that much taller than I am. "Awake. And talking, but pretty out of it. She still spends most of the time sleeping." I shrug. "It's going to be a while before she can come home."

I WANT TO TAKE a cab back, but Chazzy says he wants to walk, even with his bag and guitar—both of which he refuses to let me carry. It's cold but not too cold. More crisp than bitter. The sun is already low. It's a long walk all the way across town from Eighth Avenue to the East River, but it seems to go quickly. I start to describe my night at the debutante ball, and before I know it, the UN building is gleaming ahead, with the East River a frozen gray beyond it.

Chazzy squeezes my arm. Tiny little white flakes fill the air. "Look," he whispers. "Snow at Thanksgiving. We almost never get that. That's global warming for you."

I stare at the swirl of white motes dissolving before they hit the ground and turn to him. His nose is red from the cold. He stares back at me. It's magical, this city-turned-snow globe. If there was a moment that we were going to kiss again, this would be it. But I'm not going to do anything about it this time. It's his turn, if that's what's going to happen.

"Is that . . . is that really snow?" I ask, like an idiot.

"Are you serious?" Chazzy starts laughing.

"I'm from California," I say. "Give me a break."

"Yes, Wren," he tells me, enunciating each word slowly. "That is what we in the Northeast call *snow*." And he spends the rest of the walk narrating the physical properties of ice crystal structure like he's on some PBS documentary, while I punch his shoulder in mock irritation and something else I can't quite define.

BACK AT THE APARTMENT (home?), Ed and Ned both demand that we play for them. The whole time I can feel the heat in my cheeks more than I can hear my own voice, so I know we must not sound that good.

Then we're interrupted by a phone call. Ed runs into the kitchen to take it. When he returns to the living room, his face is pale. *Hannah,* I think, and I'm right. Ed breaks the news that the clinic in Greenland is inducing Hannah's coma again. They don't like the fluid levels in her lungs, or the slight rise in pressure on her brain tissue. If they induce another coma, they can control the recovery, put her back on a ventilator and keep her from shivering so much, so her brain and body can rest.

"This is the best possible course of action," Ed concludes, but I'm not sure if he's quoting the doctors or reassuring himself or both.

I glance at Chazzy. He gives my hand a quick squeeze and lets go.

"Does this mean she's getting worse?" I ask Ed. I can hear how panicky my voice sounds.

"No, no. I don't think so. The doctor said it's a protective measure and that she needs more time."

"How much more time?"

"They're just being conservative, Wren," Ed says. "It's just a question of the doctors being as careful as possible." He forces his genial mask back on. "So what was that last song you were playing? I like that one. It sounds familiar."

"A Glow song. 'Endless,'" Chazzy tells him.

"Right. That's an old one, right? My era?"

I nod. "Gigi's era," I say, thinking about Honor's crush comment.

Ed smiles at me as if he can hear my thoughts. "Your voice is amazing, Wren," he tells me. "I watch you, and I can't even believe that sound is you, coming out of you. How do you do that?"

"I don't know," I answer truthfully and then desperately look for a way to change the subject. "You used to sing, right?"

"Barely. They almost kicked me out of Madrigals." He nods politely to Chazzy. "You're both way out of my league. Good luck tonight. I would come, but I have a dinner, and then I have to get to the Garden in the middle of the night to see Honor ride in the big show." The way he says this, he's either poking fun at himself or his daughter, or he's dead serious—maybe a combination of all three.

"I LIKE HIM," CHAZZY says over pizza right before our show. "He's not what I expected. He doesn't really seem like a dad."

"Well, he wasn't *my* dad until a few days ago," I say. "What does he seem like?"

"I don't know. A movie star or a news anchor or something. He's, like, super polished, but relaxed at the same time."

"Like you don't trust him?" I ask.

He wipes his mouth and cocks an eyebrow. "No. I just said I like him, didn't I?"

"I think I know what you mean. He's not like Hannah, that's for sure."

"Or Honor. I hope I get to meet her sometime. Hannah, that is."

"I hope so too," I say, and a choking feeling closes my throat.

Again, he squeezes my hand. Then he tosses our paper plates and napkins into the garbage. It's time.

THE SIDEWALK IS BOTH better and worse than the coffee shop in Falls Village. Better because there's a real stage with lights; there's even a sound guy who adjusts all the levels so we sound thick and warm, like the duvet in my guest room. Worse because the room is smaller and the people here actually listen.

Some of the acts, mostly duos like us, are pretty good. Some are worse than us. The waiting relaxes me in a weird way.

Climbing onto the stage when it's our turn, I think, *What if I just go up and do this without being terrified? What would that feel like?*

Somehow that's what I do. I stand up there, with the stage lights blinding me, and sing out into the darkness while consciously deciding not to be nervous. And I'm almost not.

People clap afterward. I see Ned in the audience—I won't say crowd, because there are maybe ten people out there—and I am so happy. The last trace of my nervousness melts away. It's one forty-five when we're done, and we have played every song we know.

There's not really a dressing room, but a place backstage where you can change and leave your stuff. At this

point, it's so late that all the other bands have gone. The
floor is sticky from beer, and the sofa looks like someone
found it on the street. But it sort of feels like a real backstage, like we're a real band.

I glance at the doorway, waiting for Ned to appear. "Go,
Birdbrain. Whoo!" I say.

Chazzy looks up, but he's not smiling.

"What's the matter?" I ask, suddenly wondering if that
went a lot worse than I realized.

"Wren, with everything that's been going on, we've
never gotten a chance to . . . you know. Talk about that
thing that happened?" he asks.

"What thing that happened?" I know what he means,
obviously, but I want him to say it. I want to make sure both
of us are talking about the same thing.

"That afternoon at school. About when you . . . when
we kissed." He's looking right at me. I can see we're both
trying to see what the other person is thinking, except we
can't.

"Do you want to talk about it?" This is going in a big
circle, I think. We're like two circling chickens. I want
to smile and point that out, the chicken reference, but I
can't. I stare at the floor.

"I want to . . . I don't want things to be weird with us.
I just want to know what's . . . what you—" He stops and
looks like he's thinking about what to say next.

He kisses me instead. It's like last time. It just happens
easily, without thinking that much. The who-kissed-who
part fades, and I realize I was dumb to worry about that
so much.

"I guess I'm supposed to think it isn't worth losing my best friend if this doesn't work out," Chazzy says after stepping back. "But it feels worse not to risk seeing what happens."

"I know," I say, aware that I'm falling short on my side of the conversation, but I really don't know what I want. I want him to want to be with me. I think I might want to be with him. It's not what I pictured. And it's true if it doesn't work out, it feels like I'll lose everything, especially with Hannah so out of reach and this new crazy Gibson world. Plus I have spent all this time thinking about Nick. That feels like an investment somehow.

I have to say *something*, though. I open my mouth, ready to go with whatever comes out, when Ned barges in.

"Hey, guys." His eyes are big; he is clearly panicked for some reason and doesn't seem to take in that I'm practically sitting in Chazzy's lap. He's not here to congratulate us on a great set. "I just got a text from Eloise. You need to come with me." He's talking fast—not in the chill surfer voice he normally uses.

"What is it?" I ask, quickly stepping away from Chazzy

"Honor's missing. She's supposed to be at the show. I mean, getting ready for the show. Her warm-up time is at two forty. Eloise was supposed to meet her at the Garden, and when she got there, Honor's trainer said Honor hadn't shown up. Eloise has been trying to track her down, but she's not answering her phone."

The fact that Ned is so completely rattled is almost as troubling as Honor not answering her phone. Usually Honor is all over that thing.

"Let's go down there." I grab Hummingbird and stand up. Part of me feels sure something terrible has happened. Maybe that's natural after what just happened to Hannah.

"Shouldn't we all check our phones, though?" Chazzy asks. "Maybe it's just Eloise's phone not getting through." Chazzy, the sensible one.

"I tried to text her too," says Ned. "She's not answering."

"So let's go down there," I say, wanting to reassure him. Maybe this is what it feels like to have a little brother. "We'll find Eloise and figure out what to do. We don't have that long before her slot." I don't wait for anyone to follow, but Ned and Chazzy are right behind me when I reach the street.

"Maybe Eloise can ride Rainmaker in the warm-up," I say.

"Good idea. If they'll let her." Ned taps out a text to Eloise as Chazzy hails a cab.

Chazzy sits next to me, his arm warm against my arm. Outside it starts to snow again—big snowflakes mixed with rain and ice. I think about Honor. Why do I care if she makes it to the show? Because Ned is worried? Because of how upset Ed will be? Because you're supposed to help your sister, even if you don't like her? Because she deserves to be there for her ability, if not for her attitude?

I'm muddling through these possibilities as we get out, duck our heads as icy sleet falls down on us and run toward the 33rd Street entrance. Madison Square Garden, normally home to basketball games and huge rock concerts, has been converted to a warren of dirt-covered aisles, temporary stalls filled with the sounds of horses stamping their hooves, rustling their hay nets and making those fluttery, soft sounds through their nostrils that horses like to make.

As we walk through the stands toward the backstage prep area, I catch a glimpse of the ring, where eight kids at a time are trotting and cantering around on gleaming, expensive horses. They aren't allowed to jump the perfectly painted fences—some made of rails, some built to look like fake walls and wooden fences, others covered in shrubbery—but they can acclimate their horses to the place in the hopes that they won't jump out of their skins when they have to go beneath the lights, camera flashes and sounds of the crowd for the real thing. When we get to Honor's barn area, Eloise is there pacing anxiously in her riding clothes, while a groom holds the unfazed Rainmaker in the aisle. I put my hands flat against the horse's velvet nose and feel the soft whoosh of air through his nostrils. He nuzzles his upper lip against my shirt, searching for treats. His neck and flanks are steaming slightly.

"I don't have anything for you, sweet boy," I tell him.

"I just took him in the warm-up," Eloise says. "I told everybody that Honor will be here soon. I said her stomach was upset. Nerves."

Ned laughs. "And they bought that?"

Eloise shrugs. "She could be nervous. Deep down?"

"Maybe," says Ned doubtfully. "More likely she's wasted and passed out somewhere."

"So we have about three hours to find her," Chazzy says, trying to get us to refocus "What do you guys think? What do we do?"

"She was going to go by Francesco's restaurant for a drink," Eloise says, peering down the aisle at the riders crossing back and forth to the schooling ring as if she'll somehow spot Honor. "She wanted me to come, but I was so burnt out from last night."

"Do you have Francesco's number?" asks Chazzy.

Eloise shakes her head.

"We should go there," I say.

Chazzy thinks for a minute. "What about home? What if she went home to crash for a while and just overslept?"

"I don't really want to call Dad to find out," says Ned. "Oh, no. Dad. I have no idea what time he's getting here."

"So Ned, you go there," I tell him. "Sneak in and check. If Ed's there, you can say one of us forgot something. Chazzy and I will go to the restaurant."

Eloise nods, distracted, glancing back toward the long, dark tunnel that leads into the arena. "That's good. I need to braid and help get Rainmaker ready."

IN THE CAB, CHAZZY just holds my hand without saying anything. I feel like part of the cast of *Scooby-Doo;* what we're doing feels absurd and surreal.

"Is it normal that we're all running around New York City in the middle of the night?" I ask out loud. "Is this what kids do here?"

"I don't know. I couldn't get away with it at home. But parents, you know, they get used to other people at school worrying about where their kids are and at what time. And it's not a normal night. Your dad thinks you're all camped out safe at the Garden with Honor's trainer."

"And what does your mother think you're doing right now?" I ask him.

He cracks a smile. "I'm sure she is sound asleep, and I'm the last thing on her mind," he says. "She's from the Out of Sight, Out of Mind School of Parenting."

What's Hannah thinking? I wonder, seeing her small and still on that hospital bed. I decide right then that in the morning, I will ask Ed to help me get a passport and a plane ticket. I can borrow money for the trip and pay him back later somehow. Even as I form that plan, though, I know it's unrealistic—probably as unrealistic as finding Honor and whisking her back to the show.

THE RESTAURANT IS IN Tribeca, on a narrow cobblestone street with discrete awnings and hand-lettered signs in tiny script. You have to know where you're going to end up here.

As we get out of the cab, Ned texts NOT HERE from the apartment. He's on his way back to the Garden to help Eloise. Unless we have any other ideas? We don't. We stand under the dripping awning, texting him back.

"Do you think we should wake up Ed?" I ask Chazzy.

"Let's try this first," he says.

Considering how late it is, the restaurant is pretty busy. I was expecting Italian because of Francesco's name, but it's a trendy French bistro, small and crowded with people in expensive clothes who look like they've been here all night. I go straight to the bar, where the bartender gives me a look that says, "There is no way I am going to serve you, so don't ask."

Instead I ask him where Francesco is. Apparently

Francesco left a few hours ago. I ask him if there was a girl with him: blonde, pretty, tall. He shrugs and looks a little uncomfortable. Maybe he's thinking about how young I look and making the comparison to Honor's age. Her polish and attitude definitely put a few years on her, whereas people are more likely to guess that I'm younger than I am.

"Wren!"

It's Chazzy, calling to me from a dark hallway that must lead back to the bathrooms. When I reach him, he nods toward a leather bag sitting on a stairway: Honor's new, super-expensive Gibson store bag. There is no way she would have just left it there.

"Maybe Francesco lives upstairs?" I say. I sling the bag over my shoulder—it still smells buttery in that brand-new-leather way—and we race up, only to dead-end in a dimly lit hallway. There's only one door, so we knock. Nothing happens.

Chazzy shrugs. What would Velma do? I push at the door. It swings open easily.

The apartment is a mess—but a very expensive mess: an open loft with a platform bed in one corner and sheets in a tangle. The bed's empty, and I am relieved. But the relief fades as I turn to see what Chazzy is staring at. The bathroom light is on, and Honor's pretty, stockinged feet are sticking out the door. Chazzy and I look at each other, and I know we are thinking exactly the same thing.

Tentatively, I reach down and touch Honor's potentially lifeless foot. She twitches away and practically kicks me in the face.

Chazzy and I let our collective breath out. Conscious is good, no matter what her condition. Inside the bathroom, things are less pretty. Honor's head is propped against the tub. The room smells like vomit, whiskey and toothpaste.

"Honor. Honor." I shake her awake and start to dampen a hand towel to wipe her chin.

"What?" she mumbles. She doesn't seem very surprised that we are there.

"You forgot your bag," I say. "And you're supposed to be winning the Maclay right now."

"Oh," she says. "Is it Sunday?"

Chazzy and I help her to her feet, and I zip up her dress. With one of us on either side, she makes it down the stairs, swaying. I hold her waist with one arm and grip the railing with the other. It's dark, and the stairs are steep and rickety.

"Yeah," Honor slurs, as if answering an unspoken question. "I was just waiting for Francesco to come back. Did he come back?"

"No," I say.

"I want to take off my shoes," she says. "What are you doing here?"

"In the cab," says Chazzy, readjusting Honor to take more weight off me.

The bartender watches us as we leave. "Blondie. All good?" Not out of concern, more like he's worried about getting in trouble. "Your friends?" I glare at him for not bothering to be concerned on the way in.

Honor nods. "S'okay," she mumbles. "My sister."

My sister. She must be really wasted to admit that out loud.

"Don't tell my dad," she adds.

"Okay." *Our* dad. But let's not get picky.

CHAPTER TWENTY

Finals

Honor seems to have recovered slightly by the time we make it back to Madison Square Garden. She rides up front in the cab—which is fine by me. Her breath is toxic right now. Ned and Eloise see her and look angry and relieved, respectively.

"What the hell, Honor? I almost had to send Dad out looking for you," Ned snaps at her. She's oblivious, or pretending to be. Eloise and I help her into her riding clothes while Chazzy stands at an uncomfortable distance. Nervously I wonder where Ed is.

By the time Honor's tall, shiny boots are on, and her hair is tucked neatly in its hairnet under her riding helmet, you can't tell that only recently she was passed out on the bathroom floor of some sleazy guy's downtown loft. At least from a distance.

IN THE WARM-UP RING, even to my untrained eye, Honor's riding looks off. Eloise and I stand at the edge of the tiny ring, watching with unease. When Honor drops her crop for the second time, and a ring steward has to pick it up for her, I see him give her an odd look. When he leaves the ring, he goes over to talk to another show official, and I see them both watching Honor canter around.

I nudge Eloise, worried. She shrugs, but looks tense.

Rainmaker takes three strides—crooked strides. Even I can see that—gets to the base of the jump and then slides into it, his front legs straight and his head up, refusing to jump.

"Oh my God," says Eloise. "He stopped. Rainmaker never stops."

Honor shakes her head like she's clearing cobwebs.

"I wonder if she can do this. Do you think we should tell her dad?" Eloise asks.

I shake my head no. "Not yet. She still has a little time to pull it together."

I glance at my watch. It's 6:10 in the morning. A ridiculous time to be awake, a ridiculous time to risk getting dumped off a horse. On the other hand, Honor brought this on herself.

I glance up and spot Ed, talking with Chazzy and Ned, in our seats. He is smiling broadly; clearly Ned and Chazzy have kept him in the dark. Honor dismounts and stumbles a few steps to Eloise and me, almost throwing her reins to the groom.

"I don't even want to do this," she murmurs to Eloise, ignoring me. Over Eloise's shoulder, I see Ed giving us a thumbs-up, proud and excited. Foolish.

I whirl back around. "Honor, you might think right now that you don't care about this, but I know that's not true.

You're too good. No one gets that good at something just for her father. If you didn't care, you wouldn't have gotten this far. It's way too hard. If you don't go for it now, you're going to regret it later. For yourself. Not for Ed or whoever else you think you're trying to impress."

I don't even stay for the look of fury Honor rains down on me. I turn my back on her and head for the stands, waving to Ed on my way—"Meet you at our seats!"—hoping he stays up there and hoping Honor has the good sense not to talk to him until after her round. Eloise trails in my wake. I glance back. She looks shocked. I don't blame her. I'm shocked too.

BACK IN THE STANDS, Ned pulls me away from Ed and Chazzy as Eloise spins a lie about how Honor is just a little sleep-deprived, but she knows she's going to crush it.

"Hey, I'm sorry Honor's been so rotten," Ned says. "This is all so weird for everyone. Thanks for going after her."

"Yeah. I know. I'm sorry too. Really."

"You have no reason to be sorry. I'm sure that as nuts as it's been for us, it can't be easy for you, either."

"Thanks. That's nice of you," I say. It is. I can't believe he's only a First Year.

"Seriously, it's not your fault. Especially with Honor. Everything involving Dad seems to make her act worse than she really is. Honor's thing with Dad is complicated, anyway, even without this."

"Complicated?" I ask. Nosy question, but I'm more likely to get info from Ned than anyone else.

"Just . . . you know. She feels like nothing she does is

enough. Like it doesn't matter how perfect she is at everything, he'll still never really appreciate her for her."

"Really? Is that how you feel?"

"No." He considers. "I mean, in a way, but he's different with me. She sees it as him not getting her, seeing who she really is. I see it more as him giving me lots of space. And I like that. You know?"

I nod. It reminds me of Hannah, of how she is with me. "Thanks. I mean, it means a lot, you talking to me about it."

"I know you're not getting much love from sis." The idea of anyone calling Honor "sis" is beyond imagination, even as a joke. "But you can't take it personally with her. Seriously. You just can't."

"'Not much love' is an understatement." I laugh for the first time all night.

"Well, it'll work out. Try not to stress, okay? I'm happy you're here. The more, the merrier, right?" He gives me the surfer's thumb-and-pinky floppy *hang loose* sign. I want to give him a hug, but that feels like maybe too much.

I do it anyway. *At least I get a real little brother out of all this,* I tell myself. *That's something.*

I glance back at Chazzy, sitting against the back of our seats, his feet up on the railing. When Ed isn't looking, he blows me a kiss. I blow one back.

HONOR RIDES INTO THE ring at an unhurried walk, upright in her perfectly cut dark jacket and black hunt cap. I hold my breath as Rainmaker picks up a rocking, measured canter. They make a perfect curve toward the first jump, a gray wishing well. Centered and calm, almost not moving, Honor lets her horse flow under her, hitting the perfect distance to every jump, never varying her speed. When it looks like they will be a little tight to the narrow jumps, Honor imperceptibly closes his stride, widens her approach and gets to just the right spot. Rainmaker completes a tricky turn from the wall to a broken line, and then six strides forward to an oxer.

Even hungover, or maybe even still a little drunk, Honor makes it look so easy. And so does Rainmaker. *Push button* is what they call a horse like that, who goes like he's on autopilot and never makes a mistake.

Somehow Honor keeps it together all morning, through the flat phase, the second round and a final test. When it's all over, she comes in third.

Ed stands and claps like mad, then hugs me and Ned, one arm around each of us. I can't see any disappointment in his face even though Honor didn't win.

"She was nervous," says Ed. "She didn't even want to talk to me before she rode. But look at her!" Chazzy and I exchange a look.

"Honor! Whoo!" whoops Ned loudly, drawing a few glares.

All of us hurry down to the entrance of the arena, where Honor is finishing her victory lap, a long yellow satin rosette fluttering against Rainmaker's shiny black head as he gallops. She slows down to a jog and allows herself a smile when she sees us grouped there, but honestly, she still looks a little green.

"Hey," she breathes, winded. The sour smell of an

alcohol-soaked bar floor drifts down toward us, hitting me and Eloise, the closest to her. I turn to check Ed's expression, whether the vapors are registering. His face clouds a little, like he's remembering something, or more like he's trying not to remember something.

"Honor," he says, "come here. That was fantastic. Can I get you anything? Something to drink?"

Eloise chokes back a giggle.

If you had asked me hypothetically if I would have hoped for a moment like this, I am sorry to admit, I would have said yes. What easier way for me to be cast as the good daughter and at the same time watch Honor not get away with things for once? But in real life, my instinct is to stop it—and fast.

I see that Honor's fall from grace right now will be awful for Ed, awful for Honor and, by triangulation, awful for me. Possibly even not recoverable for me, if I want this to be my sort-of family in the future. So I surprise myself by practically flinging myself forward—cutting off Ed as I do—grabbing Rainmaker's reins and leading both of them swiftly toward the barn.

"Honor, that was incredible! Congratulations! Amazing!" I shout, while pulling Eloise along behind us with my free hand.

Honor growls under her breath. By the time we are out of earshot, she looks mad enough to bite me. "Wren, what the hell?" she barks. "What are you doing?"

"Shh," cautions Eloise.

"Your breath," I tell her.

Honor self-consciously covers her mouth. "Oh," she

says. "Okay." She slides down from the saddle. "Do you mind taking Rainmaker?" she asks Eloise. "Do you guys have any gum?" I pull some out and hand it to her like it's some undercover spy exchange. She slips it in her mouth and turns to face her father.

I watch them hug as Edward congratulates her and makes a fuss, his smile relaxed, suspicions evaporated like the alcohol fumes.

Eloise whispers to me, "Was Francesco there when you found her?"

"No," I whisper back.

"That asshole," she says. "I'm really glad you got there in time, Wren."

Honor pins her show ribbon on Ed's shirt pocket and then asks Eloise to take a picture of them together. I feel bad for a moment that it's Honor's life that I have barged into. Her world was all hers before I showed up at Hardwick.

I WOULD LIKE TO be one of those people who takes charge of her life, confronts every challenge, takes the bull by the horns, etc., but like most difficult things I leave my tuition conversation with Ed until the last minute. Eloise and Honor are still packing. Ned is helping by dragging their bags into the hall. He has one small duffel, and they have about five huge ones.

Chazzy called me last night on the way to the train. If I had had this conversation yesterday, I could have gone back to school with him. But I'm a coward and so have bought myself another long car ride with Honor. At least Eloise and Ned will be there.

I find Ed in the kitchen, making a new pot of coffee. He lobs me a welcoming smile. Honor's third-place ribbon sits discarded on the counter. I guess she's not going to bother to bring it back to school.

"All packed, you kids? Any snacks for the road?"

"No, we're set," I say. "I just wanted to thank you so much for this weekend. It's been so amazing." We stare at each other. How do you go from strangers to father and daughter? It seems like an uncrossable expanse.

"Wren, I expect it to be the first of many. You're welcome here, and I want you to feel at home. And I also want you to keep me up-to-date on everything with Hannah. I mean it. Every development. And anything you need . . ." He trails off.

Usually when people say "anything you need," what they have in mind is more on the borrowing-a-cup-of-sugar level. But I have to seize the moment. As added motivation, I picture a winter at Great-Aunt Helen's: the two of us, seated in her dim dining room, the daylight gone by four, the overboiled potatoes, the well-done, unidentifiable meat. The silence.

"There is, actually. One thing," I blurt and take a step toward him.

He looks surprised and a little worried, and gestures for me to sit at the little kitchen table. We sit.

"I can't stay at school unless someone signs my contract for next year and pays the tuition. Hannah—I mean, my mom—was supposed to, but she didn't get a chance before the accident. If I don't get the forms in by December first, which is basically Thursday, I can't come back after winter break."

"That's no problem. Of course I would be happy to sign for you." Ed looks relieved, like I was going to ask for something worse. I'm not sure he understands, he's so casual about it.

"But that would mean *you* would have to pay for it. The tuition for the spring. And if something happened. If my mother wasn't—couldn't pay for it."

"I understand," he says. "But that isn't going to happen. And you don't need to worry about it either way." My eyes well up, and the last thing I want is to cry in front him, like some pitiful orphan.

"Wren, it's fine. It's actually ridiculous that Hardwick Hall can't work something out itself and is putting you in this position. But I want you to be clear that there is every expectation that Hannah will be fine. I've talked to the clinic in Greenland every day. They are happy with her progress and not expecting complications at this point. And I am happy to contribute. Seriously. Take it off your plate."

I hug him and cry, and the ground feels solid under my feet for the first time in weeks.

"Do you want me to drive you back? I can talk to the registrar or the business office for you if you want."

"It's actually Taubin," I say, and then worry that sounds rude. I'm so used to calling her that at school when I talk about her.

"Oh, God," he says. "Nina. Well, I'm even willing to talk to her. But only for you."

"It's okay," I say. "I don't think they will kick me out right this second."

"You call, then, and just let me know what you need. Don't worry about this anymore."

"Thank you," I tell him, thinking Chazzy was right. He *is* a fairy-tale dad.

CHAPTER TWENTY-ONE

Hardwick Again

The last day of the semester, snow falls over the campus, fluffy and friendly, like in an old-fashioned Christmas TV special. Tonight is the first night of the Winter Festival and Parents' Weekend. This being Hardwick, it figures that the weather cooperates perfectly to provide atmosphere. It's a big deal for the Last Years, because they get to perform their holiday skit, usually a traditional Christmas story adapted to include the faculty, staff and popular students as characters.

If I expected my life at Hardwick to be different after Thanksgiving in Gibson Land, it is and it isn't. Honor looks me in the eye now and doesn't visibly stiffen with annoyance when I am in the suite, but she still isn't especially interested in me.

The feeling is mutual. I don't ask her what happened with Francesco. Honor doesn't talk about him. Eloise gives India a dark look once when India brings it up, and everyone drops the subject fast. India covers, obviously thrown. She hates to make anyone feel bad, but more than that, it's so rare that anyone can make Honor feel bad that it's disconcerting.

So it's not like all four of us are suddenly best friends, but sometimes now I get up early and go to breakfast with Eloise or crash an Upper or Last study break with India. At the barn, all three of them will wait for me to untack and put away Chester or whichever horse I am riding so we can walk to dinner together, even Honor.

Another big thing is that I sing one of my songs in class. Finally. I go last, but Gigi makes sure I do it. Chazzy offers to accompany me on the ukulele, but Gigi says no. I go up there all alone and sing a passable version of my new, not-quite-finished song. I stand there, feeling all the eyes in the room on me—so much worse when you know the eyes, and they know you—and I just make myself start before I can think of any more excuses not to. It's cold in the room. The heat in this building has already gone out a few times this winter, and as I sing I can see my breath in the air, rising with the song. I focus on that, and it distracts me from wondering what everyone is thinking.

I scrapped the dad/letter song. This one is a jumble of images about mirrors and Alice in Wonderland and sisters and twins, old dolls and dresses. Really not very worked out. I kind of hum the parts that don't have words yet. I'm not sure what it's about, part of the reason it took me so long to perform it. And I think it makes Gigi a little uncomfortable, given her own history—another reason maybe it takes me so long to sing it. Or she might just find it sentimental. She frowns as she listens, but she goes easy on me because she knows it is a big deal for me to sing it at all.

I say I don't know what it is about, but of course I *know* it's about Honor and finding yourself dropped into a strange world and my parents and blah, blah, blah. Obviously. But I'm singing the raw ingredients without an ending, without even really knowing what I am feeling yet.

The other kids seem to like it. Maybe more than the times I sang Cat Power or Neko Case or whatever.

"Finally," Chazzy says. "Dude, we were getting so sick of Aimee Mann."

Gigi stops me by the door at the end of class. "That was good," she says. "I know you didn't want to do that." She touches my arm lightly. "And I'm glad your mom's okay."

HANNAH MANAGES TO TAKE the train up from the city after spending the day at New York Hospital having a million tests to make sure she is fully thawed and back to normal. I guess one good side effect of her almost dying in Greenland is that she gets to come to Parents' Weekend, since she had to stop in New York on her way back to California. A cab drops her in the driveway in front of Baldwin. I catch sight of her through the window, standing alone with her one small bag, and my throat catches. I don't even recognize her.

My mother is so tiny, littler than the eighth graders I sometimes see visiting the school. She doesn't look like she could be anyone's mother. I want to run over and collapse on her, sobbing like a two-year-old, but she looks so frail I think I'm probably going to have to be the one to hold her up. Hannah insists she's fine, that she just gets tired more easily than before. Ha. Understatement of understatements.

We sit by the fire in the lobby of her hotel, drinking hot apple cider. Hannah wants to walk around and see the campus, show me the rooms where she lived and see what's changed, but she says maybe later in the weekend. She's too worn out from the trip and feels jet-lagged right now. So instead she tells me about falling under the ice, how when you really start to freeze you get warm instead of cold.

"Right, like, that's at the point when you're about to die, Mom," I say.

"I guess," she says, and blushes, as if it was silly of her to almost die.

"How's your new family?" she asks, not avoiding the topic like I expected her to. Maybe when you almost die, you realize there's no point in skirting the truth.

"Complicated," I tell her.

"I guess we have a lot to talk about."

"I guess," I agree. But I smile. Really, she's been through enough in the last two months. I feel bad about how mad I got at her right before the accident.

She doesn't mention Ed right away, so I decide not to yet. Instead she goes back to asking about Hardwick: What are my friends like? Which teachers are the best? Is Selby still so overheated in the winter that you have to leave all the windows open?

I talk about Gigi. I debate whether to ask her about Ms. Taubin, what Hannah did to hurt her feelings so badly, and then decide against it. Instead, I describe which room in Selby is mine, and she tells me she had the same room her Upper Year. She asks about Chazzy.

"You'll like him," I tell her. "You'll meet him this

weekend. He's funny and smart. He makes me feel funny and smart. Like when we're together, somehow we're both our funniest and smartest."

That makes her smile again. Then she asks how it's going with Honor. I consider telling her what really happened over Thanksgiving, but decide it wouldn't be fair to Honor. Crazy, I know. What makes me protect her?

"I know she hasn't been very nice to you," Hannah says. "It must be hard to be thrown together like this. Hard for both of you. This must have really rocked her world."

"I guess," I say, feeling a sulk come over me like a heavy weight, even though I've had the same thought myself. I don't see why Honor deserves her sympathy. I was the one Hannah kept the secret from all those years. Honor got to have both of her parents the whole time.

"Don't go all teen on me," Hannah scolds. "That will make for a long and tedious weekend."

I glare at her. I've earned the right not to be nice in this situation. "Honor has the same anchor I do. Did Ed give it to you?"

Hannah shakes her head, like it's dicey territory and she's not sure how far to wade in. "No," she says. "That was my mother's. It's a Stone Cove tradition. It's like a club. If you've been on the island a long time."

"The country club?" I'd walked past the entrance to the Anchor Club, Stone Cove Island's golf and tennis club, on my way back to Great-Aunt Helen's.

"Sort of. It's more of a social club. It's like the island's local version of the Social Register. A way for a bunch of old, snobby families to stick together. If you've been there long enough, they give you a diamond anchor. Black diamonds, because the traditional anchor is iron. The men get a signet ring with a black anchor. Edward's family was another of those families that had been on the island forever."

"He told me you weren't into rules," I say.

"Some rules. Some of their rules. I knew if they got wind of Ed and me—of you—they would never let it go. It would be like some crazy arranged royal wedding. In their minds only, obviously. The rest of the world wouldn't care. I couldn't stand the idea of being handled and managed like that."

"Even though you loved Ed," I say.

Hannah doesn't answer.

"Sorry. I just think you should have told me. It's not fair that you decided it was easier for you to keep it secret. Don't you think I deserve to have a father?"

"Of course, Wren. It wasn't that I was never going to tell you."

"No? When were you going to?"

She looks at me like she's waiting for the answer to come to her. "I don't know," she says at last. "Look, Wren, you have to remember how young I was and the point I was at in my life. I wasn't all that much older than you are now. I had just finished college. I was just starting to live my own life. That family is very controlling. Edward's family. And my family. There's nothing my parents wanted more than for me to marry someone like Edward. That's one reason I didn't tell anyone. I could never have gotten away. He could never have left New York. He had his family business to run, and he always knew that's what he would do."

I sigh. "They do have newspapers in New York, you know. I hear there's even a pretty good one."

"Wren, if I had become Mrs. Gibson, there would have been no room for that. Especially at the age I was. I hadn't even gotten started yet. Then later, I was worried about custody and getting enmeshed again . . . You won't believe me, probably, but I am glad you met him. I am glad you like him. I'm especially glad he was there when you needed him. I hadn't really thought that part through, I guess, the possibility . . ." She musters an odd, wan smile at this point, like someone in a movie. "Anyway, you do like him, right?"

"Yeah, I like him. Don't you?"

"Well, I haven't seen him in sixteen years. But I did. Yes. Of course."

"I know what you mean about the family," I admit. "It's definitely a whole scene. But I wouldn't mind being a little enmeshed. And having a family. They were nice to me. Is that okay?"

"Sure," says Hannah. "That's okay."

"I have an awesome little brother. That's kind of fun."

"Right. That's fun. And a sister your age."

"Less fun. Although I'll admit, sort of interesting. Or something. It's all so weird. It's always been just the two of us."

Without warning, my mother bursts into tears.

"Hannah! What? I'm not going anywhere. It's not like I'm leaving you for the fabulous Gibsons—"

"I shouldn't have sent you away," she sobs. "I didn't know what else to do."

"Don't cry, Mom. I'm glad." Well, *glad* might be an over-simplification, but on balance . . .

She sniffs, then laughs. "I'm a little emotional since the accident," she says, wiping away tears. "Ignore me. Actually, maybe you could sit and read to me? I still get headaches when I read to myself."

BACK IN THE HOTEL room, Hannah takes off her boots and stretches out on her bed in her stockings. It's funny that her feet are smaller than mine. Weird that you can end up bigger than your parents.

I read her every article in the in local Connecticut tourism magazine, followed by the room service menu, until she falls asleep, snuggled under the perfect flecked-linen blanket Honor picked out. *She does look better,* I think, really believing it for the first time. It's possible that life could go back to normal, whatever that means now.

I look out the window into the fading afternoon light, thinking about how nothing in my life is the same as it was three months ago.

ALL HARDWICK ALUMS ARE invited to skit night. They don't sit with the students, but in the back of the chapel. As we find our seats, the Lowers herded together on the left side behind the Last Years, I turn and see Hannah standing in the back, looking for a seat.

From across the way, Ms. Taubin is trying to catch Hannah's eye. She waves, and Hannah notices her. Hannah smiles and waves back. Ms. Taubin smiles too, though I'm pretty sure Hannah doesn't know who she is. My mom is terrible at recognizing people, and I've seen her do the same generic smile and wave before, when she couldn't place someone but knew she should. Ms. Taubin doesn't notice, though. She just seems happy to be seen.

Chazzy is way behind me, about ten rows. I wave at him, and he shrugs at me like, "Too bad we can't sit together." I shrug back.

This year's skit is a takeoff on *How the Grinch Stole Christmas*, with the Grinch depicted by Mr. Armitage, the grouchy European history teacher; Cindy Lou Who played by Gigi, obviously; and Max the dog played by Bennett Hale. Everyone laughs as the Grinch tries to steal the candy cane from the mouth of the sleeping Suki Sidwell, who chomps down on it like a terrier, and Galen Anderson, the ethereal official beauty of that grade, gets to lead the Whos in their "Fah Who Foraze!" carol, dressed in a long flannel nightgown.

After the Winter Festival skit, the Last Years lead the procession out of the chapel, wearing crowns made from evergreen boughs, and the rest of us follow in a straggly, energized, giggling throng. Chazzy is far ahead of me. The alumni have already gone outside, and Hannah has said she'll go straight back to the hotel to rest, so I don't bother trying to catch up.

Outside the cold air almost has a taste, like wintergreen. I think about what Christmas will be like in California: sunny and cool with twinkly lights on palm trees and wreaths on car hoods; thin, watercolor sky; the even sameness of every day. It fills me momentarily with longing, and then as I imagine actually returning to my life there and leaving Hardwick, my stomach knots. I feel suddenly the full impact of how much I want to come back next year, how much I want to be Suki Sidwell someday, gnawing the candy cane and growling, making my Last Year classmates and the rest of the school laugh.

I think about Christmas. I think about next summer. I wonder what Hannah will do when Edward visits us in December. (He has some business in LA so is planning a detour to Ventura to see us. I haven't told Hannah about it yet.) I wonder, but I also know it's not going to be resolved right here and right now.

"Nick, are you coming?" shouts Lauren Benaceraf from the path. When I look up, I see Nick standing right in front of me, looking expectant. I'm confused. He's waiting for me?

"No, I think I'm going to hang here. See you." He nods for her to go and turns back to me. She lingers as long as she respectably can, pretending she's looking for something in her bag, then starts to walk away.

"What'd you think?" he asks.

"The skit? Oh, funny. Really great." *Why me?* I think. *Why now?* Because I stopped thinking about him for a minute and he noticed?

"Hale makes an awesome dog, don't you think?" Nick says.

So here it is, my big chance, staring me in the face. It's like the night in the pool: this short, electric distance between us that I can cross if I want to. And then I will be on the other side with Nick. For a second I see Lauren's face, panicked and desperate as she turns away, walking as slowly as she can so Nick can catch up if he changes his mind. Students mill past us, making their way to Hale or back to their dorms.

"It's so crazy that you and Honor are sisters," he says. An observation, I think, rather than a compliment. News travels fast.

"Yup," I say. "It's crazy, all right."

But Nick keeps looking right into my eyes, like I'm the only person here. I can have what I've wanted right now, if I just reach out and take it. I expected to. But I don't. Now that it's finally here, I don't.

"You know, I should go," I say. "Chazzy's waiting for me."

It's not completely a lie. Chazzy probably is waiting for me somewhere, full of things to say, happy to see me as always, not thinking about how to act or make conversation, ready to pick up where we left off.

Nick looks surprised. "Really?" he asks. I can tell he thinks that I'm chickening out. He knows I've been a mess over him all semester. He's not an idiot. And anyway, he's used to reading the signs. He's had a lot of practice. I'm embarrassed now, seeing plainly how obvious I've been and how easy he assumed this would be.

"Okay. Don't want to keep Chazzy waiting." He reaches out and tucks my hair behind my ear. For a minute I think he's going to pat my head, like I'm a little girl. Instead he kisses me. A real kiss.

I'm so shocked, I can't move. Instead of feeling thrilled, I feel angry. I said no, and he still kissed me. Like no one can say no to him, or he can't imagine anyone could really mean it if they did. Like he just can't stand to lose any competition.

I realize at that moment what it is I actually want. And standing here, outside the chapel, flirting with Nick suddenly feels like a huge waste of time.

"I'm sure," I tell him, unsure how to back away from the kiss now that I'm standing here, our noses inches apart. Really, someone should write a guidebook. There aren't that many situations to cover, right? It would be a big help. And where are the teachers when you actually need them? I decide on a polite—I hope—smile.

"See you," I say, turning up the path.

"See you," he says. He sounds both annoyed and amused. I can almost feel him watching me walk away.

Do I tell Chazzy what just happened? No. There's no reason to hurt his feelings. And it's too late to talk tonight, anyway. I won't tell anyone. I'm sure Nick won't, either. Instead of being mad, maybe I should be grateful to him for helping me make up my mind.

Up ahead on the path, I see Honor. She turns when she hears my footsteps, and when she realizes it's me, her face clouds over. But she waits for me to catch up.

"Hey." She almost growls it.

Now what? God, she's exhausting.

Clearly Honor's mad at me again, but this time feels different. This time she's mad not like you're mad at someone you wish didn't exist, but like you're mad at someone you have to deal with every day, someone who's not going anywhere, like you would be mad at someone you've been mad at before and will be again, with other emotions and events scattered in between. This time, she is mad at me like I'm not invisible.

"You know why he didn't come this weekend, right? He didn't want to see your mother." I don't get why Honor would be mad that Ed doesn't want to see my mother. I would think she would see that as a win for her side. Advantage, Team Honor.

"I thought your mother and Ed divided up holidays and school events," I add. I had assumed that since Thanksgiving was Ed's, Parents' Weekend would be Honor's and Ned's mother's event.

"No!" she says. "He always comes to this. He always goes to skit night. He's not here because he doesn't want to see your mother. As in, he *wants* to see her."

She looks at me like I'm the stupidest girl she's ever met.

"Forget it," she says. "It's almost like you're from another planet." I know that doesn't sound like a compliment as I write it, but the way she said it, it almost sounded nice. We keep walking without talking. I can't reassure her that Ed doesn't want to see my mother, can I? I have no idea what he wants.

When we are almost back at Selby, Honor says, "So you're staying." And then out of the blue, "Ned thinks we should invite you to France this summer."

"That's nice," I reply. "You don't have to . . ."

"Obviously. It's so Ned, always thinking of others. I'm sure you have plans," she says, even though summer is still six months away. "It's not like you have anything to do with that part of my family."

"Honor. It's really okay. I'm not trying to invade your whole life."

Honor nods. "I never said thanks. At the horse show,"

she says, all brisk, like now she's in a hurry to get upstairs to our room. "Thanks."

"Anytime," I tell her. "Although not anytime soon, okay?" I follow her up the stairs, those stairs with the hollowed-out footsteps of two hundred years' worth of students' feet. From the hallway, I can hear Eloise and India giggling. We enter the room, and they burst into gossip.

"Oh my God! Oh my God! Did you hear?" India babbles.

"Nick broke up with Lauren!" Eloise reports, like she's breaking a big news story.

"I know," I say.

Everybody turns to me, a beat of surprise puncturing the mayhem, and then they dive right back in.

"We ran into her outside Hale. She's a mess. She couldn't even talk about it," says India.

"That didn't last long," says Honor dryly.

"Maybe they'll get back together," I say. "You never know."

"No way," says Eloise. "Honor, what happened?"

Eloise and India hang on her, waiting for the inside scoop. Honor shrugs and deflects their gaze by turning her face to the window and looking cryptic. "You know . . ." she trails off.

I know that she doesn't know. For once she's not at the epicenter of things. She sweeps her hair back with one hand and half-smiles. I notice she's wearing the anchor charm around her wrist again.

Eloise and India turn to me uncertainly. It's unlikely

that I would know anything, but it's worth a shot, if Honor won't spill.

I look at Honor, still gazing out the window. And then I shrug too, deciding to keep her secret. That's what sisters do, right?

ACKNOWLEDGMENTS

Thank you to my husband, Adam, and to my parents for their constant support. Sarah Burnes, thank you for your belief in this book and your willingness to reread and reread and reread. Thank you Helen Thorpe for your good advice, hand-holding and encouragement. Thanks to my great editor, Dan Ehrenhaft; to Bronwen Hruska; Rachel Kowal; Meredith Barnes; and the whole Soho Teen family. Thanks to KidLit, especially to Gretchen Rubin for creating that happy world. Thanks to my reader friends who patiently endured multiple drafts. Also to Dawn Davis, Caitlin Macy and Linda Cohen. And thanks to Neko Case and Aimee Mann for generously allowing me to incorporate some of the songwriting that sparked the girl who became Wren.